Martini Club 4:
Reckless: The 1920s
Pampered: The 1940s

by

Kathy L Wheeler

Martini Club 4: Reckless and Pampered

Cover Art by *Lisa Dawn MacDonald*

The Wild Rose Press, Inc.
PO Box 708
Adams Basin, NY 14410-0708
Visit us at www.thewildrosepress.com

Publishing History
First Edition, 2021
Trade Paperback ISBN 978-1-5092-3728-9
Digital ISBN 978-1-5092-3729-6

Martini Club 4: Reckless and Pampered
Published in the United States of America

RECKLESS...

Compressing his lips, he tugged the Luger from his trousers at his lower back, hidden beneath his jacket. "Damn thing's loaded." He grabbed her hand, its utter femininity reaching through her glove. How had he missed that when he'd hauled her into the truck? He was an idiot.

Shoving away fear that centered deep within his belly, he positioned the gun in her hand, showing her the proper hold. "If you have to shoot, try to aim it in someone else's direction. Stay behind me."

He let out a held breath at her shaky nod.

"Let's go. And straighten the mustache."

PAMPERED...

He leaned against the bar, hiding a smile, her clipped heels taking her straight by him. Of course, she ignored him. Too bad he couldn't ignore the soft scent of gardenia trailing in her wake. "Audra Faye." He tipped his empty glass in her direction. She hated being referred to by her full name. The girl had absolutely no sense of humor.

"Mr. Frisk," she murmured.

Did her steps grow faster? He'd bet on it...

The Martini Club 4 series consists of a total of eight stories by four different authors. They are intertwined and take place somewhat simultaneously, but they are best read in the following order:

Martini Club 4: The 1920s Stories:

Rebellious by Amanda McCabe
Ruined by Alicia Dean
Reckless by Kathy L Wheeler
Runaway by Krysta Scott

Martini Club 4: The 1940s Stories:

Pampered by Kathy L Wheeler
Priceless by Krysta Scott
Perilous by Amanda McCabe
Precarious by Alicia Dean

We hope you enjoy!

Dedication

To my fabulous husband who knows when to work on his music and stay out of my face when I'm furiously typing away. Bringing me water and food, cooking and cleaning. It's paying off, honey…

Acknowledgments

Our Martini Club has been a "thing" going on for some years now. Even with the pandemic and two of us moving to different parts of the country, the four of us still try to meet.

I suppose the idea to start a series of stories was a bit of joke that eventually turned into something tangible and outrageously fun. Through our many critique sessions, Martini Club meetings, and various retreats Amanda McCabe, Alicia Dean, Krysta Scott and I found a way to complete the first of these two series of truly fun novellas.

I can honestly say, I am honored to be a part of such a creative and loving group of women I will count as great friends for the rest of my life. Thank you, girls, for being the best critique partners, authors, and best friends a person could dream of having.

I don't want to forget our honorary member, Brooke Taylor, who is a fabulous writing talent in her own right.

Nor do I wish to forget the Martini Lounge in Edmond, Oklahoma who catered to our every need and want.

Martini Club 4: The 1920s

Reckless

Prologue

Eyes closed, Lady Margaret Montley glided her fingers across ivory keys of the ancient grand piano. Her voice slid into a pivotal cadence that marked the unusual piece of a 12 bar blues tune. Poignant notes that echoed against the hardwood floors and walls in the Duke of Winsome family's large ballroom. The single cheer in the form of applause startled Meggie.

Her eyes snapped open, meeting the matched pair blues of the dowager's. A force of nature, her mother. Slim, petite, and accustomed to everything in her perfect world go according to her perfect plan. And then there was her only daughter, Meggie...

"That was lovely, dear. But couldn't you sing something a bit more..." Her hand flitted out. "...a bit less..." Her mother smiled in her sweet, yet condescending way. "Something lively and upbeat, not like that new—"

"Jazz, mother. It's jazz, and it suits me *perfectly.*"

"I'm not complaining, darling. You have a lovely voice. You play flawlessly. I just don't see you impressing a man—" She cleared her throat. "—a *decent* man, singing such suggestive tunes."

Meggie bit back her irritation. It was an age-old argument. *There is no need to continue practicing, dear. Things are different now than in my day when one needed one's talents to impress a gentleman. With your beauty, all you need do is smile and they shall stampede the entry hall.*

Her older brother by a mere four minutes strolled into the ballroom, empty but for the piano. "Hey, Pegs."

The name sent Meggie's blood pressure to percolating. He knew just how to crawl under her skin. "Do. Not. Call. Me. That."

"Hi, Mums."

"Garrett, darling, when did you arrive?"

"Just this minute. Where are the others?" Garrett was stocky with hair the same blond as her own, and the same blue eyes as all of the Montleys. He was also the one sibling who knew her best. And with her and Jessie's plans to escape choke-holding England—after Jessie's sister's wedding—Meggie had to take extreme caution or their adventure would be lost before it had begun.

Garrett sauntered across the ballroom and kissed her cheek. "I heard you from the foyer, Megs. You sound good. Real fine."

Just like that her heart melted. She would miss him terribly. "Thank you, Garrett."

"Don't encourage her, darling. She has notions of singing—*in public.*" A delicate shudder wracked her mother's body.

Garrett shot Meggie a wink. "Don't worry, Mums. We'll get your girl here shackled before you know it."

Meggie's hands clenched. How easily her family dismissed her dreams, her ambitions. As if she were some emptyheaded piece to be moved about a chessboard.

Meggie's two older siblings, Samuel and Ross, meandered in. Samuel and Ross were dark where

Garrett and Meggie were fair. But all three of her brothers were over the top attractive, never lacking for feminine company.

Her mother's smile brightened. A genuine smile that stole Meggie's breath, leaving her mother looking as if she floated on clouds.

"Meggie, Mums is right. You shouldn't be singing that jazzy, blues stuff. It's much too serious and provocative."

Meggie's lips tightened as her mother gasped and tapped him on the arm. "Watch your language in mixed company, Samuel."

"You forgot *your grace*." Meggie muttered under her breath, as her sarcasm was never well received. Since Sam had stepped into their father's title some three years past, it seemed her once carefree brother's nature had been buried right along with Papa.

His lips curled. It was a weak smile at best. "Is it time for supper?"

"Yes, we're famished. I've a boxing match to attend, followed by a late night at the theater." Ross never seemed to have an opinion on Meggie's pastime. And at the moment she was profoundly grateful.

"Fifteen minutes. You know the routine. Sherry in the west parlor first. Wash up." Mother shooed them out.

So, why did Mother insist Meggie be the one to marry? This was the twentieth century. Shouldn't *she* be allowed the freedom to act on her hopes and dreams? Samuel, despite being heir to the duke, had studied law. And Garrett had been accepted to a prestigious art school in Paris. He was set to leave just after the wedding. She wrinkled her nose. Ross, however, had no dreams that she could discern. Neither he nor that lazy scoundrel, Percy, he always hung about.

The *gentleman* Mother expected Meggie to marry.

She shuddered. Just the thought of those thin lips coming near her was enough to send her swimming across the Atlantic before Lulu's wedding. She wondered if Percy was privy to her mother's designs. Doubtful, as he and Ross spent most of their time at the racetrack and gambling halls.

All Meggie dreamed her whole life was to sing—and perhaps act, but she was most careful in hiding that particular ambition. Mother would likely perish at the idea.

"Come along, Margaret. Your brothers have plans tonight."

"Yes, Mother," she murmured. Her time would be here soon enough. After all, the wedding was but two days away.

****

Three days later

Meggie couldn't believe it. She, Jessie, and Lady Charlotte Leighton, or Charli as she preferred now that she was embarking on a new life too, were just blocks from walking up the gangplank to freedom. A new start. No more innuendoes from her mother and brothers. If they could just make it to the ship without Charli giving them away.

"Don't look so terrified, Charli." Meggie tried to curb her irritation. Charli couldn't help being so shy. "This is an adventure."

Jessie looped her arm through Charli's. "You'll see. We'll have a grand time. You won't have to marry that stodgy Lord Brigdon. In no time at all you'll be baking, not just the best scones Americans have ever tasted, but the best cakes and pastries for the most lavish parties imaginable."

Meggie had to give Charli credit as she tried smiling through her fear, yet not quite managing the feat.

"I'd just feel better if we'd brought a maid or...or *some* companion." Her voice trembled.

Meggie was careful to keep her tone gentle. "You know we couldn't have dared trusting anyone." They hadn't boarded the *Empress of India* yet. Not all danger lay around the London docks. Samuel's dukedom could stifle their plans as effectively as murder.

Thick fog hovered low in the early gray morning skies. A shudder skittered up Meggie's spine. "Let's hurry," she said, broadening her steps.

Activity picked up the closer they grew to the water, along with the stench. All conversation stalled, and Meggie gripped the handle of her bag as they made their way briskly down the street.

"No!" The voice reached through the dense atmosphere a mere block from their destination.

"Come on, love. I'll be gentle," the words slurred heavily.

Meggie stopped.

"What are you doing?" Charli whispered, her voice as alarmed as the girl Meggie was trying to discern through the soupy sky.

"We have to help," she whispered back.

"Oh, Megs." Jessie rolled her eyes—Meggie could hear it in her voice.

At least Jessie would understand. If Meggie hadn't stopped, she had no doubt Jess would have.

"Let me go. Let. Me. Go." The panicked pitch rose two octaves.

"She's over there," Meggie said. "In that doorway." Meggie lifted her skirt and ran, briefly picturing her mother's horror. Jess and Charli's footsteps pounded behind. She followed the frightened sound, pausing before an abandoned shop.

A tall, lanky man hunched over a girl who tried to crouch away, his hand gripping her breast.

Meggie dropped her valise. The sound carried in the quiet street. "There you are, you silly girl. You scared us, getting separated like that."

Luckily, the girl lost no time in picking up the ruse. She shoved away the brute's hand and brought up her knee. His pained high-pitched cry erupted. To Meggie's surprise, he stumbled, tripping back and falling into a fetal position. A remarkable move, really. Something to ask the cheeky girl about later. Meggie grabbed her hand, snatched up her bag, and took off, the other girls quickly following.

A half block from the ship, Meggie bent to catch her breath, taking in the girl's matted hair and dirt-streaked face.

"Thank you, milady." Her lips trembled though she put up a brave front.

"The name is Meggie. This is Jess—" She indicated with one hand. "And Charli. What's yours?"

"Eliza."

"Well, Eliza. The docks aren't safe for a girl alone. Where are you going?"

"The same as you I imagine."

"You're going to America?" Excitement spilled from Jessie. "That's brilliant."

The girl's gaze flitted away. "Um, uh, y-yes."

Charli frowned. "Alone?"

Meggie narrowed her eyes on her wrinkled frock where something suspicious streaked across the bodice. She prayed it was mud. This girl was in trouble, something Meggie and Jess were no strangers to. "You'll come with us."

"Oh, I couldn't possibly—"

"Of course you can. We need a fourth, besides." That settled, Meggie took her arm once more, leaving Jess to handle Charli. "We're on an adventure."

Chapter One

New York City — Six months later

You don't know what you are saying, *Lady* Margaret."

That hurt. Meggie thought they were better friends than the mere acquaintances Eliza had just insinuated with her formal address. She hadn't been acknowledged as Lady Margaret—in the actual title form—since the day she, Lady Jessica Hatton, Lady Charlotte Leighton and Eliza Gilbert rushed up the gangplank of the *Empress of India* in their haste to depart England over six months ago.

"Eliza, it's after three in the morning, and you have a split lip." Just the sight of Eliza's blood drew the image of Roxy, the girl found murdered in the alley behind Club 501. "I only want to help."

Eliza's greenish-brown eyes flashed. The small, dark beauty mark on her right cheek, standing out, stark, on her pale skin. She marched across the small living area, back and forth, her slender frame seeming unable to convey her anger or worry. Meggie had trouble discerning which.

The tiny flat they shared with Jess and Charli was just that—tiny. Eliza's cropped, chestnut hair in soft finger waves swung with each turn. After her third or fourth turn about the room, she stopped and faced Meggie, hands fisted at her hips. Frustration covered her pert features. And fear, Meggie decided. Deep-reaching fear lay beneath her tough exterior.

Eliza's teeth tugged at her bottom lip—another sign of her angst. "You don't understand, Meggie. I can't let you help. This is *my* predicament, and the cost is too much." Her gaze flew to the window over the small worn sofa, fingers rubbing a pendant she wore around her neck.

Meggie rose from the sofa and grasped her friend's hands. Ice cold. "What is it? I'm certain we can help."

Panic seared her features. "No! You mustn't say anything. To anyone. Promise me, Meggie."

"Of course, I promise. Nothing can be so dire to warrant this sort of distress." She would promise anything to assure Eliza. But Meggie refused to leave her friend in peril without doing *something*. "You must tell me what happened."

Eliza pulled her hands away and went to the grimy window and looked out. "I-I fell," she said.

Meggie could spot a lie a mile away. All her and Jess's nonsense when they were at Mrs. Greensley's School for Young Ladies had taught her well. Like the time they'd stuffed glue in the locks on finals day, then batting their eyes, proclaiming their innocence to Monsieur Duclaric, who'd certainly suspected. Though, eventually, they were found out and reprimanded but good. She still wasn't sure how the French Instructor had discovered the truth to this day.

La! The bunk she and Jess handed Lady Hatton on a regular basis? Why, their half-truths and white lies kept them out of more scrapes than Meggie could count. Yes, for a *Lady* Meggie knew a thing or two about getting in and out of trouble. Eliza was not telling all.

Meggie steeled her resolve despite her heart wanting to relent and let her impatience through. "Blast, it, Eliza. If you don't tell me the truth right this minute then I shall call the constable."

"You wouldn't," she whispered.

"I would. Now, spill."

Eliza turned from the window, eyes glittering with tears. "The-the job with Oscar isn't quite as...as grand as I first believed."

Meggie was afraid of that. "Is he the one who hurt you?"

Eliza lips tightened, but she didn't speak.

Meggie's heart went out to her. "Oh, darling, he is, isn't he? Please, tell me what's going on. I can't help if I don't know." She tugged her friend to the tattered sofa.

Eliza swooped her pocketbook from the cushion and gripped it, knuckles white. She worked the clasp open and closed, over and over, sniffing back tears. "It's fine, truly. I just thought it would be..."

A chill stole up Meggie's spine. "What, Eliza? You never answered my question. *Did* he hurt you?"

"No, it's just as I said." The words came quickly. "I f-fell. I just believed the work—the work would be a little more...glamorous." She glanced out the window again, inhaled deeply, then turned back. Squared her shoulders. "Truly, Meggie. I'm fine. It really is a grand o-opportunity." Her stutter was another sure sign there was more to that story.

"But?"

Eliza gazed out the window again, but Meggie felt certain she saw nothing beyond the sheer curtain. It was dark, and no moon filtered through the thick clouds. Her gaze grew unfocused, as if her mind had drifted elsewhere—somewhere unpleasant. "I didn't realize I would be expected to…" She took another deep breath. "…to…to date…some of the guests." The words ended on a whisper and her gaze fell to the purse in her lap. She seemed surprised to see it there.

"Date," Meggie repeated slowly. "Eliza, you're not—what I mean is, you aren't—" The ghastly thought stuck in her throat, but she forged on. "—you haven't been—" She inhaled deeply. "Are you—*prostituting* yourself?" The last came out in a horrified whisper.

Eliza's hazel eyes darkened with anger. She shot to her feet, knocking her pocketbook to the floor. "Of course not! How dare you suggest such a thing."

Meggie dropped to the floor to help gather—she picked up a fat wad of bills, looked up at Eliza, whose already pale face turned bloodless. Meggie stood slowly and held the money in her outstretched palm. Eliza snatched away the wad and squatted to swoop up the rest of the contents that had spilled.

"It—it's my pay for last week," Eliza mumbled, standing.

Shock then certainty ricocheted through Meggie. She'd never seen so much cash. "Oh, Eliza." She took her friend's cold hands in hers, forced her to meet her eyes. "I know there is more going on than you are sharing." Meggie pulled herself up, infused her voice with her usual confidence. "You must leave his employ immediately. We'll help you. All of us. Charli, Jess, and I, until you find some other position."

The tears shimmering in her eyes broke Meggie's heart. "You've done so much for me already. I'm the daughter of a *housekeeper,* Meggie. The three of you—you're ladies. You've taken me in, helped pay my way." She shook her head, and the tears slid down her cheeks. "How can I bear not doing my part?" She dashed them away, drew in an audible breath, and dropped her eyes. "Besides, I-I can't just…leave any time I choose."

"Don't be ridiculous. Of course you can. He doesn't *own* you." Meggie was furious. How dare Mr. Cummings treat one of Meggie's friends like a common…common harlot!

Eliza shrugged away, shoulders hunched, looked out at the dark night again. "Actually, he does. I…I signed a contract. I'm obligated to remain for two years. Unless I can pay the termination fee." She turned back to Meggie, her bottom lip trembling.

The sight incited Meggie further. "That's bunk, Eliza. The man is treating you like a slave." This is what came for people who were taught no better than to believe they should be indentured for life. Meggie pulled back her shoulders and lifted her chin. "It's probably less trouble to just pay his damned extortion fees. All of us will chip in, and with the funds you have there…" Meg nodded toward her pocketbook. "How much is the scoundrel demanding?"

Eliza grimaced, tiny lines appearing around her lips. "A thousand dollars."

Meggie fell back onto the sofa, feeling faint. "A-a thousand?"

****

Club 501 was hopping. The tucked-away speakeasy on the lower end of Broadway in Manhattan with its soft ambience in muted gold lighting splayed against dark grained wood was most elegant. Flappers and socialites decorated the arms of dapper young men. A crowd of aristocrats, upper echelons, and a theater throng, all of which had hit the doors less than an hour ago. A small grin touched her. If only her mother and brothers could see her now. Not everyone in this speakeasy was here just for the hooch. They'd come to see her too. Take that lovely Harry Dempsey for example. He sat at his regular corner table barely drinking at all. Eyes the color of whiskey with depths of promised secrets that had her crooning her deepest desires in his direction.

Meggie let out a stream of air, her feet already aching at their first break of the night. "I'll be back in a jiff, Freddie," she said to the young trumpet player. She hurried to the bar and called out, "Ginger ale, Ira."

Worry gripped her. She had to somehow find a way to help Eliza. Though Jess, Charli, and Meggie had found Eliza near on the London docks, there was a certain innocence about her that drew men in her direction. Men like that awful Oscar Cummings. Meggie pushed her way through the crowd to the ladies' room. Not an easy task, navigating such a mob.

She reached for the handle but was snagged by the waist.

"Where's you headed, doll face?" Gin-saturated stench that could likely take out half the crowd as quick as a round from Machine Gun Kelly's chopper hit her nostrils.

Something about Joey Keagan raised the fine hairs at her nape. The weasel's short black hair was parted on one side and slicked down. Sure, some might find him attractive enough, but Meggie thought him a bit off. Like tonight, wearing knickers that fell just below his knees, but the perfect match between his red and green argyle socks and sweater were a bit of a stretch.

Well, Christmas was but a month or so away…

She shoved against his chest and stepped back. "Retiring room, Joey." Confusion covered his drunk-filled gaze before understanding set in. She rolled her eyes.

"Ah, the john." He leaned in and licked the lobe of her ear. She gasped but he spoke over it. "I'll bet the swells never tire of that purty English lilt you sprout. Go on then. I'll be here waitin' for you when you come back."

"Perfect," she muttered under her breath, making her escape. Despite the speakeasy clientele being upscale, there were still the creepers. Meggie cringed at her snobbish thoughts. Unlike her mother's beliefs, class was something a person should be able to earn. Not be handed to them due to their circumstances of birth. Just look at Percy.

She took care of business quickly, scrubbing away the touch of Joey's disgusting thin lips, and shuddered. It would be a cold day in hell before that bastard touched her again. She'd flatten the sap, just see if she didn't.

Her reflection in the mirror showed her blonde curls a little worse for wear, so she fluffed them up. The new sleeked down styles didn't flatter her heart-shaped face in the least. Not that it mattered. She wore her hair to her shoulders—a style that would send her mother into an apoplectic fit—in curls that acted of their own accord. She reapplied her red lip-stain, carefully maintaining the Cupid's bow effect. After adjusting her dress, straightening her stockings, pinching her cheeks—until surely, she'd dawdled long enough to outwait Joey-the creep-Keagan, she went to the door and peered out, looking both left then right.

Relief rushed out in a quick breath. Joey was nowhere in sight. The club crowd was thicker. The shows in Times Square must have let out, and patrons kept piling in. She edged her way to the bar for her ginger-ale. Before she made it, some corked sot plowed into her, upsetting her balance in her uncomfortable T-strap pumps. The drunk's hands closed around her upper arms from behind. Joey's nasally pitch sounded in her ear. "What's eatin' you, doll face?"

Hysteria clogged her throat with an onslaught of nausea as Joey's gin-reeked breath reached her nostrils. Another shudder skittered up her spine. She'd thought him nice enough as blokes went, but that sentimentality flew away along with her calm demeanor as she struggled against his tightening grip.

Her glance snapped to the corner, to Harry Dempsey's regular spot. Empty.

He was always there when the set started. Not only did his tranquility center her before each performance, and she suspected he had a hand in keeping the Joey Keagan's at bay, she was utterly and completely enthralled with him. But where was he when she needed him?

She squelched her panic, swallowed her screams. "You shouldn't call me that." Joey was always tossing out the odd innuendo she rarely understood.

He spun her around, his smug grin shifting her panic into fury.

"What makes you think something is 'eating me'?" The leer he turned on her set her cheeks aflame. "Let go of me."

"Come on, doll. You don't mean it." Joey's dark brown eyes softened with desire. He leaned in, breathed on her neck. "We'll make a great team. With your body and my smarts, we can't lose."

He couldn't possibly mean—embarrassment flooded her. Was this what happened to Eliza? Meggie brought her hands up and shoved, but his hold firmed, and he nipped her neck. If he were a poisonous viper she'd be dead. "I'll pass, thank you."

He licked the place he bit, making her skin crawl. "Come on, doll. Just think of it. We could make hundreds, thousands—"

Alarm skittered up her spine. She slammed the pointed heel of her shoe onto his foot. His arms dropped so suddenly she flailed back. A push, then drunken slur "hey, watch it" sounded behind. The sot managed to right her, and she grabbed the opportunity, slipping through a paneled door and ran. She flew past stacked boxes of crates, past darkened rooms through a winding hallway that made her dizzy then breathless. She paused at a staircase leading up and listened for him.

Heavy footsteps echoed on the clapboards, and she darted up the stairs of Club 501's inner sanctum to another hallway with very little light guiding her path.

The corridor seemed eerily quiet compared to the mob in the club. Meggie clung to the wall, cognizant of the danger she'd just put herself in. Thoughts of that dead girl, Roxy, raced through her head with startling clarity. Just over a week ago. Had she been dragged through these very halls first? Fear spiked her pulse along with the sound of the increasing footsteps. She spotted a light ahead and increased her pace.

Meggie paused outside a darkened doorway and slipped off her heels, then tip-toed by. All she could see was the back of Butch Weaver's shiny bald head, hunched over, counting a stack of bills that took her breath away.

Money that could help Eliza. Where had it all come from? Butch murmured something to someone she couldn't see. Joey's footsteps pounded the wood planks. Meggie slipped past the office to the next door and twisted the knob. Locked.

She hurried on. A second later she stumbled into the large open area of an abandoned warehouse. She glanced around and spotted several stacked casks lining the end of the hallway near open doors where a large truck was backed in.

Meggie ran over and squeezed between the first two casks she could fit between, certain her red dress rivaled a beacon. She would leave screaming for help as the last option. Nothing irritated her more than having to shriek for help. Having three brothers did that to a girl.

She plastered against the large barrels just as Joey filed into view. She held her breath.

"Come on, doll," Joey called softly.

The bastard. How she wished it had been his face she'd stomped instead of his foot. She'd rub his nose in his own blood. Gads, her brother always accused her of being somewhat more bloodthirsty than the norm.

Meggie's heart pounded so hard it vibrated through her spine to the wood barrels at her back. The breeze whipped through the casks, stirring her skirt. She tried to snatch it back, but it billowed out like a cape before an enraged bull.

Joey's maniacal chuckle chilled her inside out, his steps gliding toward her. Now she was well and truly trapped.

"Keagan. What the fuck are you doing back here?" the dark, growling voice demanded.

Meggie leaned forward. The light was too dim to make out the expression behind that deep pitch, but not the sound. Listening to him left her feeling alive, tingling from head to toe. Its timbre coursed through her the same as it had since the first night she'd invited herself to his table and sat down.

From his private corner, he'd watched her each night, sipping on his illegal whiskey, piercing her with eyes that matched his drink. Never having more than one, and always alone except for times she would meander over and tease a smile from those firm lips.

When the music hit her veins, the words that flowed from her mouth were directed to him. No wonder his regular seat was empty. Harry Dempsey must have been the man with whom Butch was speaking.

"Dempsey." Joey's tone held an edge of fear. "The…uh…dame took a wrong turn."

Harry moved in her direction, his gait slow, deliberate, until he stood within touching distance. "Dame?" That single word rang through the abandoned space.

Oh no. Meggie launched herself from her hiding place and threw her arms about Harry's neck. Locked in his muscular embrace, she rested her chin on his shoulder. His arms tightened around her. "Oh, Harry. I came as fast as I could. Just as we'd planned." The words she'd intended to carry came out breathless.

"Fast, huh?" The whisper was against her ear where no one else could hear, raised goose prickles over her entire body. "Guess I'll have to do something about that." He lifted his head. "What are you doing with *my* girl, Joe?"

Joey's hands flew into the air, indicating his surrender. "Sorry, Dempsey. Had no idea she was anyone's quiff—"

Meggie's cheeks burned, and she stiffened at the insult. Harry's one arm gripped her closer. The other shot up, jerking her body like a rag doll. She couldn't see Harry's face with her own now buried in his neck, but she felt the corded muscles contract. A split second later, a sickening crunch sounded followed by a deathlike groan.

Meggie let out her breath and felt a slight shudder ripple through her defender.

"What's going on here?" Butch demanded. "You know this part of the club is off limits, Miss Montley."

Meggie lifted her head from Harry's shoulder and looked into his eyes.

"I requested Lady Margaret's assistance." Harry's gaze never wavered from her.

Meggie's voice caught in her throat. She couldn't have spoken to save her life.

"You there," Butch barked. "Drag this piece of shit out back."

Meggie dared a peek and saw Joey Keagan's limp body being hauled out by the arms, legs dragging the ground, by two huge ruffians. She turned back to Harry where a slight sardonic curl lifted his lips.

"Cash or check, doll?" he said.

She swallowed. "W-what?"

He chuckled, setting her cheeks aflame. "A kiss now or later," he said for her ears only.

Meggie wet her lips before answering. "Ch-check," she stammered out in a husky whisper.

"Check, it is." He loosened his hold, and Meggie slid down his hard body. When her feet touched the floor she realized she still clutched her shoes by the straps.

Harry, tall, deliciously handsome, quietly strong was the most tempting of men. She met those whiskey-colored eyes wanting to drown in them.

He set her away from him and stepped back. "Isn't your set about to reconvene, Lady Margaret?" His serious tone belied the twinkle of mischief she was certain she detected.

Meggie started. "Oh, yes. Yes, it is." She backed away, taking in her surroundings. The overhead door open to the club's alley. The large delivery trailer set for loading or unloading, she couldn't discern which. Two more gruff men guarded more barrels as the original two skirted by lugging Joey's unconscious form. Hooch. Heaps of it if she wasn't mistaken.

As she moved into the darkened hall Harry's voice went hard, sending a shiver up her spine. "We need another man, Weaver. Keagan's useless to us now." He flicked his wrist, shaking out his hand that flattened that slime Joey Keagan.

"Yeah, yeah. I'll have someone meet you out back. Tomorrow night. Three A.M."

Meggie cast one last glance to the office where she'd seen all the money stacked on the desk. After shaking her head, she turned and fled the way she'd come.

****

Harold Evan Dempsey narrowed his eyes on the provocative English miss's exit and groaned. Meggie Montley was up to something. It wasn't Prohibition or Legs Diamond that was likely to kill him. That honor went to the sweetly curvaceous Lady Margaret.

That little maneuver she'd just pulled triggered a desperate need burning through him. He could still feel her breath on his neck, smell the faint scent of roses he'd learned to crave.

Every Friday and Saturday night the past few months when he'd first heard her sing at L'Argent, and now Club 501, he nursed his single whiskey and reveled in the sultry tones that struck something he'd long believed dead deep in his chest. His lust for her platinum locks and voluptuous body were the reasons behind his bloodshot eyes and worn-out demeanor. And Harry wasn't a man easily led by the head in his pants.

No, it was Meggie Montley's joy for life, that sparkle in her eyes and small smile that made a man forget his father and brother were lost to him forever. Murdered.

Her spare time spent at his table, night after night, teasing him slowly back to life. God, how he wanted her. He wanted her to infuse him with her passion. If he didn't have her soon, he was sure he'd self-combust. Something he knew he'd be a fool to attempt. Harry ran a hand through his hair, frustrated.

How had he wound up appointing himself her personal guardian angel? Devil, more like. But he couldn't seem to help himself from keeping a close eye on the crowd any given night, assuring her safety. But tonight something had gone terribly wrong.

Apparently, he and Frank Markov were due for some words. Joey Keagan shouldn't have even been in the club. The bastard should have been out back, waiting on the arrival of the latest rum shipment. His lip curled involuntarily, and he flexed his hand. The one now sporting torn skin and Keagan's blood. Satisfaction surged through his veins. Keagan was a done deal. If Harry saw him again, he'd probably kill him.

"What the hell was that all about?" Butch demanded.

"Hell if I know," Harry muttered under his breath.

"Let's get this shit finished up before Markov comes back here demanding answers. And keep your girlfriend out front where she belongs."

Harry couldn't agree more and followed the homely bookkeeper back into the office determined to wrap up the evening's business. Meggie Montley had another set left for the evening's entertainment, and Harry had no intention of missing it.

Chapter Two

The next morning Meggie stretched and glanced over at Jessie's bed and smiled. It was a jumbled mess as usual. The scent of fresh scones brought her fully awake. Breakfast may come too early in the cramped quarters of the Gables Boardinghouse flat she shared with Jessica, Charli, and Eliza, but thank heavens for Charli's bake house dreams.

Eliza. Meggie jumped out of bed and darted for the small kitchen. Charli and Jessie sat at the small round table perusing the *New York World*, each holding their coffee, nibbling on Charli's latest concoction. "Um—" Meggie started.

"Tally ho, Megs. Coffee's on, and Charli's outdone herself. Lemon and basil today." Jess pointed to the tiny counter without lifting her head from the newspaper she was devouring.

"They smell wonderful, Charli. And, Jess, "Tally ho" is a ridiculous word. Remember my Uncle Bartie?"

"Ah, yes. The uncle whose disgusting moose head hung over the hearth. As I recall we managed to deface it one Christmas and barely escaped with our hides intact."

"Yes, that's the one. His favorite greeting was—"

"Tally ho," she and Jess said unanimously. Jess giggled. "You make a good argument."

Meggie reached over the sink and pulled out a cup. "Eliza still sleeping?" She kept the question casual.

Charli glanced up. "No, her bed is made. I'm worried for her. I think she might have a new beau." She frowned. "She shouldn't be staying overnight with him."

Not good news. Damn Eliza for her silly gag order. Armed with coffee, Meggie went to the small, rickety table and sat. "Can we talk?" She tipped a spoon of sugar into her cup.

Jessie looked up quickly. "Is something wrong, Meggie?" Her question drew Charli's attention.

Meggie stared down into her cup. "Yes. I—" She sucked in a deep breath. "I-I'm concerned about my finances."

Jessie laughed. A tinkling, feminine sound that she'd shared their whole life. One that meant she believed nothing bad could happen. Life meant laughter. In the old days, at least. If only that were the case now.

"Is that all?" Jessie shook her head. "Darling." She snatched the section of the paper Charli was reading and flipped to the entertainment section. Slamming it down, she turned it to Meggie with one perfectly manicured nail covering the headline. "*You* are a sensation. Well on your way."

Meggie frowned. "On my way to what?"

Jessie grabbed the paper and read. "A rising new star is on the horizon. Lady Margaret will make your heart weep with those husky, sultry tones of hers. Small appearances in the Broadway productions of *The School of Scandal* and *Betty, Be Good* have not deterred this deliciously attractive young *lady* from singing gigs around Greater Manhattan. No. These bit-parts Lady Margaret is accruing seem to be serving her needs well.

Mark my words, ladies and gents, you would do wise in catching this rising star—if you can."

"Let me see that." Meggie's breath caught and she snatched it back.

"And that's not all," Jessie said smugly. "Paul Whiteman was at Club 501 last night with some new composer. Gershwin something or other."

"Paul Whiteman?" she squeaked.

"Do you know of him?"

"Know him? Know him! They refer to him as the King of Jazz. Dear God. He heard *me*? The man played at Aeolian Hall last year. I heard tell he's receiving five thousand dollars for a single broadcast." She felt faint and fanned herself with the paper. The one small broadcast with Bernie and Edison at WHN had netted her nothing. Of course, she hadn't cared. She was on the radio. But now…she needed money, fast.

"May I have my paper back, please?" Charli shot them a pointed look. Meggie thrust it at her.

"Are you singing tonight?" Jessie asked.

"No. Alyce Kutcher is the featured guest." Meggie rolled her eyes, disgusted.

Jessie laughed. "Don't they refer to her as 'The Kitchen'?" Charli covered a fit of giggles behind a string of coughs. "She's awful. How in Hades did she get in with Bernie's little orchestra?"

Meggie snorted. "You have to ask?" She jumped up from the table, knocking her coffee cup askew, barely saving the teetering cup from disaster.

"Careful." Jessie smirked. "See? Soon, you'll be *rolling* in the dough."

They'd strayed way off topic. Like finding Eliza before she turned Dumb Dora on them and went and did some John, *if she hadn't already*. Meggie curled her hand and studied her painted nails. "Where…um…do you suppose Eliza is this early?"

"I'm sure I don't know." Jess, already distracted by her portion of the paper, had her head down.

Meggie couldn't very well tell her Eliza didn't have time to wait for Meggie to become a star. She let out a frustrated sigh. "I'm going to shower. I have errands to run." *Like locating their missing friend.*

"Congratulations, Lady Margaret," Charli said.

Meggie dipped a useless curtsey, since neither saw her, and escaped to her room.

Chapter Three

The dread in Harry's gut was not new. He pushed open the door to his mother's quaint house in Queens where a mixture of gin and stale cigarettes greeted him. And, thankfully, coffee. He stepped over litter that cluttered the path to the kitchen. "Hey, Ma. Is there enough for me?"

Her smoke-rasped cackle barked in what he decided was a yes then cascaded into an emphysemic fit. "Git me that bottle," she demanded between hacks, pointing to a silver flask next to the stove. Disheveled and frayed gray hair hid her aged face as she hunched over today's copy of the *World*.

Repressed fury roiled deep in his belly and rose like bile. He pushed it back and snatched up the flask. Vile stuff. Pa's and Lewis's murders had sent her spiraling into oblivion. His idea bank in helping Ma was depleted. The grip on his own control was taut.

"What are you reading, Ma?" He set the bottle on the table. He snatched up her cup and turned to fill both.

She pulled a long swig from the flask and let out a satisfied sigh. A crooked index finger tapped the paper. "That shoulda' been me," she huffed. "I was at the top of my game 'fore yer daddy stole my career."

Harry set fresh coffee in front of her and leaned in to see what she was rattling on about. The first few words had him biting back a groan. *A rising new star is on the horizon. Lady Margaret...*

"I thought you were happy, Ma," Harry said quietly.

But she was on her rant, and there was nothing that could stop her. "I coulda' been a star. I was on the brink." Tears filled her eyes. He left us destitute. Destitute, I tell ya."

Her tears always did him in. Harry turned away.

He didn't need a reminder that Meggie Montley was on the brink of taking the world by storm. He'd known it the first time he'd heard her sing. When her voice transitioned into that seductive contralto, it was like she'd melded through to his bones...his soul.

He had no business fantasizing about her. He was a business owner out for justice, and she was young, about to hit her prime. Disgusted at the constant unrealistic fantasies, he flipped on the faucet, surprised at the slight tremble in his hand.

Determined to shove away such distraction, he concentrated on the matter at hand and surveyed the tiny kitchen. Dishes covered the sink and countertops. He hadn't been home in two weeks. "Ma, when's the last time you ate, huh?"

"Yesterday."

Yesterday. He snatched up a dish towel, went to the back porch, and opened the icebox. The ice had long since melted. He pulled out a jug of milk and sniffed. The sour odor hit his nose with a vengeance. He jerked his head back, banging it against the doorframe. Moldy cheese and some kind of vegetable he couldn't make out were the only other items in the box. *Hell.*

"Yoo whoo."

Harry glanced up. Dixie—or doxy as he'd never been able to resist referring to her—Ward lifted one hand in greeting and started across the yard. Her short, bright red hair was plastered in waves against her head, full hips squeezed into a tight skirt, generous breasts bouncing, unconfined. The woman had less subtlety than the lighted signs on Broadway.

"Hello, Harry. How is that sweet mama of yours today?" She held up a covered dish. "I brought her some lunch."

"Much thanks, Dox—er, Miss Ward." Her anxiousness in asking after his ma was suspect. He doubted she'd been by since the last time he'd made it home. He swallowed a muttered oath. It wasn't Doxy's place to feed Ma. "Would you care for coffee?"

"Oh, that sounds lovely." One of those large breasts brushed his arm. It did nothing for him. Just sent his thoughts spiraling to Margaret Montley and that red dress she'd performed in the night before. How she'd clung to him in the darkened depths of Club 501, breaths rapid and unsteady when she'd thrown herself in his arms. Then slid down his body, reminding him just how long it had been since he'd been with a woman.

Shaking his head, he stepped back, allowing Doxy through the door.

"Hello, Dixie," Ma said. "I see you done cornered Harry." Dixie's face turned as red as her hair which sent his mother into another fit of hacks.

Harry got her some water and set it on the table, retrieving the flask at the same time. He glanced at her coffee. Full. "Ma. Miss Ward brought you lunch."

His mother wisely said nothing. She rose from the table and went through to the living room.

Doxy, however, planted herself at the table, preparing for a long visit it appeared, and glanced over the paper. Harry ignored her and started on the dishes.

"We miss you around these parts, Harry." Her husky tones told him exactly what she missed. He and Dixie had had a thing way back. Years back.

He just grunted.

"Oh, Harry." Her shrill laugh sounded like rusty nails on a sheet of metal.

"Been pretty busy with the marina since Pa and Lewis…" His voice trailed.

It took damn near an hour to get Doxy-Dixie to leave. Harry made a trip to the market, loaded up the ice box with fresh ice, and fixed Ma a few meals to last her a couple of days. Two weeks was too long between visits home.

He woke her from a long nap and sat at the table, making her eat at least half of what he'd put on her plate. Still, Lady Margaret devoured every thought. With an index finger he slid the *World* over and, unable to resist, read the article that spelled out reason after reason why Harry should stay far, far away from Lady Margaret Montley.

She wasn't singing that night, but on her off nights she occasionally showed up at Club 501 with her friend Jessica Hatton.

Thirty minutes later, Harry was back on the subway bound for Manhattan.

Chapter Four

Meggie swiped the finishing touch of paint across her lips then checked her appearance in the full-length glass on the back of the bathroom door. Her knee-length dress of black crepe accentuated her waistline perfectly. She abhorred those sacks the flappers were wearing these days. She spun in a circle then drifted into the kitchenette where the entertainment section of the newspaper still lay open to the article depicting her future. She picked it up, smiling. But worry for Eliza seeped in, and she dropped the paper.

Eliza hadn't returned to the flat before Charli left for her shift at Club 501 hours ago, and Jessie was off scooping the lead for her next big story. Meggie shuddered, praying Eliza didn't end up found hidden somewhere in a clump of debris no better than tossed out garbage like Roxy.

Blast it, where *was* Eliza? She hadn't been accounted for all day. Meggie had tried searching for her near the sewing factory, then the coffee shop where the four sometimes met on the rare occasion their schedules allowed. Meggie glanced at the wall clock in the kitchen. Nine o'clock.

Waiting around an empty flat for Eliza was doing no one any good. She grabbed her used ermine wrap and matching clutch then darted out the door just in time to see the backside of the trolley whipping around the corner. She let out a frustrated sigh. The evening was balmy enough for her six-block walk. She just didn't fancy the streets off Broadway where there were very few streetlamps. Any tiny noise made her jump, reminding her of Roxy's unfortunate end.

A block from Club 501 Meggie caught sight of a tall attractive man assisting Eliza from a newer Model T. Meggie sagged, relieved. He gripped her friend by the chin and planted a facer on her. How exciting! Eliza *did* have a new beau. Everything was fine. In the morning, Eliza would downplay her romantic adventures between the four of them over fresh baked scones and coffee.

Meggie started forward. The man grinded himself against Eliza—in plain sight of anyone, then grabbed her breast and squeezed. Meggie froze as he kissed her again, hard, before striding to the driver's side of the auto. He climbed in, slammed the door, and drove off without so much as a wave in Eliza's direction.

How could Eliza allow him to treat her like that on the street like a common…common harlot…or—

Eliza wiped her mouth with her forearm, her eyes wild.

"Eliza," Meggie called out.

Eliza spun.

"*He's* not your new beau, is he?" Meggie demanded.

Tears filled Eliza's eyes. She stood stockstill, hands clenched at her side.

"Tell me," Meggie pleaded. "I wish to help. But I can't if you aren't honest with me."

"I don't know what to do," Eliza cried. "I promised my mum."

"Promised your mum what?"

"That I wouldn't be any man's—" She choked, unable to finish.

"You aren't." Meggie took her by the arms and shook her. She pulled in a deep breath.

Eliza shrugged from Meggie's hold, drew her shoulders back and looked around, before meeting Meggie's gaze. "What am I to do?" Her voice was low and shaking. "A thousand dollars is an impossible amount."

Meggie swallowed. That was indeed a fortune. She reached again for one of Eliza's fisted hands. "I'll…uh, admit the cost is astronomical. But surely there's a way. Between Jessie, Charli, and me—"

Eliza jerked her hands away. "No! You mustn't tell anyone. You promised me, Meggie."

"But Eliza—"

"No! No. I'll work this out on my own." Eliza turned and disappeared down the stone stairs to the entrance of the club, an ominous silence filling the atmosphere with her departure.

"How, Eliza?" Meggie whispered to the night air. *One thousand dollars.* How on earth could they come up with that kind of blunt? The thought crossed her mind to contact Sam, but she tossed that away just as quickly. Sam would certainly have helped before, but Papa's death had turned her eldest brother into a stodgy old man by the day of the funeral. Lady Hatton would help. She was always generous, always willing to assist those less fortunate. But Lady Hatton posed two problems. The fact of the matter was that Jess, Charli, and Meggie had run away, and Lady Hatton was sure to tell Meggie's own mother. More importantly, if Eliza caught wind of Meggie going to Jessie's mother, Eliza might choose to disappear.

Meggie turned in a slow circle at a loss. There must be *something* she could do to raise some money. Damn Eliza's silly promise in not letting Meggie ask for help. Stacks and stacks of crates flashed through her mind, followed by the stacks of cash Butch had been counting. There must be lots of money to be made. But how? How could she, a mere woman—*Wait*. Wasn't Butch sending someone to help Harry with a shipment of illegal liquor?

She had friends. Lots of friends. Actor friends, costume friends, *make-up artist friends*. Eliza might keep her from telling anyone the real issue, but there were other ways to get help. Meggie spun around and marched down the street. Straight to Broadway.

****

Harry leaned against the wall near his regular table, one arm folded across his chest and sipped at his single whiskey, glaring at Theodore Clifford. Someone should shoot the bastard for some of the items the man stretched the truth for in his sensationalistic approach to news story-writing.

Harry glanced at his watch, disappointed. Eleven-thirty, and no sign of Meggie Montley. He'd caught sight of one of her roommates over an hour ago. She'd looked upset, but Vince Taggart swooped in, and Harry turned his attention back to the entertainment. Alyce Kutcher. The woman had nothing on Lady Margaret. He tuned her out, morosely, watching newcomers stream in. Once the theaters let out, there wouldn't an inch in the place to maneuver about. The joint would be packed despite its size.

"Hey, Harry." The come-hither pitch could barely be heard above the hum of the crowd.

"Alyce." He nodded once in her direction.

"I finish up at one. What do you say we meet right after?"

Harry's gaze roved over her short, dark, wavy hair, to blood red lips that were too thin for his tastes. A myriad of necklaces were draped around her neck designed to draw the eye to an impressive cleavage. He lifted his drink and sipped. "I'm working, doll. Sorry."

She leaned in, and her voice dipped into a husky timbre. "Then how about you and me for ten minutes? Care to meet in the Green Room?"

He couldn't help it. He laughed and shook his head. The Kitchen never did understand the word no.

Chapter Five

"What do you think, Georgie? Will I pass?" Meggie stared at her reflection in the mirror, stunned by the transformation. She wrinkled her nose. "This mustache tickles. How do men stand it?"

Georgie, a tall, slender make-up artist she knew from *Betty, Be Good* at *The Globe,* wore his black hair slicked back. "It's a sign of masculinity, dear. Besides it's the best way to hide your delicate features. It's not easy turning a beautiful, rising star into a bootlegging thug. Now, stand still. Are the bindings too tight?"

"Unbearable," she muttered, feeling the heat crawl up her neck.

"Don't worry. As soon as I adjust the suspenders, we'll add a jacket. Just don't take it off. Anyone with eyes could spot there's more there than should be for a young, thin man." Georgie turned her and adjusted the straps that were designed to hold up her knickers.

"These trousers seem a bit short," she said.

"That's the style. The boys are quite proud of their silly argyle socks." He spun her about again and knotted the necktie.

Meggie slipped on the jacket then studied the overall package in the mirror.

"Really, darling, we should cut your hair." She watched him eye the smoothed back version tied at the nape of her neck with anticipation.

"Forget it. It's bad enough that we put this brown rinse on it. You're certain it will wash out after a day or two?" Her voice trembled.

Georgie chuckled. "Don't cry. That emasculates the entire picture of what we are trying to portray." He grabbed her hand then frowned. "We'll have to cut your nails."

Meggie groaned. "Gloves. I'll wear gloves." From the corner of her eye, she caught the time on Georgie's desk clock. "Good heavens, is that right?"

"Two fifteen? I'm afraid so, love." He held out a pageboy cap and a pair of brown gloves.

"Blast." She snatched both items from him. "I've got to go."

With a quick hug, Meggie scrambled out the door. After a colossal failure at flagging down a cab she began the brisk walk to Club 501, running over the conversation between Harry and Butch the night before.

The truck was scheduled for three A.M., which should give her plenty of time to get to the alley and hang back. *The alley in which Roxy was found, dead.* She didn't know what she would do if Joey's replacement beat her there. Bopping him on the head was an option, she supposed, scanning the ground for a weapon. *Weapon.* She needed a weapon. This hair-brained scheme was certain to get her killed. If not this one, the next. How did she keep ending up in these foolish situations time and again?

Shadows loomed, and every so often a match struck, and the red-tipped glow of a cigarette illuminated a face. Meggie pulled a deep breath to steady her jumpy nerves. Adapted her mind into her stage persona mode. Forced a casual stride. It occurred and surprised her in how comfortable the oxford-styled uppers were compared to the toe-choking heels she wore nightly. She shoved her hands deep into the pockets of her tweed coat.

The closer she grew to Club 501 the tighter her stomach knotted. She reached the block and crept around the building, nerves taut as the gory details relayed by Jess and Charli in her head like the film with Ramon Navarro she and Jess had seen. Only the scene in her head appeared in vivid colors. The most dominant being red.

Fingers clenched to stop their trembling, she hugged the side of the building. Nothing.

She didn't know whether to be relieved or furious after all of her and Georgie's painstaking efforts.

Just as she let out a dejected sigh, a truck rolled in with the lights cut. Meggie sank to the ground behind a row of bushes and watched. An overhead door to Club 501 raised and Butch hurried out, Harry following in his more deliberate gait. A hundred bats flew into motion deep within her abdomen. Could she do this? *Eliza. Eliza needs help.*

Meggie was an actress, wasn't she? An accomplished actress. Newspaper articles attested her acclaim, and this was her most important role to date. Rising to her feet, she squared her shoulders.

"Where the fuck is he?" Harry demanded. Meggie fought an urge to run the opposite direction. "We need another man."

"He'll be here. He'll be here," Butch snapped.

"What the hell is his name?"

Butch barked out a laugh. "What the hell's wrong with you, Harry? I've never seen you this out of sorts.

Ah, need a boff, do ya? I saw you talking to Alyce. I'm pretty sure—"

Meggie cringed. Did Harry have a thing for "The Kitchen"?

"That's enough," Harry growled. "His name."

"Sid. Flash is sending him over. Keep an eye out for him. I'll be in the office if you need me." Butch slipped inside.

This was it. Now or never. Meggie pulled her cap down over her brow and stepped from her hidden place among the bushes.

"Sid? 'Bout damn time," Harry said. "Let's go."

With a steady pace, Meggie edged her way to Harry, knees threatening to give way. Harry's mood kept her quiet and watchful. With the grace of a mountain lion, he leaped up in the bed of the truck. Her first real attack of fear slammed her when she gaged the height at which she'd need to somehow maneuver *and* appear masculine. She stole a glance at Harry, who watched her with curled lips. She threw out a gloved hand. The curled lip shifted to a disgusted smirk, but with a grunt he hauled her up. Just like the Harry she believed him to be.

He banged on the ceiling, and the truck jerked into motion, tossing her to the straw-covered floor.

****

Lightweight. Harry turned his gaze out to the street. The boy couldn't have been more than sixteen, though that mustache was pretty full for one so young and slight. "You been doing this long, Sid?" His shirt was too damned white.

The kid just grunted, leaned back, and pulled his cap farther over his face.

Harry decided to do the same. No sense wasting unnecessary words. These weren't the assignments where a man made lifelong friends. Pelham was an hour's drive. They'd catch the boat out to the Long Island Sound. Hell, he'd be lucky to make it home by six.

The depth of night meant less traffic and faster time. The usual sixty-minute trek took forty-five. The truck lurched to a stop, and Harry jumped out. The kid attempted the same, barely avoiding a conk on his head but for Harry's grab on his arm. The maneuver sent his cap flailing. Jesus, the kid needed food, he had no muscle.

Harry narrowed his eyes on the brown, lackluster hair tied back with a black strap. Sid jerked his arm from Harry's hold and swooped his cap from the ground.

A whiff of something vaguely familiar—soft and floral, flowers of the hothouse variety, tingled his nostrils. A not-so-good feeling started deep in Harry's gut. The kid jammed his cap on his head, stepping back. *Roses.*

"Meggie," he whispered harshly.

The kid whipped his head around, facing him, mustache slightly off center. Angled like the Leaning Tower of Pisa.

"What the fu—" He stopped himself from letting his vulgar language touch such delicate ears.

"Boat's ready for you, cap'n."

Harry jerked ramrod straight. "Give us a minute, Marco."

"Sure thing, cap'n, but time's a wastin', they won't give you too long. You know the score."

"Yeah, yeah. I said a minute," he growled. He turned back to his companion, fury surging through his veins. "What the hell do you think you're doing?" He kept his voice to a whisper. The danger temperature just hit the hundred mark.

Her brilliant eyes flashed. "I need blunt. And this seemed the quickest way to obtain it." Her clipped British accent was low but definitely the same distinct voice that haunted his dreams night after night.

"The butt of a cigar? What the hell are you talking about?" The effort to keep his voice low was building the pressure in his skull.

"Money. Cash. Currency," she said just as hotly.

"For what!"

"For—" She stopped, mouth gaping. It snapped shut. "Never you mind—*cap'n*—I-I have my reasons."

"I'll give you the God damned money. How much?" He glanced over his shoulder.

A figure stood on the bow of the boat. "What's the hold up, cap'n? Time's a'wastin'."

She followed his gaze. "One thousand dollars."

"One thous—are you out of your fuc—" Harry pulled himself up. "What the hell for?"

"Keep your voice down." She raised herself up. She looked magnificent, despite the crooked mustache. Only where the hell were her curves?

"What for?"

Her gaze dropped to her feet. "I can't say."

"God almighty. Do you know what kind of people these are? What kind of danger you're putting yourself in? *Me* in?"

That jerked her head up.

"These men don't give a shit whether you are the biggest star on the Silver Screen or the lowest life in the subway."

"I-I'm sorry." Tears glinted on her lashes.

"Oh, for God's sake. You'll damn sure give us away if you blubber like a girl." He squinted out in dark. "I can't very well leave you here. You'll have to come with me." He rested his gaze back on her. "Keep that hat low on your head and don't say a fucking word. If they kill me, you can bet when they find your body there won't be anything recognizable left." He felt like an ass letting the curse words fly. But if something happened to her—it didn't bear thinking about. Then, to see her lips tremble. *Hell.* "I don't suppose you know how to use a gun."

"I-I used one on stage once," she whispered.

Compressing his lips, he tugged the Luger from his trousers at his lower back, hidden beneath his jacket. "Damn thing's loaded." He grabbed her hand, its utter femininity reaching through her glove. How had he missed that when he'd hauled her into the truck? He was an idiot.

Shoving away fear that centered deep within his belly, he positioned the gun in her hand, showing her the proper hold. "If you have to shoot, try to aim it in someone else's direction. Stay behind me."

He let out a held breath at her shaky nod.

"Let's go. And straighten the mustache."

Chapter Six

Meggie stared at the heavy metal in her hand, feet rooted to the ground, shock coursing through her.

"Sid!"

Harry's fierce bark startled her forward. Was she supposed to hold it? Put it in her pocket? Stuff it in her pants like Harry had? She shoved the gun in her pocket, carefully keeping it pointed to the ground, and hurried her steps.

The moon was but a sliver in the night sky, only offering up the others in shadowed depths. She darted after him, staying close on his heels. Her fingers moved to the hair above her itchy lip and pressed the piece firmly in place.

"Where's Keaton?" The gruff growl pierced the night.

Harry's sudden stop caught Meggie by surprise, and she plowed right into him. He responded with a chuckle that sounded more like an evil menace. "Indisposed." He jerked Meggie by the scruff of her jacket, pulling her from behind him. "This here's, Sid." He shot her a flat grin. "He's mute."

Mute? She glared at him. Not that it affected him. He'd switched his attention back to the figure in the boat.

A long pause ensued, and Meggie felt the weight of the man's stare. "We ain't got all night."

Harry strode down the pier and jumped in a boat no larger than the loo Meggie and her flatmates shared with their neighbors at the Gables Boardinghouse. Every feminine sensibility she possessed was offended by Harry's actions from stomping off ahead of her to his crude language. His head dipped from sight and a flutter of panic pulsed through her veins.

"Come on, Sid," he taunted. "I'll help you in. This is the kid's first time on a boat," he directed to his companion.

Meggie gritted her teeth. This was *not* her first time on a boat. What of her trans-Atlantic crossing on the *Empress of India*, just six months ago? Besides, that thing he'd just boarded could not be considered a boat.

Oh. He said he'd help her. She ran forward; he was so clever.

****

"Where'd you find this green boy, cap'n? If'n he's worth his weight in gold, we're in trouble." The cigarette in Marco's mouth bobbed around the words, yet surprisingly the fag never fell. Just the ashes. He stood at the back near the motor, his hands at his hips.

"Keagan landed himself in some trouble. Lay off Sid," Harry said. "We gotta job to do." *Like find Legs Diamond and put a bullet in him and keep Meggie Montley from getting them all killed.*

Harry moved to the side, hoping he blocked Marco's view. How the woman thought anyone would believe her a man was beyond him. Despite the masculine attire, she was one hundred percent woman. One who'd filled his dreams since the first night she'd taken the stage at Club 501. His vision conjured up the sultry moves as he'd seen her sway to soft percussions that filled the air, eyes closed. Once her voice let loose, the sweetest sound touched him, making him almost believe there was a heaven.

If they got out of this alive, he promised himself, he would take a kiss from those full lips once and for all.

Meggie reached the boat, and Harry stepped back, clenching his hands into fists. Grabbing her by the waist would be a dead giveaway to her gender. If Marco realized she was a woman, what was to stop him from pulling out a gun and shooting Harry in the back, or both of them for that matter? He didn't trust Marco any more than he did the bastard who'd killed his father and brother.

"Hurry it up, cap'n. They won't wait all night."

Meggie's feet had no more than touched the boat before Marco gunned the engine, throwing her into Harry. He landed on his ass, her on his lap. A small squeal erupted from her. Harry glanced quickly at Marco. Harry set her aside. "Hold on to your hat, boy."

She glared at him, but a gloved hand plastered the hat against her head, drawing his chuckle.

Between the wind and the motor, neither Harry nor Marco were inclined to speak. Just as well, as Harry couldn't conceive of any idea in how to keep Meggie safe. God damn, Diamond was supposed to be on the big boat. This was the opportunity he'd been waiting for. Take the bastard out, feed the fish in the Sound. He flicked a look in her direction—no way could he take the chance on her getting hurt. A vise squeezed deep inside his chest, making it difficult to breathe.

The night air on the boat in early November was cold, and everything he'd fantasized about Lady

Margaret Montley seemed to fall in line. Her quick assessment of the danger they faced to the lack of complaining of the frigid weather most likely chapping her lovely nose and cheeks. Everything about her sang to his dark soul. *Everything* except the idiocy of dressing like a man and traipsing about the city in the middle of the night, that is. Which begged the question again—why? Why the hell did she need that much money? Christ, what a poser. An unmitigated disaster.

"Up ahead, cap'n." Marco's thick accent barely sounded over the motor.

The engine cut, jarring him back. In the distance ahead, a shadowed vessel sat low in the water with at least two masts. It was long and dark. From this distance Harry couldn't see anyone aboard, but he knew they were watching for him. He glanced out at the black night, but with Meggie in the boat the last thing he needed, or wanted, was gunfire.

Once the boat was drifting, the wind died down. But the November air was biting. Water slapped the skiff, rocking it gently.

"That you, cap'n?" The voice came from the schooner, echoing in the night.

"Who else you expecting?" Harry called back.

"Come on up, then."

Harry glanced at Marco over his shoulder and gave him a sharp nod. Marco cranked up the motor and guided them around the bow. Harry leaned over to Meggie, fear clawing at him. "How you doing, Sid?"

She looked at him, eyes wide. She hid her emotions well, and thankfully kept to the "mute" story. Her eyes flashed to Marco then back to his. He took her one blink as a sign and moved away.

Dread weighted, as deep as a block of iron, in his gut. He latched onto the roped ladder and climbed aboard the schooner, straight into the pit of vipers waiting, and tossed another useless glance over his shoulder in the depth of the night.

At the top rung a pair of stout hands hauled him up and over. Harry caught himself before he stumbled to his knees. The deck was dotted with a few lanterns for light, but not many.

"Who's in the boat, Harry?"

"Marco and Sid."

Legs Diamond stepped into view, his light color fedora low on his forehead, expression stoic and cold. "Heard Keagan got the shit beat out of him."

"Damn sure did. Bastard messed with the wrong girl." Harry savored that tidbit.

Legs chuckled. "You liked to have killed him, Harry."

Keagan slid into sight behind the savvy gangster. *Ah, shit.* Too late. Harry fell into the trap like a starving kitten going for food. So the bastard had been working for Legs all along.

"Yeah, you dick, and now it's my turn to repay the favor." He laughed. "And then I'll go back for the quiff."

Harry started toward Keagan pleased with another opportunity to beat the shit out of the weasel. Maybe this time he'd finish the job.

Legs laughed again. A malicious menace that filled the Long Island Sound. "Not so fast." He jerked his head to the bulkhead. "You remember Alphonse Milano, don't you, Harry? Perhaps better known as Shaky-hand Alphonse?"

Alphonse lumbered into the meager light, dragging a ragamuffin of a figure by the collar. Yeah, Harry remembered him, and his gut tightened at the sight. No lips, large nose, ears sticking out so far from his head if the wind caught he'd catch flight and drop in the Sound. Shaky-hand Alphonse—the bastard who'd killed his father and brother. A numbing sensation started at the base of Harry's neck and wrapped his brain.

Alphonse tossed the slight figure at Harry's feet.

"Harry." His eyes were swollen shut. Bruises covered his face to unrecognizable, one hand missing two fingers, the remaining fingers deformed, bones broken. Yet the voice. A most recognizable voice. "It's me, Harry."

"Lewis." Raging fire surged through Harry, shoving out the surrealism, choking him along with the shock learning his brother wasn't dead after all. Harry jerked the Luger from the position at his lower back and fired. Alphonse dropped to the deck in a heap.

"Ah, now, Harry, why'd you have to go and do that?" Legs clucked his tongue.

Harry pointed the gun at Legs then swung it toward Keagan. "You next?"

Keagan's hands flew to the air as he backed away, fading into the night.

"Throw down your gun." Harry aimed his words at Keagan, but his focus was on Legs from his peripheral vision.

"I ain't got a piece, Dempsey. I swear." Keagan was a begging weasel.

Legs' arm came up, extending a tommy. "Ho, shit." Damn thing must have weighed some twelve pounds. Harry threw his body over Lewis, firing off a round at the same time. The machine gun's rapid shots flew wild over Harry's head, stopping as quickly as they'd begun as the Tommy thudded on the deck. Silence filled the air. Harry jumped to his feet, threw Lewis over his shoulder, and backed to the bulwark, Luger pointed out. Legs lay still, slumped over his gun, and whereever Keagan had slithered to, Harry refused to contemplate.

"Marco, catch," Harry called out softly and dropped Lewis into the skiff below. A soft grunt met his ears, and he leaped over after him. His landing rocked the boat hard enough that water sloshed in. "Hit it, Marco."

The engine roared to life, the noise deafening in the cold night air. An unconscious Lewis lay in the muck, and Harry touched his fingers to the pulse at his neck. It was faint, but there.

Meggie shifted over and lifted Lewis's head to her lap. Harry met widened eyes that reflected the sliver of moonlight. Her bottom lip trembled, and he resisted reaching over to squeeze her hand.

Emotions suffocated him, stabbing him from every direction. He scrubbed a hand over his face, stuffed them back. So much could still go wrong, and now he had two fragile lives to guard. He looked to the heavens. *My hands aren't big enough.*

The engine cut, snapping Harry to the situation at hand. They were halfway between the schooner and shore. Silence once again roared in the night. Harry narrowed his eyes on the old man.

A portable, lantern-style flashlight burned to life next to Marco. He struck a match, lighting the cigarette that appeared permeated to his lip. He tossed the match overboard and sucked deep, then blew out a stream of white smoke. "Well, cap'n. Guess there ain't to be no cabbage fer us tonight."

"I guess not, Marco. Sorry."

"Dammit all to hell. My moll won't be happy."

"You know there's more to be had, Marco. Plenty of trouble boys to hang with if you want easy dough."

"What!" Meggie gasped. "We aren't to be paid? At all?"

Marco froze, shock painting his scraggly features. His gaze darted to Meggie's sitting form. Harry swallowed a groan.

"Huh. You ain't so mute then after all." The faint light beamed off a pistol in Marco's hand. His arm moved slowly and stopped, pointed at Harry.

****

Fear stopped Meggie's heart, the breath caught in her throat. Why did she always have to open her mouth at the wrong time?

"Put the gun away, Marco. This here's Lady Margaret Montley."

Meggie lifted her chin. "I sing with the Bernie-Edison Orchestra."

Marco chuckled, the gun never wavering in his hand. "Who's ta stop me from killing you, cap'n, and makin' a bit of a profit off yer *Lady* Margaret Munt…Munt…whatever her name is? Why, I could sell her off and make double what I should'a took ta'night."

Terrified, Meggie slipped a trembling hand in the pocket of her jacket and wrapped her fingers around the gun Harry slipped to her earlier.

50

"No one, I venture to say, cap'n. Now, drop yer piece over the side. Real nice an' slow like." Harry hesitated, and Marco raised the gun.

Fingers shaking uncontrollably, Meggie raised her gun in his direction. "No." Her voice cracked. She forced an impossible calm. "No," she said again.

"I said, drop it, cap'n."

"I'll shoot. I-I will." But she feared her trembling endangered Harry's life. The man whose head rested in her lap stirred. His hand slipped over hers, fingers lining hers, and squeezed. The gun went off, jolting her whole arm, ringing her ears. She screamed, dropping the hot metal, and slumped back.

In an instant Harry had her wrapped in his embrace. "Meggie." She burrowed deeper, shaking uncontrollably.

"It's okay, sweetheart. You had no other option."

Meggie clung his warmth, his voice.

"She didn't do it, Harry. I had to do something to keep her from killing one of us." The raspy tones indicated a distinct lack of use.

"Are you all right? Meggie?"

She made an effort to pull herself together. She straightened out of his hold. "Yes. Yes."

He took her chin and lifted it. Forced her gaze to his. "Don't worry, the worst is over now, Lady Margaret." He spoke softly. "I need to take care of that bag of bones. Are you sure you're okay?"

With a deep breath, Meggie nodded.

Harry made his way to the back of the skiff and bent over Marco. "He's not dead." He went to the seat near the engine, lifted the cushion and pulled out a rope.

"Well, Marco, you fucked with the wrong man." He laughed. "And the wrong woman."

"This is quite a dame you've got, Harry."

Shock held Meggie silent. The words in her head refused to form into any sort of coherent sense. Like "who was this man too weak to sit? How did Harry know him?" And "how had *she* shot a man?"

"I think I'm going to be ill." She launched herself to the side of the boat, flinging the man from her lap, uncaring that his head landed hard on the boat's bottom. A second later not a thing was left in her already empty stomach. A large hand smoothed the hair from her brow, the tie holding it back long gone. Tears filled her eyes. She couldn't face Harry's wrath, though she deserved it, every last word. But his set-down would do her in.

"Are you crying, Lady Margaret?" She was trying not to, but his gentle question sent the tears spilling over.

She shook her head. But he had to know she lied, as certainly her training as an actress hadn't granted her such skills.

He chuckled softly, which only added to her emotional outburst.

"Here, sweetheart. Take a sip of this." He took her head and held a small flask to her lips. "It will help with the shock. Dispel that nasty taste from your mouth."

With a small nod, Meggie accepted the peace offering and took a healthy swig. It burned all the way down her throat. Another bout of tears surfaced. "Where did that come from?" she coughed out between words.

"Marco has a pretty dependable stash hidden. I just happen to know his hiding places. This stuff will kill damn near anything."

"Who's your friend?" she said once she caught her breath.

"My once-thought-dead brother, Lewis. Lewis, meet Lady Margaret Montley."

She glanced over her shoulder to the man.

"Ma'am. The pleasure is mine."

He was a charmer.

"You all right now?" He spoke against her ear.

Meggie inhaled carefully then nodded.

After squeezing her hand, Harry moved to the back of the boat, kicking Marco's feet out of his way. "There's coppers crawling all over Pelham Bay. We'll turn Marco over to them. Someone should be able to give us a lift back to the city. We need a croaker to give you the once over, Lewis." He flashed the light three times then fired up the engine.

The cold air against Meggie's face did much for her constitution, and she shifted back to Lewis and leaned over him. "I'm sorry about your head, Mr. Dempsey. Can you explain what a 'croaker' is?"

A groused laugh erupted from him, followed by a short groan. "The doc. Lady Margaret—*the* Lady Margaret? The one from the radio? WHN?"

"Well, yes, I suppose that's so. We did do a broadcast early on, once I'd joined Bernie's."

"How the hell—er, pardon, Miss Montley. Jeepers—how, uh, did you hook up with my bluenose brother?"

Meggie frowned. "Bluenose?"

"Killjoy. Harry's not the greatest fun to be had."

She cast a glance over her shoulder at Harry, who steered the motor with his large, efficient, most capable hands. "I beg to differ, Mr. Dempsey. Harry is the furthest thing from a killjoy I know of."

"Please, Miss Montley. I'm on my back here. Might you call me Lewis?"

The first real grin of the night touched her. "I'm happy to make your acquaintance, Lewis. And I insist you call me Meggie. May I assist you up?"

"I'd be right grateful, Meggie."

She slipped an arm beneath the thin shoulders and lifted him. He weighed but a feather. "What happened up on that bigger boat?"

"I think my killjoy brother offed one of the most famous bootleggers of the decade. Did you kill the bastard, Harry?"

"I don't know."

"I don't understand," Meggie said. "I thought we were just supposed to pick up a shipment of...of..." She threw out a hand. Blast. She hadn't any idea what they were supposed to have bootlegged, which was obviously nothing now. Thoughts of Eliza engulfed her. She'd failed her friend. Utterly and completely. And now they weren't to be paid.

"Gentleman Jack ain't no gentleman, cap'n. He'll come after you," Marco piped up.

The old man's voice startled her, his words stirring confusion along with the thread of unease through her. "Who is this Gentleman Jack? And if he is a gentleman, why would he come after Harry?" Meggie's head began to throb with all the innuendoes.

"Gentleman Jack is another name Legs Diamond is well-known by," Lewis told her. "I don't know where they came up with the name 'Gentleman' for the bastard, but he got the name 'Legs' for flaunting his money and…uh…er…women all over town. Hell, all over New York for that matter."

She glanced back at Harry, concerned. "Will this 'gentleman' try to hurt Harry?" Meggie couldn't imagine singing at Club 501 without Harry sitting in his usual corner. Without those dark, fathomless eyes pinned on her. He brought out a side of her she'd never realized existed.

She snapped her gaze back to Lewis's harsh laugh. "Oh, yeah. He's likely to cut off his ba—er, pardon my French, Miss Montley, Meggie. I forget myself."

Meggie should have been mortified. Instead, fury raged through her. "Why should this Legs-Gentleman want to-to—" She couldn't form the phrase.

"He murdered our pa. And by the look I saw on my brother's face, he thought Legs had done killed me too." Lewis leaned against the side of the skiff and closed his eyes, exhaustion seeming to have claimed him. "As it turns out, he only wounded me a little and starved me a lot. Damn, I'm hungry."

Chapter Seven

The relief that spilled through Harry in finding Lewis alive and delivering Margaret Montley home safe was overwhelming. The wait to get Lewis home to Ma left Harry fantasizing he possessed some magic artifact he could rub for three wishes. Wish number 1: Lewis's health, of course. Nothing could dim the joy in Harry's heart than seeing his brother hadn't perished at the hands of Legs Diamond via Shaky-Alphonse. Wish number 2: Ma's elation so complete at having her younger son back, her craving for bathtub gin quashed forever. The shit was poison. Wish number 3—Harry's gaze flew to Lady Margaret and he took a deep breath—Wish number 3: Stealing the blinding smile she turned on Lewis, to keep for Harry, and Harry alone.

What a pipe dream. Meggie Montley could never belong to just Harry. Not with her talent and the momentum of that talent. The lady's career was on the verge of exploding, and no way in hell would Harry be the one to hold her back.

He squinted behind him into the inky night. The faint shadow of the lighthouse guard was moving in on the schooner. Harry let out a relieved breath. One step closer to getting Lewis and Meggie out of danger. He glanced toward the woman who kept his dreams captive. Any ordered semblance of her previously contained hair had long since dissipated.

"What are you planning on do with me, cap'n?"

Harry tore his gaze from the locks whipping across Meggie's face and focused. "I ought to drop you in the Sound. That hunk of metal lodged in your chest in place of a heart would drag you straight to the bottom. You could feed the marine life for weeks."

"Ah, cap'n. I wouldn'na shot you." The man put whining babies to shame.

"Shut it, Marco." Lights dotted the shoreline. He counted at least twelve. He lifted the flashlight and signaled the coast. A few minutes later he dropped the engine into a lower gear. "Sid," he barked. A nudge of pleasure shot through him watching her gaze shoot to him. "Get that hat on and grab the rope. Toss it up on the dock when I give the word." He bit back a laugh at her scowl but inordinately pleased that she did as he asked. She slammed her newsboy cap on her head as he guided the boat alongside the dock. "Now," he said.

On the first try the rope slid back into the boat, but she snatched it up and threw over a second time with an aggravated force. "Mute time," he told her, dragging Marco with him. He stood him nearby before hoisting Lewis up carefully. He moved to the ladder. "Hey, Warren. Got some good news. Shaky-Alphonse is dead."

"Good job, Harry."

"But my brother, Lewis here, he needs medical attention. You got someone who can get us to the city, fast like?"

"Of course."

After handing Lewis up, Harry hauled Meggie, none too gently, to the ladder. Unable to help himself, his fingers molded her waist, and he lifted her halfway up. She scrambled from his hold much too soon. "This is Sid. He's mute."

"He ain't mute," Marco yelled out. "He's a she. Some big-time, famous singer—"

Harry's fist shot out. Marco's slight figure crumpled like a rag doll. Harry tossed him to up to the pier, no heavier than a sack of potatoes, then bounded up after him.

"What's this about a famous singer?" Warren's eyes narrowed on Meggie.

Harry stepped in front of her, cutting off the man's sharp scrutiny. Another fellow moved into sight from the shadows. His fedora sat way back on hair slicked away from his forehead, beady eyes taking in every detail. Shit. Theodore Clifford. No need for the usual twist the man gave his stories that bordered on outrageous lies. In this case, Lady Margaret managed to hand him the story of the century.

"Warren," Harry snapped. "That ride?"

"Right. Sure. Marvin will get you to Mount Sinai straight away."

Harry shot Meggie a look over his shoulder. Lips pressed tightly together, she pulled her cap down to her eyes and moved up behind him. *Good girl.* He put his arm about Lewis, whose breathing had turned harsh and labored. "Let's go."

As they moved down the pier, Warren called out. "Harry, a man's been shot."

"Yeah, well he pulled a gun on the wrong man. The bastard's lucky he's not dead."

****

"Lady Margaret? Lady Margaret Montley?"

Newshawk. Meggie recognized him from the club. Always standing about, small eyes set too close together, darting from socialite to shyster to any goose he might find newsworthy. More times than she could count did Bernie and Eddie have something nasty to say when Mr. Clifford drummed up a non-existent row between the combo orchestra's—in her opinion— skirmishes that amounted to nothing more than slight artistic differences.

Take for instance their appearance at WHN. Eddie was adamant the band stay true to their calling, singing before live audiences, where Bernie argued the more people who heard them the more likely the crowd would grow. Meggie tended to agree with Bernie and had a sneaking suspicion that just Eddie feared new, unproven avenues or worse, failure. The whole idea was silly given how successful they'd become.

Not to mention Jess's reaction to every article that appeared in the Gazette. Her sniff of disgust when Mr. Clifford's latest fabricated piece showed up regarding the Bolsheviks. Meggie's stomach dropped, and she tugged her cap down farther almost covering her eyes. The man could destroy her career with the stroke of a pen.

Tendrils of panic started in the tips of her fingers and toes and converged in her chest, squeezing the air from her lungs. Her gaze flicked over a greasy lock that had slipped loose. She quickly dropped her eyes.

"What a pickle you must find yourself in, hmm?"

She forced a low grunt passed her clogged throat and started around him.

"Back off, Teddy. This here's Sid. And he don't talk much." Harry's hand flattened against Mr.

Clifford's chest and he pushed. Not so hard as to knock him to the ground. But Meggie knew Harry held himself back with tremendous effort.

"Say, what is this?" someone yelled.

She spun, momentarily caught by the excitement from behind. A large boat—well, not as big as the *Empress of India*, mind—eased into her view. Then upon closer scrutiny, a smaller vessel making its way in quickly.

"Hold up there, Harry."

"Christ," Harry muttered. He turned back toward the water. "What now, Warren? I gotta get my brother to the hospital."

"Looks like the Lighthouse Service might have a question or two for you."

"Marvin, get Lewis and Sid to the car. I'll only be a minute."

Once the smaller boat eased in to anchor, Harry pushed Meggie, none too gently, on the shoulder in Marvin and Lewis's direction. Meggie didn't hesitate. She ducked her chin and darted past the sleazy bloke and hurried after Lewis and their new chauffeur.

Just as Harry promised, he wasn't long. Fifteen minutes later they were on the bumpy road back to the city.

Harry scooted onto the backseat next to Lewis, and barked, "Let's go, Marvin," before he'd even shut the door. Marvin hit the gas, throwing up dirt and rocks in their wake.

"What'd they want, Harry?"

Meggie longed to hush Lewis. His raspy voice, a painful reminder of his ordeal. But she was glad he'd asked too, as she certainly couldn't.

"They had Legs and wanted the details. I gave them the short version," he said.

I want the details. Meggie wanted to shout.

Lewis gave a short laugh. After a moment he slumped against Harry and fell silent.

From the corner of her eye, Harry's clenched jaw looked as if it would break if the car hit a hard rut. But now that they were on their way back to the city and away from that newshawk, Meggie could feel the tension lifting from her as quickly as the rising sun.

The sky, though still a deep dark blue, was brushed with the softest pink edging over the horizon. It offered the promise of an unusually crisp and bright November day. Nothing remotely similar to England's standards.

She reached across Lewis for Harry's hand then remembered the driver and pulled back. Her eyes flashed to the mirror where Marvin's were pinned on her.

Cheeks heated, she inhaled deeply and relaxed against the seat, cutting her gaze to Harry. She wasn't certain, but she could swear his lips twitched. The effect lessened the tightness about his mouth.

She released her breath with a vow. After this harebrained scheme, all future adventures were to receive a thorough plan of attack. The thought hit her hard in her chest. With all the danger she'd place herself in, *Harry in,* she'd still managed to not come up with the blunt Eliza needed to be free of indentured slavery. Her head fell back, and she closed her eyes, defeated. It was barbaric.

A warm hand covered hers and squeezed. Tears filled her eyes, and she refused to look at him. Most especially when all she desired was to throw herself in the man's arms the way she had two nights ago. There she'd felt the promise of a different sort of adventure, a promise of warmth and protection. Nothing remotely close to that fool Percy. A cold Englishman her mother seemed determined to force on her for life.

God, she was exhausted. Meggie willed the past few hours from her mind and took in deep, steady breaths. She reveled in Harry's presence despite the barrier his brother provided sitting between them.

****

Lady Margaret Montley's fingers went slack against Harry's, and he glanced over. Her forehead rested against the windowpane, her chest rising then falling in a slow rhythm. He marveled at her ability to live in the moment. God, how he wished he shared such a gift, because sleep was a gift. One he'd embrace in *his* life.

Marvin must have realized the same. "Sid is an attractive fellow," he piped up. "All those soft curls and full lips are enough to turn a man."

"That's enough, Marvin." Harry's voice had lowered to a growl that bellowed deep.

"You seem awful possessive of this Sid." He chuckled. "Out cold, is she?"

Harry shook his head, refusing to answer. Harry couldn't deny it. Meggie was his—for the moment, anyway.

"What'd those lighthouse boys have to say?"

He met Marvin's eyes in the mirror. All mischief pushed aside, voice serious.

"Just what I said to Lewis. Legs was shot. Not dead, the lucky bastard. Guess they'll haul him to jail?"

"Hope they can make something stick this time. He's as slippery as they come."

"Kidnapping," Harry said with a bite. It was all he had. The problem, as he saw it, was that the hand who'd actually pulled the trigger, murdering Pa, belonged to Shaky-Alphonse. He glanced at Lewis. The morning sun, though still low in the eastern sky, showed his ashen pallor. When was the last time he'd had a decent meal?

God, had it been six weeks already since Pa had sent him on that fool's errand to check on Ma? Right at, he thought. On a day just like this one was shaping up to. No clouds marring a brilliant fall morning, unseasonably warm.

"I need you to run out to Queens, Harry." Pa hefted an outboard motor on his shoulder that had to weigh fifty pounds.

"Pa, let me handle the heavy lifting around here." Irritated, Harry took the motor from him. "Better yet, let Joe take it. What the hell do we pay him for?"

"Put it over there and get out to Queens. I have a meeting."

Harry hauled the motor to the table Pa indicated and set it down. "What kind of meeting? I can handle this shit, old man. You need to start looking at retirement." It was a strange request. Ma was probably soused already, besides.

"Damn it, not this again, Harry—"

"Hey, there, Pa. Harry."

Harry glanced over. Lewis was leaning on Roscoe, their head mechanic. "Shit, Pa. Lewis is drunk. We gotta do something about him. He's gonna hurt himself or someone else before all is said and done."

"Just get out to Queens," Pa snapped. *"I'll take care of your brother. Now."* Pa stormed off in Lewis's direction, jerked him by the arm and dragged him to the small office, slamming the door behind them.

What the hell? Harry forced himself to let it go, promising to address the matter with Pa again later. *That night, at home.*

But Pa and Lewis never made it home. Shaky-Alphonse, and most likely Legs Diamond, had paid Pa a visit, demanding Protection money. But Pa was a stubborn old man and refused to buckle. And, Harry learned, he was proving just as stubborn as his pa.

The car jerked to a stop, jolting Harry from the past, knocking Meggie's head against the window. "Ow."

He winced at the definitely feminine outburst and shifted his gaze to Marvin's. The twinkle of mischief was back. Harry shoved the door open and climbed out, sweeping Lewis up in his arms.

"I can walk, Harry. Put me down."

"You're more likely to faint like a girl," he retorted, carefully setting him to his feet.

Meggie slid along the seat and exited next, eyes narrowed on them. Harry held out a hand to assist her. Her gaze widened slightly, and she shot the driver a glance over her shoulder.

"Marvin's great deductive skills saw past your 'soft curls and full lips,' Meggie." Harry smirked. "He's sharp, that Marvin." She sniffed her disdain at his outstretched hand. He ignored her rebuff and snatched her by the wrist, pulling her up and out of the car and into him. Her eyes flashed in surprise. A deep chuckle erupted from Harry. "Thanks for the ride, Marvin."

Marvin flashed a short wave, gunned the motor, and took off.

****

Meggie stumbled back from Harry's hold, trying desperately to right her senses. She focused on a five-story building before her, constructed of brick and limestone. An elaborate carved cornice decorated the upper edge. The wrought iron fence surrounding the property added charm but looked to serve a second purpose with spiked tips on each post, spaced merely inches apart. Each level had its own balcony, the top one lined with bushes of greenery, though somewhat brown and thin, considering the time of year.

With his arm about Lewis, Harry strode to the portico. Meggie followed quickly, realizing the hospital was not too far from home. She reached Harry and Lewis as they stepped between two large columns that supported the protruding, flattened roof.

Once inside, Meggie found the noise deafening. She'd never actually visited a hospital before and the amount of people in this one was staggering. The entire scenario seemed a chaotic mess. Nurses darted about, some ushering patients; others attempting to calm screaming children; another rushed by carrying a stack of linen; yet another wielding a broom and dust bin. Meggie shuddered.

Harry snapped his fingers and, irritatingly, two—make that three nurses, who, of course, couldn't possibly be of the aged, homely variety—rushed over. A lovely brunette, sizing up the situation, snagged a wheeled chair and headed in their direction.

Meggie stood back, half tempted to rush back out the door. As if Harry read her mind, his hand snaked out and gripped her upper arm. Beautiful woman No. 1's eyes went wide as they roved over Meggie's unusual attire before stepping up to assist Lewis into the chair. After attempting to mask their giggles, No.'s 2 and 3 drifted off to assist others.

"Hello, doll," Lewis rumbled, and Meggie bit back a smile. "I'm yours for the takin'."

She turned a brilliant smile on him that moved swiftly to Harry, surprising Meggie with an urge to scratch her eyes out.

"The doctor will get with you as soon as possible, Mr. Dempsey." She spoke directly to Harry, forcing Meggie to swallow a groan. "Possibly an hour or so. As you can see—" Palm out, she indicated the ensuing disorder. "—we are a bit understaffed. If you follow this hallway to the fourth door on the left, there is a waiting area that should be a bit quieter."

"Thank you. That is much appreciated."

The nurse wheeled Lewis in the opposite direction. "Don't desert me, Harry," Lewis called out.

"Never again," Harry said. But the words were spoken softly and sounded like a promise to himself. Once Lewis disappeared from sight, Harry, still holding her arm, guided them to the waiting room the nurse had mentioned.

Meggie tried pulling her arm free to no avail. His grip tightened. Honestly, the man had no say over her nor any right to still be angry. They'd made it back unscathed, hadn't they? He probably wanted some simpering miss who jumped at the snap of his fingers, doted on his every word. Not a headstrong English Lady who took it into her head to dress as a boy—

"We're going to talk, Lady Margaret."

"Fine," she bit out. "But there is no need to manhandle me. I am not some unruly dog to be taken to heel."

"Someone needs to take you to heel." He reached the door and opened it.

It was somewhat quieter, but there were hordes of people sitting and standing about. Harry let out an expletive and shut the door. His hand slipped down to hers, and he pulled her after him, checking other doors along the corridor until he located a supply closet devoid of anyone. It was a good-sized room, stuffed with shelves stocked with bandages, linens, cleaning supplies, and other items Meggie couldn't begin to identify.

The minute Harry shut the rest of humanity away she jerked her hand from his and moved into an area out of direct sight of the door. A nearby window with opaque glass let in light. Not that it distanced Harry. He just stalked her into a small open area that served as a place to hang things, a cubby of sorts.

"What the hell where you thinking? Dressing like a boy? Attempting to run with a bunch of thugs?"

Exhaustion, fear, frustration, and finally anger caught up and overwhelmed Meggie in the beat of a second. "I don't know." She swallowed back the tears. "I-I'm worried for my friend. She started a new occupation. I think she's in way over her head. She needs money to buy her way out of her contract."

"Contract! So instead you came up with some brilliant plan of your own. One that puts you in harm's way? Where's the logic in that?" Harry pushed a hand through his hair.

"I just wanted to help her."

"Damn it, Meggie. You need a keeper."

Fury roared through her, usurping her exhaustion. "I need no such thing, you-you *beast.* I had enough of that from my brothers." She lifted her chin. "Which is exactly the reason I sailed to America. To get out from underneath the domineering thumb of my overbearing family. Not to mention my mother's unrelenting matchmaking machinations."

"Dear God. Are you telling me that you took off for another country *on your own?*"

"Don't be ridiculous." She gave him her haughtiest look down her nose. "I came with three of my friends."

"And I'll wager not one of the four of you bothered sharing your plans with anyone."

"I'm a woman grown. I don't *need* anyone's permission to live my life, thank you very much."

Harry took her hand and tugged the snug glove from her hand one finger at a time.

Nice and slow, sending a thrill racing up her spine and other unmentionable places.

His pitch dropped, reverberated through her like a tightly stringed instrument. "Not even to keep you from gangsters like Legs Diamond or Shaky-Alphonse?"

He pocketed the one glove, then started on the other. "Who is Shaky-Alphonse?" The words came out in a tremble, husky and warm.

He grabbed her, pulled her into his hard body. "A dangerous man like me."

"You? You aren't dangerous, Harry." Her voice came out a whisper despite her attempts to appear unaffected.

He leaned in, his breath touching her lips. "Ah, but I'm very dangerous, Lady Margaret." His lips slid over hers, stealing her breath. He took her bottom lip between his teeth and bit down gently. Startled, her lips parted, and his tongue scraped and danced over hers. It lasted but a second before he pulled back. Her fingers gripped the lapels of his coat.

"Yes," she said. "I-I see what you m-mean."

Chapter Eight

God. She tasted as sweet as his dreams promised. "I want you, Meggie Montley. I want you so badly, I ache." He tugged her closer, her eyes widening. No doubt, at his erection pressed against her abdomen. He took her mouth again, pleased at her enthusiastic response. Harry fumbled with the buttons on her shirt then reached for those luscious breasts. "What the hell?" He drew back frowning.

"What?" Her husky, breathless, yet puzzled voice threatened to send him over the edge. She glanced down then back up with a cheeky grin. "Oh. That."

He smoothed a palm over a wide strip of fabric that wrapped her chest that began just under her arms and spanned her ribs. "Yes, that," he growled.

"Well, I couldn't very well pass as a male with…with…"

He passed a hand over her flat stomach. "No, I don't suppose you could. Men certainly don't have such—" He turned a wolfish grin on her that set a deep blush in her cheeks. He dropped to his knees. "—enticing curves."

"W-what are you doing?"

He laid his lips on the silky skin of her stomach, dipped his tongue in the shallowed indentation of her navel. Her fingers latched into his hair, holding his head in, what he considered, the perfect position. "Have you ever made love, Lady Margaret?"

"In a supply closet?" Her voice hitched high.

His fingers gripped her waist, extending over slim hips. "Anywhere," he murmured against her stomach.

"N-no."

Harry fluttered light kisses over her exposed belly. With one hand he reached for the top fastener on her trousers.

The door flew back, and two chattering voices entered. He froze. The grip on one side of his head loosened while the other tightened, entangled in his hair.

"The bulls are everywhere. Who do you suppose he is?"

"Grab some of those linens, would you? I heard Dr. Welks tell Nurse Thompson it was Jack Diamond. You know, Gentleman Jack. *Legs Diamond.* They worked him over in private."

A sharp gasp sounded from one of the intruders, and Harry's fingers tightened on Meggie's hips. He glanced up and saw Meggie's hand covering her mouth, eyes squeezed shut. He forced his fingers loose. Her eyes opened and met his. Hell, he'd probably left a mark.

With luck, their two intruders would leave as quickly as they'd appeared.

"Lord, have mercy. The man is not so difficult to look at, is he?"

"Heaven's, Agnes, the man is a menace to society. He *kills* people." That shrill, nasal tone announced to the world how precarious Harry's own situation was.

As if he needed that reminder.

"Look at it this way, Eleanor. The man keeps us employed." She giggled, and Harry wanted to throttle her.

"You are twisted, Agnes. Twisted." Their voices faded, the door latching with their exit.

Harry let out a breath, then rose to his feet. Desire slipped away, replaced with fear and, finally—common sense. Taking Meggie's shoulders, he shook her lightly. "Damn it, you could have been killed. Legs Diamond isn't even dead."

"Who *is* this Diamond person? And why should he want to kill *me*?"

"Because he wants *me*." The urge to shout was overwhelming, but he bit it back. "He murdered my father and kidnapped my brother. I'll wager I'm at the top of his hit list." The words spilled from him like volcanic ash.

Meggie's face paled as his words struck home. She shook her head. The tears filling her eyes tumbled over. "No. No. Nothing can happen to you, Harry."

He felt slightly nauseous in terrifying her so. But such rash behavior could only lead her into deeper trouble. How else was he to get through to her? Taking her head with both hands, he brushed her tears away with his thumbs.

"Nothing will happen to me." He kissed her gently. "But how am I supposed to keep you safe?"

Meggie's large blue eyes flashed in something like fury. Her hands flattened against his chest, and in one swift move, shoved. Shoved him hard, catching him off guard. The whole ridiculous scenario happened so fast, he found himself flat on his backside. Quickly rebuttoning her open shirt, she stuffed the shirttail in her trousers as if she were no stranger to wearing men's garb.

"What is it? What did I say?" Puzzled, he rose to sitting.

Meggie leaned down, outrage emanating like a fog. She poked a tapered nail in his chest. "No one appointed *you* bodyguard." She stepped over him, flung open the door, and stormed out.

What the hell just happened? By the time Harry recovered his wits, two nurses reappeared and started at his presence. He had no idea if they were the same women from before.

"Sir, this room is off limits to the public." At least one of them was, he decided. He didn't think he'd ever get that high-pitched shrill out of his head.

"Of course, ladies. My apologies." He darted around them and down the corridor. He reached the front doors in time to see Meggie's shapely buttocks disappearing down the street in a crush of people. Slowly, Harry turned back the way he'd come. Meggie was safe enough now in the light of day. He had other priorities. He needed to look after Lewis.

****

Tears streamed down Meggie's face. Blast that Harry Dempsey. She shoved them away only to be deluged with recurring rivulets that refused to dry up. Who did he think he was? Another one of her bossy siblings who'd never see her as an adult? Or worse, someone like her mother, set to see her married to some pasty-faced noble with no inclinations other than sitting about drinking day-in, day-out with his school chums. Or gadding about the globe, playing grown up with no meaning or yearning for life other than the next horse race? She'd throw herself off the tallest building in New York before allowing that to happen.

Meggie marched to the corner of Lexington and 67th. The man treated her like a recalcitrant child. Not like a woman who would adore him, cherish him, set him afire as he did her. She slumped against a light post, gulping back an outburst of sorrow.

"Get out of the way, Jobbie."

She glanced up, wondering where her hat had disappeared. Her hair blew free in the cool November breeze.

"Can't you see anything, Ralph? That ain't no jobbie, despite her outlandish attire."

An elderly woman whose height was lessened by her hunched shoulders reached out and patted Meggie's hand. "What is it, dearie? Man trouble?" She cut a look to the old geezer beside her. His thin, gray hair poked out from beneath a cap similar to the one Meggie had started the night with. "I'll wager it is. Take it from me. They're more trouble than they're worth."

"Then what in Sam's hell is she wearing boys' clothes for?"

Meggie's attempt at a smile fell short, but truly she was grateful.

"You know, I hate admittin' Ralph's right about anything," the old woman said, stuffing a tissue in Meggie's hand. "But if'n the boy means that much to ya, ye might try wearing things a little more feminine like. Why, a pretty little thing like you—" She narrowed her faded blue eyes. "In fact, ya look a teeny bit like that canary—"

Meggie wiped her nose. "Canary?"

But the woman would not be blustered. She wanted her say, and Meggie admired her for it. "That new up-and-coming singer. I heard her on the telegraphy."

"It's a radio, Doris. Let's go. I want my lunch."

"And I saw her picture in the newspaper. She was mite prettier than you with her light hair and smiling face."

Meggie's spirit lifted a little. "She was?"

Doris patted her hand again. "Ye take my word for it, dearie. Just dress like a girl—" Her eyes fell to Meggie's chest. "And, well, for most men a pretty face will do the trick."

The urge to giggle tickled Meggie's throat, but she maintained a straight face. She straightened from the light post and lifted her chin, a stubborn resolve setting deep inside. Harry thought of her as a child who needed looking after? Undisciplined, misbehaving, headstrong? Ha, the bloke will never know what hit him. "Thank you, Doris. May I call you Doris?"

"O'course you can, dearie. Me? I don't stand on no ceremony."

"I'll take your comments under advisement." Meggie glanced over at the scowling Ralph. "You'd best get Ralph fed, Doris. He looks hungry enough to eat a bear."

Doris peered at her companion. "Ain't it the truth. Ye take care now." With a short wave, Doris turned to Ralph who growled at Doris, but he took her hand and placed it on his arm. The sight melted Meggie as she watched them walk away, her heart suddenly full. With a lighter step she walked the two blocks east to Madison Avenue and caught the Fifth Avenue Coach to The Gables. Harry could wait until she'd had sleep.

Meggie stumbled into the flat, her light mood gone. Exhausted, frustrated, and failure weighed her down. What would she tell Eliza?

The smell of burnt scones assaulted her. Charli, shoulders shaking, stood bent at the tiny kitchen sink, hot pad in one hand clutching an empty baking sheet.

Meggie rushed and wrapped an arm about her friend, pushing a strand of her red hair from her tearstained face. "Charli, it's just a batch of scones. The next group will turn out fine. I'm certain of it."

Charli shook off her hold and stepped back. "No! It won't. Nothing will ever turn out right for me. Ever," she shouted. "You. You don't know anything, Lady *Perfect*." The baking sheet clattered in the sink. She turned and dashed to her and Eliza's curtained off bedroom.

Meggie stood there, stunned. Even at Meggie's and Jess's constant razzing at Mrs. Greensley's Charli had never reacted so...so vehemently. And Lord knows, she and Jess had certainly deserved Charli's wrath, or worse, on more than one occasion.

Tears pricked Meggie's eyes. *Lady Perfect indeed.* God, if only. Meggie made her way to her room and jerked the curtain closed. She wished she could curtain off her thoughts as easily. Collapsing down on her perfectly made bed, she listened for sounds from Charli's and Eliza's room. She caught a sniffle from Charli, but nothing else. No chatter from Eliza, and Jess was clearly working late.

Charli would not welcome her intrusion, and fatigue robbed Meggie of further coherence. She tugged the coverlet up from the side of the bed without rising and closed her eyes. She would rest, just for a moment, then talk to Charli...*just for a moment.*

****

Harry had no choice. Meggie Montley was out of his league. Not only was she scads above him in class, but her career was set to take off for the stars, and he refused to be the one responsible for standing in her way. The woman lived and breathed a sensuality that knocked him senseless. Just look how Ma had resented Pa. Harry would rather cut off his arm than have Meggie sneer such resentment in his direction.

"Mr. Dempsey?"

Harry glanced up at the petite nurse who had wheeled Lewis down the corridor earlier.

"The doctor will see you now, Mr. Dempsey."

Harry pulled himself to his feet and followed her past a desk which several volunteers sat behind. Past a large room lined with beds protruding out from the walls along both sides, each separated with a chair. There must have been forty beds in that one room, and not a single empty. They passed another three rooms, each the same. Only the faces were different. At the end of the long hall, she turned into another room, this one devoid of the number of people. Antiseptic hit him full force.

"Where is Jack Diamond?"

The pretty little brunette kept walking but threw over her shoulder, "He was released."

"I'd heard he'd been shot." Harry almost laughed, but it wasn't funny.

"Just grazed, sir. He was treated, then released with a police escort."

He grunted, somewhat relieved at that bit of information. But, hell, some of the coppers were more crooked than the criminals.

"Here we are," she chirped. "Mr. Dempsey?"

"I told you, doll. I'm Lewis. Mr. Dempsey is the flat tire standing behind you." Lewis laughed a grousing sound that despite his words made Harry feel better.

"And I told you, *Mr.* Dempsey, the name is Nurse Gladys, not doll." She snapped the covers up to Lewis's neck but tucked them around him more gently than he deserved.

"Mr. Dempsey? I'm Dr. Jolston. Your brother here, I'm surprised to say, will live. He hasn't taken much care with his body, I daresay." His clipped British accent reminded him of Meggie's. "He's malnourished and bruised. But insists upon leaving. Can't say as I recommend it, but being short on beds, I'm willing to place him in your care."

"Thank you, Doctor. I'll see that he is well-provided for."

The doctor scribbled something on a board he held, then ripped the page away and handed it to Harry. "There you are then. Just show this to the women at the desk on your way out." He gave a short nod and disappeared as quickly as he'd appeared.

Damn, croakers. Harry didn't trust the lot of them. "Come on, brother. Let's blow this popsicle stand. It's time to send a little happiness Ma's way."

****

"Where's Meggie!"

Truly? Jessie's screech could wake the dead. Meggie squinted into the waning light from a crease in the curtain, head pounding. Maybe she was dead. Her mouth was dry like she'd imbibed too much gin. The single overhead light bulb flickered to life, and Meggie blinked against the intrusion.

Jessie was still dressed in her office attire that consisted of a plaid pencil skirt, topped with a hip length mulberry cardigan. "Is this true?" She rattled the paper she held in one hand.

"Is what true?" Meggie's voice croaked with sleep as she pulled herself to sitting.

Her eyes flicked over Meggie. "Oh my God. It is." She sank down on the bed beside her. "You're wearing boys' clothes. You've made the papers—again!" She snapped the paper out and read:

"*Lady Margaret turned Lady Bootlegger? Or Lady Copper?*

"New York City is in for a surprise. The sultry canary, English Miss, Lady Margaret Montley was spotted early this morning dressed in boy's garb accompanied by none other than Harry Dempsey. You may remember Mr. Dempsey's father who was allegedly murdered by Shaky-Alphonse in recent weeks, believed in some circles that Gentleman Jack "Legs" Diamond as the culprit behind the hit when the elder Dempsey refused to pay out protection money for his Marina Supply Company.

"Seen with Harry was his thought-dead brother, Lewis Dempsey. Sources refused to confirm that Legs was shot sometime in the early morning hours. But he was taken into custody by the police from the US Lighthouse Service. Rumor has it that Mr. Diamond was treated and released from Mount Sinai Hospital in police custody as this story went to press.

"Several questions beg asking: who shot Legs Diamond this time? Has Lady Margaret turned Lady Bootlegger? Was Harry Dempsey out for revenge?

"Your faithful news reporter — Theodore Clifford"

****

Jessie lowered the paper. "Is it true, Meggie?"

Meggie flopped back on the bed and covered her eyes with the crook of her bent arm. "I never saw this Legs Diamond."

"It is true." Jessie whispered. "You reckless girl. You could have been killed. What on earth drove you to do such a thing?"

Meggie sat up again. Charli and Eliza appeared in the doorway, and Meggie smiled wryly at Charli. "I guess I'm not so perfect after all, am I?"

"I should have never said that, Megs. I'm so sorry." Her mouth turned down, regretful.

Jessie rolled the paper and smacked Meggie on the arm. "Don't ever do something like that again. At least not without me."

"I'm sorry. I didn't mean to worry anyone."

Jess hugged her. "We know you didn't, darling. Now, I have a date tonight." Eliza stepped in the room, allowing Jessie to leave with Charli.

Alone with Eliza, seeing her pasty face, tears clogged Meggie's throat. "I'm so sorry, Eliza. I wanted to get you the money, but I completely failed you."

"No. No, don't ever say that." Eliza hugged Meggie. "I can't believe you did that—*for me*."

"Don't you see? It was all for nothing." Meggie raised her gaze. Pools of moisture shimmered in Eliza's eyes.

"No. Please, Meggie," she whispered. Eliza straightened then squared her shoulders. "I have wonderful news. The contract's been paid. Mr. Taggart paid it. He paid the entire thing off. I'm free and clear."

Meggie narrowed her eyes on her. "That sounds quite marvelous. Almost unbelievably so."

Eliza returned Maggie's stare, blinking only once. "Yes, quite. I was surprised myself, but he's English. He was delighted to come across a Brit with housekeeping experience." A soft smile touched her lips. "You may meet him if you wish."

That was a surprise. Meggie studied her friend's wide, hazel eyes carefully. After a long moment, she let out a long stream of air, convinced Eliza was telling the truth. She pulled her in another hug. A second later she felt Eliza's relief escape in a shuddered breath.

"Thank God, Eliza. Thank God."

Chapter Nine

Meggie worked her way past the slew of cheers, well-wishers, and exclamations of shock of having survived her ordeal from the previous night. Her step was lighter. Eliza was okay, and that was the most important thing. Meggie eked her way through the crowd, bound for the stage. Bernie's shiny, bald head was lowered, and his fingers tapped the cymbals lightly. He glanced up, and a smirk tilted his lips. "Well, if it ain't our own Baby Vamp."

The other boys chuckled but continued with their warmup. She scowled at them. "I hate to even ask what that means."

"Ain't nothin' but a popular female, doll. What the hell were you thinkin'? Did you shoot Gentleman Jack?" The others stopped what they were doing and peered at her, interest obvious.

"I never saw Gentleman Jack. Blast, there's no proof it was even me! You didn't see my picture in the paper, did you?"

"Lady Margaret?"

Meggie spun and found herself standing a few inches over a portly fellow with a double-chin and thick, black mustache. A receding hairline made him appear older, but his youthful face attested him somewhere in his early to mid-thirties.

He took her outstretched hand. "Allow me to introduce myself. I'm Paul Whiteman." At her gasp of surprise, he went on. "And this here—" He indicated another man beside him, tall, slender and attractive with light brown, wavy hair. "—is George Gershwin."

Mr. Gershwin gave a short incline of his head. "A pleasure," he murmured.

"You've created quite the stir, Lady Margaret." Mr. Whiteman laughed, sending a blush of heat that spread from her neck up.

She'd donned the silver-sequined number she'd worn for the masquerade aboard the *Empress of India* and was certain her skin, red and mottled, clashed horribly. "It's a pleasure to meet you, Mr. Whiteman. I-I don't know what to say." Surely, he would forgive her unrefined stammering. He was renowned, and he *knew her by name.* Meggie felt a little faint at the notion.

He led her to a nearby table, shooing away patrons already seated, and guided her into a vacated chair. "I like your moxy. I have a proposition for you."

Indignation curdled her stomach, and she started to rise.

Mr. Whiteman's hands came up, palms out in a defensive motion. "Calm yourself, Lady Margaret. George here will be playing with my orchestra at the Plaza on election-Tuesday. One of the largest Voting Parties in the country, and we'd like you to sing."

Stunned and speechless, Meggie could only stare at the two men.

"You are already a sensation, Lady Margaret, but quite frankly, I can catapult you to the moon and back. So, what do you say? The Plaza on Tuesday?"

Unable to utter a single word, Meggie just nodded.

"Excellent. That is just excellent, Lady Margaret."
Mr. Whiteman took her hand and pressed his lips to her
knuckles. "Until Tuesday then."

By the time Meggie croaked out a "thank you" they
were gone.

"Megs?"

She blinked, and Charli was standing before her.

"Megs, you're going to have to move." Charli
looked over her shoulder. "Ira is getting angry. This
table is for paying customers."

"Oh, of course, Charli. Sorry." Meggie stood
quickly, but her path was suddenly blocked by another
gentleman of a stocky and broad, muscular build. His
nose was crooked like he'd spent a lifetime fighting.
His newsboy cap was pulled low over his face.

"You a friend of Eliza Gilbert's?"

"Yes." She spoke slowly, the fine hairs at her nape
rising. His aggressive stance had her taking a step back.
She glanced around, but Charli was already at the bar
refilling her tray with drinks. "What do you want with
Eliza?"

"I want information."

Her chin went up. She gave him her Mrs.
Greensley's coldest stare. "Today is not your lucky day,
sir. I don't give out information on my friends."

"P'haps I should start again, ma'am."

"Perhaps you should."

"I'm trying to find out something about a missing
girl."

Meggie swallowed. "N-not the …dead girl found
in the alley?"

His lips pursed. "No. Not Roxy Gould. I'm looking
for Cynthia Yost, my ex-fiancée," he said harshly.

"Your friend, Eliza, knows something, but she won't come clean, bein' quite the skilled fabricator she is."

Meggie's hand landed in a solid crack across the bounder's face. His cap flew to the ground, revealing a shock of dark-blond hair that was a tad too long. The instruments behind her screeched to silent. He shocked her with a smile, showcasing a dimple that creased the right side of his face.

****

Harry tossed back his whiskey, welcoming the burn down the back of his throat. He signaled for another, pissed that a blonde, sultry bearcat had the ability to knock off his carefully managed existence. Her silver gown did nothing to stem his careening desire. The low-cut bodice that shaped her bust so perfectly had him wishing she still wore the bindings and buttoned-up shirt and bowtie from two nights ago. Those assets should be for his eyes only. He groaned. And this was exactly the reason he should stay away from her.

She should have already been crooning *It Had To Be You.* But no. Some short, fat man had led her to a table, talking ninety to nothing. Harry couldn't make out the egg's words, but when Meggie's lips tightened and hands fisted, Harry rose.

A second later, the gent's hands lifted, palms face-out, and her expression softened into something rhapsodic. The second whiskey appeared on the table. Harry lowered back down and snatched it up. And he damn sure didn't like the looks of the younger man who nodded to her. *Meggie was his.* He swallowed another hit. *But she wasn't, was she.* He'd already made it clear he couldn't keep her safe.

85

His lip curled. As if she'd cared.

Meggie's eyes grew wide at something the round man said, then she nodded. A minute later the two men were making their way through the crowd. Harry's eyes followed them to the door but not before Markov hurried over to them in all his elegance, shaking their hands. By the time Harry's gaze settled on Meggie again, another man dressed no better than a dock worker had her cornered. Enough was enough. He threw back the rest of the whiskey and stormed his way over.

He made an effort to stuff the envy. Seeing the two in a standoff, sparks flying, was somewhat reassuring. He reached Meggie's side just as her hand landed upside the gent's face to stun the surrounding crowd into silence.

Rather than anger, the man smiled at Meggie, sending Harry's blood surging.

He swooped his cap from the floor and tipped his head. "I do hope Miss Gilbert appreciates such loyalty." He spun on his heel and disappeared through the gathering mass of onlookers.

"Miss Gilbert?" Harry took Meggie's trembling hand and followed her gaze after the hulk. "If I'm not mistaken, that's Vincent Taggart."

"I don't care who he is. He had no call to insult my friend." Meggie bit her bottom lip, and damned if Harry wasn't tempted to drag her back through the secret hallway and have his way with her. "Who is Vincent Taggart?"

"Vincent 'The Fist' Taggart. Only the best prize fighter, next to Dempsey—a…er…cousin of mine…" Harry cleared his throat.

She tossed her unfashionable curls, the fire back in her eyes. "Still—"

Harry cut her off and snagged her arm. "Come on. I have something for you." He led her to the bar, then touched the panel to the side, dragging her through the secret door.

"What are you up to, Harry? I have to sing in another fifteen minutes."

"This won't take long," he growled. At the first open room, he pulled her inside. And because he couldn't resist, slid his mouth over hers. He savored the sweet taste of mint before his tongue demanded the same. His palms curled Meggie's slender neck. Her pulse beat against his thumb, his erection pressed against her. If he didn't stop, he'd find himself unable to at all. He pulled away.

"Harry?" Her whisper slid over his skin like the finest silk. That pulse against his thumb, fast and erratic.

"I have something for you, Meggie." He pulled the folded envelope from the inside pocket of his coat.

She took it with shaking fingers. "What is this?"

He watched her expression, waiting for the moment she threw herself in his arms. It was everything he had in the world.

"Cash?" Shock colored the one word in something like a hiss.

Not quite the reaction he was expecting. "What is it? What's wrong?"

She slammed the money in his chest along with the realization that he couldn't put her from his life. He needed Lady Margaret Montley as a permanent fixture in his life.

"How dare you! I am *not* for sale, Mr. Dempsey!" She tore from the room as if Legs Diamond suddenly appeared pointing a pair of Smith & Wessons on her.

"It's for your friend." But he was already speaking to an empty room. Damn it. That girl belonged on Broadway. Her exits were spectacular.

Chapter Ten

Three days later

Meggie, you have got to stop crying. We only have three hours before you are expected at the Plaza to perform in front of all those people. Important people, Meggie. It's their big election day. Georgie is on his way over. He's bringing every arsenal in his bag of tricks."

Meggie sat at the rickety kitchen table with Jessie standing behind her, holding her favorite silver-handled brush. Jessie stuffed a dainty lace handkerchief in her hands, and Meggie pressed it to her eyes. The tears flowed like the river that's dam had burst.

"Those circles beneath your eyes are as deep and dark as the English Channel," Jessie went on. "That damn Harry Dempsey. I have half a mind to bop him on the head the next time I see him."

Her sobs slowed to hiccups, and she peered in the table-top mirror. Jess was right. She looked like the devil. "You and me both. But I'm sure I've seen the last of him…" The words trailed off into another onslaught.

"What I don't understand is why he had an envelope full of cabbage."

Meggie looked at her.

Jess shrugged. "That's what the boys at the *World* call blunt."

"That's the dumbest thing I've ever heard in my life," she muffled in her tissue.

"Tell me, Megs. Why would he attempt to pay you?"

The question infuriated her all over again. "Because he thinks I can be bought like some cheap floozy—" Meggie's back stiffened.

Jess pulled the brush through her hair. "What?"

"He must have thought I still needed—" Meggie dropped her head in her hands. "I'm such a fool."

Meggie raised her head, meeting Jessie's narrowed eyes in the mirror. "Why would Harry think you needed that much money? Did you even count it?"

"No," she said softly. "But I'll wager it equaled a thousand quid."

Jess's hand flew to her chest, and she stumbled into another chair. "Dear God, Meggie. A thousand dol— why, that's a fortune. Why? Why do you need that much money?"

Meggie squirmed under Jess's scrutiny. "It wasn't for me."

"Then who?" Jess fairly shouted.

"Eliza!" she burst out. Her hand flew over her mouth. At Jess's puzzled expression, Meggie drew in a deep breath. "Eliza got in a bit of a bind."

"What kind of bind, Megs?"

"It's okay now, Jess. Really, it is. Eliza told me yesterday everything is taken care of. I need to find Harry. Apologize to him. He was only trying to help." Meggie stood quickly as the tears gathered and fell once again. "I have to find him."

The door flew back. Georgie stood there blocking any exit, make-up satchel in hand. "Darling, *you* are going nowhere looking like the drowned rat you do. We have work to do. Now, sit!"

****

Harry shoved his hands in the front pockets of the only black suit he owned and ignored the politicians, newshawks, society bigwigs—all a bunch of swells and high-hats in his book—while they meandered about shaking hands and kissing asses. His gaze was locked on the orchestra members making their way to the elevated stage setup, instruments in hand. Not the six-piece combo of Bernie and Edison's little six-piece orchestra. No, this was the big-time. At last count there were seventeen pieces, not including the shiny black grand currently being rolled out onto a pink marble floor. He snorted. *Pink.* The elaborate ballroom suited Lady Margaret, right down its ornate chandeliers embellished in gold and the mirrored surfaces decorating the walls. Harry felt as if he'd stepped into a French Chateau straight out of the early 1800s. Close to a hundred white, small, round tables were placed strategically back from an area reserved for dancing. Each adorned with a single, long-stemmed rose—*red*— in a crystal vase.

The sight of those roses filled his head with images running amok. Meggie throwing her body into his, sliding down his own hard body, his hands clasping hers as he tugged her into the darkened hallway at Club 501. Dropping to his knees, where his lips found the silky, bare skin of her belly. Every thought screaming what could have been. What should have been.

Knots cramped his stomach. He hadn't seen her since Saturday night when she'd mistaken his intentions of handing over every last dime of his savings. He'd been so angry he'd stormed out of Club 501 and high-tailed it home, deciding to check on Ma and Lewis. Regret had him rushing back. But by that time the band was tearing down and Meggie was long gone.

So here he stood, at Frank Markov's invitation, who had also disappeared. Waiting, *hoping* for the opportunity to share just a few words with her. Explain how he'd only wanted to help her friend. Tell her—tell her that *he loved her.* If she blew him off after that, then he would let her go—*bullshit.* No. No way in hell was he prepared to walk away.

He scanned the ballroom as more patrons crowded their way in from an opulent foyer, frowning when Teddy Clifford ambled in flashing his press pass as if it were the key to the city. The man was still a sleaze, no matter how decked out he was.

As the band members tuned up, Paul Whiteman's thick mustache seemed to twitch, his movements agitated. The whole scenario set the hair at Harry's neck rising. There was no sign of Meggie. Nothing strange about that, but Harry ventured closer. He couldn't quell the sensations. Sensations that rang all too familiar when Pa sent him on a fool's errand just before he was brutally murdered.

The need to see Meggie surged through him. His skin pricked with apprehension, and he hastened his steps. A scrawny fellow brushed by reaching Whiteman just before Harry.

"What the hell do you mean she left?"

"I'm sorry Mr. Whiteman. I-I was checking on her as you asked, but she was halfway down the hall with some palooka. Looked like he been done over but good. Face was all banged up."

"Son of a bitch," Harry hissed.

The two men's gazes jerked to his.

"You know anything about why my star canary would scram fifteen minutes before showtime?" Whiteman demanded.

Harry sucked in a deep breath. "Keagan," he said.

****

The dressing room door opened then clicked shut. Meggie glanced in the mirror to see who else had come to wish her well. First, Jess, then Charli had visited. No sign of Eliza *or* Harry. She froze. Alarm hit her veins. But it felt as if her movements were hindered, like swimming through molasses. She stood from the vanity table and turned. Long gone was Joey Keagan's neatly slicked back hair and dapper matching argyle socks and sweater he'd sported the last time she'd seen him. He still wore them, but now they were ripped and soiled beyond repair. The stench emanating from him reminded her of something vile dredged up from the Thames.

"I've nothing to say you, so you may as well leave." Damn her shaky voice.

He sneered. "You think you're better than me? I told you before—you and me, we could make thousands. Instead, you throw yourself into the arms of the closest lug. Fuck that Harry Dempsey. In fact, I'm guessing you already have."

Meggie's cheeks burned, not because she had been with Harry, but because she so wanted him in that very way.

Joey ran a hand over his bruised jaw. "Well, I'll take my due with or without your say so."

Fury poured through her. "Are you insane? I'm singing in fifteen minutes. I'm not going *anywhere* with you."

He blocked the door, standing with legs spread, arms folded over his chest. "You're nothing but a quiff, and I'll have my way with you yet."

Meggie's anger began to give way to fear. "You think I'm going to just walk out of here? With you?" She forced a laugh, suddenly realizing her mistake in hesitating. She'd given him too much time to ensconce himself. She should have lunged at him, gouged out his eyes, brought him to his knees with a pointed kick. Yes, Eliza *had* taught her that little maneuver. She tamped down her panic. She would just have to wait out the next opportunity to execute the move.

He straightened and slipped his hands into the pockets of his tattered tweed jacket and pulled out a small gun. "I happen to think that's exactly what you'll do." His gaze swept from her face to her feet and back, settling on her cleavage. "That blue sequined stuff looks mighty fine, but I expect you'll need a coat for our little adventure."

Someone pounded on the door. "Five minutes, Miss Montley."

She opened her mouth to call out, but the hammer on the pistol clicked, and the words stuck in her throat.

He let out a low chuckle that would haunt her dreams for life. "We'll have to do something about your name. After a while we can set you up like one of those courtson's." He inclined the gun toward the coat tree in the corner. "Let's go."

Meggie snatched up the dark, blue and black tapestry weaved coat with fur cuffs and collar she'd found in a second-hand store somewhere near 6th Avenue and 42nd Street and slipped it on. "Courtesan. If you are going to use the word, you should at least make an effort to pronounce it correctly," she snapped.

Joey stepped closer and fingered the collar, his wrist brushing her chin. "Nice."

She jerked back.

"We'll have none of that *Lady* Margaret," he said, gripping her arm. "By the time I'm done with you, you won't be a *lady* anything. Well, perhaps a lady of the night." He laughed at his silly joke, lifting her chin with the barrel. He pressed it into her skin.

Terror speared her spine, racing up then down.

"We'll just quietly make our way out. There's doors all over this place. But one wrong move, and I'll knock you off and anyone who comes close. I may not live through it, but neither will you. You understand?"

She could barely nod. She buttoned her coat and put her chilled hand in her pocket. *The pocket that held her flat key.*

Still gripping her other arm, he jerked her to the door. He slipped the gun into his pocket and eased the door back. After checking the corridor, he tugged her out, strolling just as nice as you please.

"Miss Montley?" The words sounded behind.

Joey picked up their pace and snarled, "Not a word."

Another wave of anger surged through her. She refused to make it easy for him. "You'll never get away with this, you know. I'm not even wearing a hat. Women just do not go about without a hat."

"Shut your trap," he bit out.

But Meggie was afraid. She clutched the clunky metal between her fingers, praying for an opportunity, *any* opportunity, because just ahead on the left were doors facing the north, and across the street from that, Central Park. At this time of year, he could stash her anywhere. That was if he didn't kill her first. At least there were people around now—

"Hold it right there, Keagan."

The deep, menacing voice was so low Meggie stumbled over it, her fear reaching the clouds. All she could envision was the man she loved bloodied and sprawled at her feet. "Harry. He's got a gun." Her trembling voice squeaked. She gripped her inadequate, but only, weapon tighter.

"So do I. Move away from her, Keagan, before I blow your brains out all over her pretty dress."

"You fucked with my life enough, Harry. Now I'm gonna fuck with yours—"

Meggie didn't wait another second. She jammed the spiked heel of her T-strapped shoe into his foot. Her motion caught him by surprise enough to loosen the grip he had on her arm. She threw her elbow into his stomach, then spun. With a pained grunt Joey bent forward. Then with the key positioned between her index and middle fingers she went for the kill—but missed his eye, only managing to clip his neck strong enough to draw blood.

She was flung against the wall like a rag doll but somehow managed to stand on her own two legs. Joey slid to the floor out cold. Blood trickled from the side of his head co-mingled with the wound on his neck.

Chest heaving, her pulse raced, her cries whimpered. "Is he d-dead?" The words landed in the warmth of Harry's neck, and she shuddered in his hold. Perhaps she should rethink this being famous business. Between the coppers who'd raided the 501 and some brow-beating bully accosting her at the Plaza—she shuddered.

"Not from lack of trying," Harry growled. "Nice work, Lady Margaret. You are quite resourceful." His breath teased the hair at her temple.

"I have three b-bothersome b-brothers." Things would be fine. She just needed to stay calm. *And here was Harry, coming through yet again.*

"Come on, you have the performance of a lifetime to give. And you're already late." His gentleness brought tears to her eyes. "And then? We need to talk."

Chapter Eleven

"Oh. My. God." Tears pooled in Jessie's eyes, along with the words that had Meggie sniffing back her own. The problem, as Meggie saw it, was that once she let loose a river, then all was lost. Not one who cried prettily or, in most cases, often—just lately.

Jess was waiting in Meggie's dressing room when she'd arrived. "You were fabulous." She threw her hands in the air and spun about like a ballerina in a perfect turn. All those dance lessons Lady Hatton had forced on her paid off. She stopped and lifted her chin—another Lady Hatton inheritance. "But then, I knew you would be."

Meggie grinned, because she just couldn't help it. "I was, wasn't I?" She faced herself in the mirror, snatched a tissue, and dabbed at her tears, refusing to turn into another blubbering mess before her face-off with Harry. She needed every arsenal for the talk he was demanding. Her premonitions for these things were quite reliable, and she would not let him brush her away. *Not again.*

"What did Whiteman say afterward? I saw him tell you something. You looked positively vapor-struck when he walked away."

Meggie's hands flew to her mouth, and she spun back to her friend. "Oh, Jess. He's been asked to compose music for a new Broadway show and asked that I audition." With each word her voice went up an interval until it ended an octave higher and on a squeal.

The room filled with stunned silence, Meggie's eyes meeting Jess's. A second later Jess's screams met Meggie's, and Jessie pulled her into a hug. "You did it, Megs. You truly did it. You made it without any help with your interfering brothers and your mother's disapproving airs. You'll never have to marry that icky Percy. Or anyone if you don't so chose."

The words caught Meggie by surprise, reeling her back from the clouds she'd just been floating on. *Harry. I would marry Harry.*

Someone banged on the door, startling them. "Everything all right in there?"

Before she could answer the door crashed back. An attendant was righting himself then skittered off. Harry moved into the doorframe, then like a cat strolled inside. Serious and unsmiling, solid—steady, strong. Tempting Meggie to throw herself into arms that would always keep her grounded.

Jess squeezed her in another hug and slipped away, leaving Meggie on her own to fight the battle of her life.

****

Harry couldn't get a read from the wide, blue, unblinking eyes peering at him. "Huh. So you never wish to marry? And who the hell is Percy?" The statements had thrown him. How the devil was he supposed to convince Meggie that he was the man for her? The *only* man for her.

She blinked.

Unnerved and off his game, Harry blundered in, pushing the door to until it latched. Meggie's eyes widened slightly. The only sign showing she was not as confident as she pretended. She dropped into the chair before the mirror and picked up a silver-handled hairbrush, fingers trembling. Another encouraging sight.

"I believe I mentioned that before."

"No. No, I would have remembered you saying that." He sauntered closer, relieved and itching to run his fingers through locks that were once again the blonde, soft curls he loved, the brown rinse completely washed away from her adventure several nights ago.

"Oh. For years I've been living under the pressure of being manacled to some pale-faced noble with no ambition. Something of which I have no desire."

He took the brush from her hand, surprised at how heavy it was. "I see." He slid it through her hair, met her eyes in the mirror. "I'm glad you don't sport that short wavy 'do most of the young women are wearing these days."

"But I could," she said softly.

He set the brush aside and fingered the softness of her hair while he considered her response. "Yes, you could. But it wouldn't stop me from wanting you in my bed every night for the rest of my life."

Her eyes went wide again, then narrowed on him. "What exactly are you saying, Mr. Dempsey?"

As stern as she tried to appear, her bottom lip trembled, touching something deep within his chest. He felt a smile play about his lips, desire spiraling through him. His hands moved to her shoulders, and he swiveled her around. He lowered himself to his knees where they were face to face.

"I mean it, Harry. Despite—" She paused, took a steadying breath. "I can't be bought."

He opened his mouth to explain. Tell her that the money was just a misunderstanding, but she stayed him with an index finger to his lips. His own pulse tripled. He resisted, with great effort, of sucking her finger into his mouth, but couldn't keep his tongue from one irresistible lick.

Heat flooded her cheeks, coinciding with her sharp intake of air. Another thread bonded her to him. An unbreakable tie.

"I realized later that the money…the money was most likely for my friend."

He nodded.

"Still, my brothers would hunt you down and dig your heart out with a dull spoon if they caught wind of—"

"Stop. I've heard enough." His tone came out darker, harsher than he'd intended. "Do you really believe I'd want you without binding you to me forever?" He snorted, disgusted. "Leave you an easy way to escape?"

Her eyes softened and the block in his chest gave way.

"Hell, no. I want you with me. Always. Inevitably tied by matrimony."

Her eyes shimmered, and the sight filled him with hope.

"I'm not an easy man, Lady Margaret. But I'll never stand between you and your dreams."

One tear spilled over. Only one.

He wiped it away with his thumb. "I love you. I didn't need to be at Frank's every night. I was there because I couldn't stay away from *you*."

She launched from the chair and into his arms. "Don't ever scare me like that again." Her sobs soaked his collar, and he tightened his arms around her. "Ever."

"No," he whispered. "Never."

Martini Club 4:
The 1940s

Pampered

Prologue

Martha's Vineyard, Summer 1935

Audra Faye Dempsey folded down one white, lace-edged sock then the other and slipped her feet into her shiny black Mary Janes, buckled them, and hurried from the bedroom she shared with her best friends in the whole world: Iris, Sophie, and Maddie. Her friends had ducked out ages ago in worn dresses and *sensible* shoes. But then their mommies weren't famous singers like Audra's mom, Lady Margaret, whose agent expected her child to dress in a way that reflected her mother's glamourous image.

Mommy didn't usually mind that Audra's pretty dresses might end up ruined with dirt and grime by the end of the day. She said that it was Mr. Frisk who was so image-conscious. He was a stodgy old man, and Audra didn't much care for him. He fawned over Mommy way too much. Daddy hated it too, even though he didn't really say it out loud. It was something she just knew.

Audra pushed away her irritation and let the excitement flow through her. This was her favorite time of year—when all Mommy's English friends and their families met for their annual holiday in Edgartown. Audra darted down the hallway and down the stairs, passing the library.

"Damn it, Meggie."

An icy chill crept up Audra's spine, and she slowed. Daddy never raised his voice. Most especially to Mommy. They loved each other more than anyone in the whole world. Even her, and that was saying something. She crept closer to the door.

Her mother let out a sigh. "Harry, darling, you know I've no choice in the matter."

Even though Mommy had been in America since 1924—one year before Audra was born—her English accent was still strong, just like her aunts Charli, Jessie, and Eliza. They weren't really her aunts, but Mommy said they were the sisters she'd never had. Audra often wished *she* had a pretty accent too. She did get Mommy's pretty, blue eyes, everyone said so.

An exasperated huff erupted from her mother. Something that, lately, seemed more the norm. "I *must* go. Surely, you see that."

Go where? Audra's stomach dropped. Mommy was already on the island. Everyone was. It didn't make sense for her to go anywhere. It was that stupid Mr. Frisk. He was always trying to ruin something or other.

"It's time to let go of New York, Meggie." Her father fairly growled. Audra had never heard him sound like that before. "We need this. *Audra* needs this. You know I won't be handed another opportunity of this magnitude again in my lifetime."

Audra peeked through a crack. Different gun variations lined the walls. She didn't really like them, but Daddy did. He said he was an avid collector, whatever that meant.

Mommy bristled, and Audra's eyes snapped to her. "Harry. This isn't like you. You know I can't just up and move from New York to Boston. Not with all my pressing obligations."

He stormed to the terrace doors where Audra could make out his reflection clear as day as he glared out, hands shoved deep in the pockets of his brown trousers. He turned and faced her mother. "It's always about *your* obligations, *your* career, Lady Margaret." His mocking tone was not something Audra recognized from her usually collected father. Audra brought her shaking fingers to her trembling mouth.

Her stomach was a riot of nerves watching as he ran a hand through his hair, seeming to weigh his words. Something he always did when he was frustrated. "Damn," he breathed. His light-brown eyes looked harder and colder than the cliff rocks in the height of winter. He squared his shoulders. "I'm making a stand, Meggie, whether you decide to go or not is up to you." His tone was resigned like he was tired.

Mommy's face turned white. She clutched the edge of the huge mahogany desk that took up one end of the large room. "You would leave—me and Audra?"

His eyes narrowed, and his voice etched harder than steel. "Oh, no, my dear. I won't be leaving Audra." A peculiar calm oozed from him that sent a frisson of fear surging through Audra.

Mommy's eyes shimmered with tears. "Harry, what are you saying?" she whispered. She fell back into one of the two chairs before the desk as if her legs could no longer hold her up.

"That your contractual obligations—your *singing career*—mean more to you than your own family."

A flash of fury Audra had never witnessed in all her ten whole years erupted from her mother. She shot from the chair and jabbed her index finger in Daddy's broad chest, catching him by surprise, forcing him to stumble back a step. "Don't you *dare* think to intimidate me, Harry Dempsey. I had enough of that from my toplofty mother and brothers my entire life. They still telephone weekly, only to let me know what a disgrace I am to the family, the *title* I abandoned—no—should have married, and I refuse to fall victim to yours or anyone's threats." Each word was punctuated with a poke to his chest until he winced.

Daddy's compressed lips parted. "Meg—"

Mommy's hand flew up, palm out. "I've heard enough. I implore *you* to remember your own par—"

Audra didn't wait to hear more, somehow holding back a wrenching sob. A desperate need to talk to Maddie, Sophie, and Iris squeezed the air from her lungs. She bolted for the front door and swung it back to find her way blocked by a man with lightish hair and gray eyes, fist poised to knock. "Oh. Hello," he said in that condescendingly fake sweet tone people used when Mr. Frisk introduced her as Lady Margaret's only child. She couldn't tell how old he was. She wasn't good at that sort of thing. "You wouldn't be Audra Faye, now would you? You must be. You're as pretty as your mama. You have her eyes."

In a blinding flash of fury, fear, and intuition, her life as she knew it was about to change. The words stuck in her throat, suffocating her; apprehension pounding through her. "Who are you?"

He raised a forefinger to touch her nose, but she turned her head forcing him to miss. Red stained his cheeks at the abrupt awkwardness. Her whole body rebelled. Good. She hated when people treated her as if she were nothing but a walking-talking "Lady Margaret" doll one could purchase at Woolworths. She glanced down at her pink-pleated dress trimmed with white embroidered flowers suddenly hating all its femininity.

"Um." He cleared his throat. "I'm Leo Frisk. I'm here for Lady Margaret. We have an appointment."

He was lying. She knew Mr. Frisk, and this wasn't him. "She's busy. She can't talk to you. I guess you'll have to leave."

"Audra Faye! What the devil." Mommy stood in the arch of the library with her hands on her hips. "Leo, darling, I wasn't expecting *you*." Audra steeled herself against her mother's stern gaze with a stubborn lift of her chin. "Please come in, and please forgive my precocious daughter."

Darling? Audra bristled, narrowing her eyes on the intruder, then quite deliberately stomped past him, his foot under her sturdy Mary Janes.

The morning air failed to cool her flaming cheeks. She took off in a run unable to grasp a breath, tripping at the edge of the drive. A sharp pain shot through her knee. But she ignored the pain, feeling *his* eyes burning her back through her shoulders. Tears stung, but she refused to let them fall, doing her best to shove away Mommy's and Daddy's words, and darted for the garden.

Dante, the caretaker's son, was supposed to show them how to shoot arrows today, and now she didn't even want to. The angry words her parents hurled at one another swirled in her head. And now Leo-Frisk-

darling had to show up and ruin *everything*. He was there to take her mother away. She sniffed, and she dragged her sleeve across her nose. Why did Mommy want to leave? *Your singing career means more to you than your own family.*

She scraped a fist over her eyes, pushing away tears that fell anyway. Panting, she stopped at the backyard that faced Major's Cove and scanned the area for her friends. Sophie sat at the base of the old elm tree, fingers darting quickly over her sketch book and—

Oh, no. Dante stood rigid as a wood post. His stance spelled big trouble as his hands closed into tight fists at his side. He drew himself up to his full height. Which was really tall. He was fifteen, practically a grown man. His lips were pressed into a thin line, facing off with that mean ole Thomas Killman. Thomas's family owned a summer house right down the road. Why couldn't Thomas have just stayed home? He was always saying things Audra didn't understand.

One thing was certain. Dante didn't dare risk a fight. Uncle Vince didn't tolerate such confrontations, which was funny since he was a boxer. Audra took off in another run, ignoring her pained knee. She might be small, but she was fast.

Sophie tossed her drawing book aside and rose, apparently sizing up the situation just as quickly.

From the corner of her eye, Audra spied Maddie and Iris sitting, heads together, on a wrought iron and wood bench situated in what Mommy dubbed the "field of flowers." Neither seemed to have yet noticed the unfolding drama.

Sophie pulled up next to Audra in front of Dante. Audra grabbed Sophie's hand. "Dante, you know you can't get into a fight," she whispered. "Uncle Vince said he'd send you and your daddy away if it happened again."

He ignored her, addressing Thomas. "You watch what you say about Iris, Killman, or I swear I'll flatten you." Dante's teeth were so clenched the words barely passed through. He looked fit to kill, and Audra's dread rose.

Thomas glanced over at Maddie and Iris and shrugged. "I'm not saying anything that ain't true. Her mama serviced my pa."

Audra spun around. With her hands on her hips, she drew up, defiant. "Aunt Eliza wasn't your pa's maid, Thomas Killman. She left that position when she ran away from England with Mommy and Aunt Charli."

Thomas's laugh bounded through the yard, against the cliffs. He tapped her nose, and Audra jumped back, scrubbing away the vile touch. He turned back to Dante, taunting. "I'm just saying, that girl's gonna grow up prettier than her mama, and I plan to continue the tradition."

There he went again, saying things Audra didn't understand.

Before Audra could blink, Dante's fist shot out, clipping Thomas's chin, snapping his head back, sending him slumped to the ground in a heap. An unnatural silence filled the yard. Even the waves hitting the rocks seemed to lose their constant roar. No birds twittered. No wind stirred.

Then Maddie and Iris were there, all five of them surrounding the unconscious, mean Thomas Killman.

Audra should feel bad, but she truly didn't. She *hated* Thomas Killman more than ever.

Maddie, Aunt Jessie's niece, the oldest of all the girls, was twelve. She peered closer and wrinkled her nose and said in her snootiest British accent, "Do you suppose you've offed him?"

Butterflies fluttered deep in Audra's stomach as more tears blurred her vision. "You have to run away, Dante. Uncle Vince will *kill* you."

"I'll be fine," he grated out.

"But—"

Iris reached over and touched his knuckles. "You're bleeding."

He glanced down at his injured hand then back at Iris. "Promise me something." He spoke softly, and the air grew uncomfortable.

No one said a word, and after a long moment Iris nodded uncertainly.

"Don't ever let anyone tell you that you are anything less than you are. Do you hear?" he said roughly. "*Ever.*"

"O-okay. I-I won't."

Dante kicked Thomas in the ribs, and he groaned. Audra was glad. "Get up, you piece of shit." He didn't move, and Dante hauled him up by the neck and threw him over his shoulder like a sack of grain then strode from the yard without a backward look.

"Audra, your dress," Sophie said, breaking the silence. "It's torn. And you're bleeding too?"

Audra glanced down at her knee, now noticing how it throbbed. Sure enough, blood oozed from a large scrape. Her pink dress was ripped and covered in dirt.

She looked back up at her friends. Friends she'd known her whole life. All ten years.

"Mommy is leaving Daddy and me." Her voice shook, and she burst into tears.

Chapter One

Club 501 — Boston, 1947

Leo's tonic was tart and the gin smooth, exactly as he liked it. He slung it back keeping his eye on the door.

Half a minute later, and like a well-oiled clock, it swung open. Audra Faye Dempsey swept in like the force of a hurricane. He couldn't draw his gaze away from the pert nose in her heart-shaped face framed by soft, short, dark curls. He didn't have to look at his wristwatch to see that it was 4:13. She rolled through every afternoon that exact same time, rarely a minute earlier or later. Sometimes, the compelling urge to meet her on the corner just to throw her off her meticulous timetable overwhelmed him. But Leo had the unfortunate plague of desiring Audra beyond redemption.

He leaned against the bar, hiding a smile, her clipped heels taking her straight by him. Of course, she ignored him. Too bad he couldn't ignore the soft scent of gardenia trailing in her wake. "Audra Faye." He tipped his empty glass in her direction. She hated being referred to by her full name. The girl had absolutely no sense of humor.

"Mr. Frisk," she murmured.

Did her steps grow faster? He'd bet on it, as she hightailed it past the large orchestra's stage to the hallway behind, bound for Harry's office. Leo forfeited the urge to follow as was his custom, knowing how it pricked her temper. But for some reason, he didn't feel up to her usual prideful censure today.

Leo set his glass gently on the bar and left. He'd had his Audra-fix for the day. *For now*, he thought a little morosely and walked the two blocks to his office, taking the stairs two at a time in an effort to expel some of the restless energy that plagued him when he came within touching distance of the little minx.

He was not a normal man. Oh, sure the sexual urges were there, but he hadn't acted on them, with *anyone*, since he'd attended the little prodigy's college graduation the year before. She stole his breath. He wasn't so sure he hadn't fallen a little bit in love with the obdurate Audra that day she'd stomped by him all those years ago. Back when he'd shown up in place of his father to escort Lady Margaret to a quick fundraiser for war widows. He'd never garnered an explanation of Audra's anger that day. How furious she'd been. At the time, Leo had wisely choked back his laughter at her measly attempt to crush his foot.

Now, Leo let out a grunt as he pushed through the front door of his office. "Good afternoon, Mrs. Jones. Any messages?" The question was rote as he rounded past his secretary's desk to his own through another door located behind her.

"Only one, Mr. Frisk," she said, holding out a soiled envelope.

He stopped and turned to her. Frowning, he pinched the edges between his index finger and thumb. "What's this?"

She wrinkled her nose. "I'm sure I don't know."

He moved on through and fell into his chair, studying his name scrawled in a shaky scratch across a stain he prayed was coffee. He pulled the letter opener from its woodblock and slit open the envelope.

Dear Mr. Frisk,

Our mutual friend, Evelyn Payne, has met with an unfortunate end. It was Evie's dying wish that you see to all she held dear. Unfortunately, I can only offer you two days before releasing her belongings to the highest bidder. I can be found in South End where East Street meets Tufts. Ask around, everyone knows me. I urge you to think carefully before disregarding Evie's wishes... Two days, Mr. Frisk.

Vera Clay

What the hell? He hadn't seen Evelyn Payne since he'd gone overseas in 1940, some seven years prior. And, yeah, he'd gotten Evelyn's letters. Even wrote her back once or twice. Once Leo's father had passed from this world unto the next, Leo had been forced to return home and step into his role at the agency his father had founded full-time. Then seeing Audra all grown up...well, he hadn't given Evelyn another thought.

His eyes roved over the words again. The sense of urgency raised the hair on his neck.

Damn. This was all he needed.

****

The burn from Leo's stare eased between Audra's shoulder blades the second she entered the hallway that wound behind the stage and out of his direct gaze. The man drove her crazy despite his physical appeal. Every day, he sat on that very corner watching her. It unnerved her, though she'd never admit it aloud. She reached her father's office and dropped her head from one side to the other to loosen the tension in her neck. What was it about that man that had her running like a skittish filly? Infuriating. As if she had the time or inclination over something—no, *someone*—as trivial as Leo Frisk. Audra straightened her spine and braced for the real battle. The one with her father. It saddened her how close they'd been at one time, but since she'd graduated from college he'd become an unreasonable bear. Uncompromising. And, downright…stodgy!

A quick glance over her shoulder showed Leo hadn't followed her this time. Jeeps, he was so annoying. If she didn't know any better, she'd swear he did it to get under her skin, reminding her of Tommy Clover from third grade. Always pushing her on the shoulder, dogging her steps, and tugging on her braids until she'd begged Daddy to let her cut her hair.

"He just likes you, pumpkin. Boys do dumb things when they like a girl as pretty as you. Are you sure you want to cut off all that beautiful hair?"

"Yes! I never want long hair again."

Good grief. Was she comparing Leo to a kid in her third-grade class? Worse, did his actions indicate an attraction? *That* was the most laughable thing that had gone through her head since she'd met the man when she was ten years old. Besides, it wasn't *Audra* he was attracted to, she reminded herself.

The old fury pulsed through her, compounding her anger. She couldn't stomach Leo Frisk. He still harbored feelings for her mother. How could he not? Lady Margaret was a larger-than-life persona Audra could, and would, never deign to compete with. Ha! Compete with Meggie? Another laughable idea.

Audra ran her fingers through her short curls, let out a breath before clasping the knob of the closed door. Sometimes, she wasn't so sure Daddy didn't pay Leo to keep an eye on her. Couldn't any of them— Mother, Daddy, *and* Leo—see that she'd grown up? She stifled her aggravation and entered her father's domain.

Her father looked up from the small gun he was cleaning. The worry in his gaze squeezed the oxygen from her lungs like an iron-band torture device straight out of one of her college history books.

"Hi, Daddy."

He stuffed the small pistol in a side drawer and gave her a hard look. "Damn it, Audra."

She moved farther into the room and plopped down in one of the two uncomfortable chairs across from his desk, rolling her eyes. "*Now* what's wrong?"

He slapped a newspaper down on the desk and slid it across the desk to her. "Another body was found near the railroad tracks in South End."

"Daddy—"

"It's the fifth one in the last six months." He snatched up the paper and shook it out. "They've dubbed him the South End Slayer. I don't like you going down there, Audra." The paper fell back to the desk, and he shoved a hand through his hair. "I mean, do you have to go? Every damn day?"

In his late fifties, her dad was built as sturdy as a locomotive. Sometimes it was all she could do to keep from throwing herself into those powerful arms as if she were still four years old and let him right every wrong in her world. Given any opportunity, he usually did just that. Unfortunately, it never seemed to occur to him that she was now twenty-two and graduated from college—two whole years before the other girls her age. He pierced her with eyes the color of aged whiskey.

The argument was old. But she was his daughter. The stubbornness that flowed through her veins came straight from him. "I don't want to argue anymore, Daddy. I'm doing what I have to do."

He let out a resigned sigh. "I know, I know," he said. "I just don't have to like it." His eyes moved over her black collared blouse opened at the throat. The lines about his mouth tightened.

Another bout of aggravation flitting through her waged war with gnawing guilt. But what did *she* have to feel guilty about? Audra stood and smoothed her hand over the pleated trousers she wore and raised her chin. "Katherine Hepburn wears trousers, Daddy. It's all the rage."

"If your mother—"

Enough. She sure didn't want to get into that discussion. Audra breathed in through her nose to stem more rising anger. "I didn't come in here to discuss Mother, as you well know."

"She'll be home over the weekend."

The steady stream of air seeped from her pursed lips. Her gaze dropped to the floor. "So?"

A long pause ensued before he said gruffly, "Just don't wear those things at dinner Saturday night, please."

"I-I have plans Saturday night."

His hands flattened on the desk in a bang that startled her eyes to his. "Yes. You do. Dinner. Eight-thirty sharp. That should give you plenty of time to finish up at that godforsaken soup kitchen," he bit out.

"It's not enough time to change," she mumbled, stepping back.

"Make the time." His growl startled her, then made her angry. *Always your bidding, Lady Margaret.* Those words had haunted her since that summer in 1935. Always close to the surface. Always ready to suffocate her.

Audra swallowed her hurt—no, her fury—fully aware she'd won the first battle. Dinner, however, was another matter. Mother's travels had taken her to Europe the past two months *this time,* and Audra could already feel the tension gathering in her neck. "Fine. Who's coming?"

Her father reclined, the chair squeaking in protest to his solid bulk. "Leo, of course."

Why? She wanted to scream. *You know what they did*! But she lost her nerve to voice those fears like she always did and swallowed her...annoyance and the tart rejoinder, *of course he is.*

"A couple of other Hollywood bigwigs. Someone from Look Magazine. They're doing an article."

Another eye roll to the ceiling.

"That's enough, Audra Faye." He sat forward, the chair moaning dangerously. He held out an envelope. "I need you to run this by Leo's office."

"He's at the bar, Daddy. I don't know why you don't give it to him yourself. He'll probably be here in a minute, anyway." God, she sounded sulky. What was wrong with her?

He lifted a brow.

She snatched it from his hand. "Fine. I'll hand it to him on my way out."

Her father lowered his eyes to a stack of papers and started flipping through them, amusement creasing his cheeks. He couldn't hide it. Not from her. "Thank you." Ah, there it was. His customary dismissal.

Audra spun on her heel and reached for the door, trying desperately to rein in her temper. Everyone was forever trying to run her life. But *that* would never happen, she vowed. Someday she would meet someone who loved her for herself and not because she was *Lady Margaret's little girl.* Resentment burned her lungs making it difficult to breathe. And that somebody was not Leo Frisk, Jr.

Her groan filled the narrow hallway. Where were these stupid thoughts coming from? She hated Leo Frisk. He was nothing but a bootlicking salesman who catered to the rich and famous. Number one on his list? Lady Margaret.

So what if Daddy and Mother were still together after all these years? Their whole relationship was just a front for the eager-beaver news reporters wanting something juicy for their reels. Hadn't she'd learned that truth twelve years ago?

"Audra," he barked.

Exasperation finally won out. She spun on a heel, facing her overbearing father. "What!"

"Be careful. You know how I feel about South End." He let out a sad, resigned sigh. "I'll see you tonight."

"I'm twenty-two, Daddy. Not ten." She would never be ten again. Tears pricked her eyes as she stalked back out to the bar—where, blast it all—Leo Frisk was nowhere to be seen.

Chapter Two

Audra frowned. "Hey, Pauley. Do you know where Leo disappeared to?"

"Nah, Miss Dempsey. He done skedaddled."

Leo wasn't usually in such a hurry to leave, most times stopping her for some mundane idle chat she was certain Daddy put him up to. A ruse to keep her time in South End as minimal as possible. But Audra had her reasons for working at the soup kitchen. And no one was going to stop her. Especially some idiotic monster dubbed the South End Slayer. She was smart enough to stay in the populated areas.

Ugh. With Leo gone, she really would have to go by his office. While it was only a couple of blocks away, it was located in the opposite direction of the bus she needed to take. That would put her fifteen minutes behind schedule. She *hated* being off schedule. This was Leo's fault for not following her down the hall like he usually did.

Seven and a half minutes later she stalked through the door of his office. "Hello, Mrs. Jones."

"Oh, Miss Dempsey." Her iron-gray curls bounced with enthusiasm, and Audra took a step back. Mrs. Jones was one of the "star struck" ones. Audra being the only child of Lady Margaret made her a favorite of Mrs. Jones. "How lovely to see you...and wearing..." She swallowed. "...trousers." She seemed to have difficulty getting the word out.

Audra hid her grin in a spin. "Aren't they adorable? Katherine Hepburn wears them."

Mrs. Jones cleared her throat and beamed Audra a bright smile. "You missed Mr. Frisk by just a couple of minutes, dear. If you hurry you should be able to catch him."

Oh, good. Luck was with her. With a little more, she shouldn't have to see Leo again until Saturday night. Audra returned Mrs. Jones's smile with a bright one of her own and held out the envelope. "I'm only dropping this off for my father. I'm in a bit of a hurry."

Her thin lips turned down. "I suppose you're off to that nasty soup kitchen," she said with a disapproving sniff.

"Mr. Ruthers keeps a clean kitchen, Mrs.—"

But Mrs. Jones was on a roll. "—a pretty thing like you should be married by now with a couple of children. Why, my own daughter has two, and she's twenty."

"How marvelous for you," she murmured. Worse than the star-strucks, were the do-gooder matrons of the world who believed only that a woman's place was in the home.

"You know, Mr. Frisk would be per—"

Truly? Audra spun to the door desperate for a quick escape. "My apologies, Mrs. Jones, but I really must be on my way."

"South End is too dangerous for a young wo—"

Audra shut the door firmly, cutting her off and hurrying down the stoop. She glanced at her watch. Nine minutes. Now she would be forced to take a cab, costing money that cut deeply into her pin money.

The ride took another twenty minutes due to the five o'clock traffic. Two blocks from the soup kitchen, she tossed the driver a five. "This will do, sir." She jumped out to stride quickly the remainder of the way.

Less than a block from her destination, she put her hand on her heart, spotting the small figure she'd been watching for. He sat cross-legged beneath a large oak with his loyal companion glued to his side. Audra made her way across a field of patchy grass, uncaring of her heels that sunk into the ground with every step. "Hi, Jamie. How are you this afternoon?"

"Hungry, Miss Dempsey."

She frowned. "You didn't have lunch?"

His light-blond hair was in its usual disarray. He dropped his head and smoothed a hand over the matted coat of his dog.

"You did eat, didn't you?"

After a long pause, he nodded.

"Then what—oh. You must be feeling Willie's hunger pains," she said gently. Willie was a mutt with the softest brown eyes and floppy ears. Cleaned up, his coat would be the perfect strawberry blond hair women would kill for. He was skinny and malnourished, and Audra could count the poor dog's ribs.

Jamie looked up, big tears pooling in his eyes. "I can hear his tummy growling."

Audra leaned over and rubbed Willie's ears, and indeed, also heard the rumblings coming from the pooch's stomach.

"Mr. Ruthers looks at me funny when I tell him Willie is hungry too. Mean like."

"I expect it's more that he's concerned with the humans in the neighborhood getting fed first, Jamie. I wouldn't pay him any mind."

A tear slid down his cheek. "I can't eat anymore. Not until Willie does. It's not fair."

The sight broke Audra's heart. "Hm." Audra glanced across the street to the soup kitchen where the regulars were already lining up for dinner. On the corner across, a local prostitute was gripped by a fierce man who jerked her arm and tugged her down the street. It took everything in Audra to go home at night, knowing Jamie lived in such a horrific environment. Other than snatching him up and stashing him away where no one could find him, she didn't know what else to do but check on him every day. If she couldn't hide him to keep him from harm, then she could at least reassure herself by seeing him. The woman's brassy blonde hair bobbed with her pronounced limp, having likely turned an ankle in her impractical stilettos.

Audra wished she could help her as well, but she was only one person. *Baby steps.* She let out a sigh, watching until the couple disappeared around the corner. "Suppose you wait around behind—by the back door. I'll see what I can rustle up." She ruffled Jamie's hair. It was in desperate need of a wash. "But we'd best keep this between the two of us, okay?"

Jamie blinked quickly, nodding, his smile lighting up the late afternoon sky.

Willie looked up too, and she'd swear his smile was a big as Jamie's, his pink tongue hanging out, tail wagging so fast she thought he might take flight.

"As soon as the two of you have eaten, you go straight home. Will you promise me?" He nodded, and her heart sung. Somehow, she refrained from hugging him, them. She had a feeling it wouldn't be appreciated.

These two. These two were the reason Audra braved South End day after day. "Now scoot. I'll see you soon."

****

Leo kept a watchful eye on his surroundings. Difficult with low powered gas lamps that still marked the street corners of South End at ten o'clock at night. City officials must have felt the better use of the newer mercury vapor electric lamps belonged only on Boston's major intersections.

A late start in South End was never wise, especially after sunset. He made his way down East Street toward Tufts, uncertain why he didn't just let Miss Payne sell Evelyn's belongings as she'd threatened. But for some reason he felt taking care of Evelyn's last wishes might ease his guilt at how he'd let her fade from his life without the slightest explanation.

Closure. Perhaps it would bring closure.

Evelyn, while a bit brassy, had taught him plenty. Things a young man of nineteen or twenty might never have had the opportunity to learn. How to touch and tease a woman to completion, he thought, as an image of Audra's face and petite stature floated past him. Once Leo had joined the war effort, more important things had taken precedence. He truly believed he and Evelyn had both accepted things for what they were. Short term.

He'd been doomed regardless. The exact moment plowed through his memory. The one where he and a couple of the boys had a few days leave. They were in Paris, the city of love. *The French lovely sidled up beside him and whispered in his ear, her cheap perfume filling his nostrils. He hadn't understood a single word. Hadn't needed to. Her hand brushing his raging hard-on said plenty. He splurged and took her to the cinema. Times were tough for everyone, but he could afford more than most to be generous.*

1944 would surely go down as the worst in history, but in six months he'd be home. God, he missed home. But that was wrong. Unpatriotic.

Her hand pressed harder. He groaned. Yes...just the right place, just the right pressure. His eyes fell shut. A shudder racked his unused body. God, it'd been so long. But he was in a public place. His buddy's rasped breaths breached Leo's conscience, bringing him out of his sensual stupor. Lurching him back to his surroundings. His gaze swept the patrons' faces lit up by the film projected on the screen in the darkened movie house.

"On a lighter note—" The reporter's tone on the newsreel turned jovial. "Lady Margaret was spotted coming out of Sardi's in New York City." Leo's eyes snapped to the screen. "Them lucky navy boys! They're crowdin' around. Ooh, that Lady Margaret. Still as fresh as ever. And that daughter of hers... mm...mm...mm. Why, she's quite grown up and quite the looker herself. One can see how she is her mother's daughter."

Audra? Leo's fist wrapped the French girl's wrist and pulled her away, her protest lost in the announcer's words.

"Word on the street is Miss Dempsey's upcoming graduation from Radcliffe. And no beau in sight. At least so far," the bastard chuckled.

Leo let out a curse but couldn't summon the will to follow his angry date out of the theater. Couldn't tear his eyes from the larger-than-life screen.

Audra stood rigidly beside her mother in a light-colored, formfitting evening gown. Her dark hair atop her head, curls trailing down, sucked the air from his body as if he'd been whiplashed by an unseen enemy. Harry stood behind the two, lights flashing all around. Lady Margaret wore her practiced smile, but Leo recognized the strain.

For whatever reason Leo couldn't fathom, Audra and Meggie had never been close in his recollection. Audra's elfin features hadn't changed much over the years. Fuller lips perhaps, kissable now at the age of twenty-one. Slender, curves slight yet perfect.

The stench of stale cigarettes hit him, and he blinked, surprised to find himself standing in front of a darkened doorway. "You looking for a good time, mister?" The man's raspy timbre alerted Leo to his surroundings. Not wise to lose sight of one's senses. Not in this neighborhood.

Hands squeezed into fists at Leo's side, tensing at the insinuation. "Er, no thanks."

He chuckled. "Not for me, lover boy. I got a girl for you. Vera's pretty enough—"

Leo paused. "Vera, you say? I, uh, take that back. Yes. Yes. I'm interested."

"It'll cost you. She ain't cheap. Quite experienced, she is."

Leo glanced up at the windows of the dilapidated building. "She lives here?"

A match struck from the darkness, a second later blown out. The man sucked in, and the red-tipped end of his cigarette glowed bright against a large diamond on his pinky finger. "That, she do. Like I said, it'll cost you. Twenty bucks before you go up, and ten when you leave."

"I see." The temptation to walk away tugged at Leo. Twenty dollars was a lot of dough for some men. This Vera woman must be in desperate straits. *Closure.* What the hell. It wasn't like he didn't have the money. "I, uh…pay you?"

"That, you do."

Leo fished the cash from his pocket.

In a flash, the money was snatched away and tucked out of sight. The man stepped aside. "4B," he said, slinking into the inky night.

No use wasting time. Leo took the stairs by two to the fourth floor. He found 4B easily enough and knocked softly.

A hacker's cough sounded from inside, and he waited.

And waited. He knocked again.

"Hold onto your britches." The door flew back revealing a woman, not much older than himself he'd guess, but wearing every one of her thirty-something years. She stood before him, cigarette in hand. Frayed lace trimmed her satin peignoir. "Well, well, well," she drawled. "Looks like my luck is about to change." She looked him up then down. Her gazed landed on the crotch of his pants. "For the better." She ran her tongue over her lips.

"Vera Payne?"

She lifted a narrowed glare on him. "Who's asking?"

"It's Leo Frisk. You sent me a note regarding Evelyn—"

It was subtle. A shift in her body that signaled Leo her senses had gone on high alert. "I told you to meet me on the corner." The sulky tone didn't match the sharpness of her gaze and did nothing to enhance her attraction. A second later, she croaked out a laugh. "You fool. What did he charge you to get up here?"

"Twenty. Ten when I leave." A survey of his surroundings indicated a host not so particular when it came to cleanliness. Dishes covered countertops in various stages of use. And an unusual amount for one person. He counted at least six piles of clothes. No books or shelves holding knick-knacks decorated the small, cramped space.

Her gaze ran over him again. "Evelyn sure didn't exaggerate your assets. No sir-ree, not one iota."

Heat crawled up his neck. It carried a layer of grime.

She stalked over to a low table and stubbed out her cigarette. "Well, I can't reimburse you—not with cash anyways."

"Uh." Leo cleared his throat. "I appreciate the offer but—"

"Right. Forget I asked."

"I can't stay long—"

"Get out here!" She cut him off. Again.

His annoyance climbed. "Excuse me, Ms. Payne, but..." His voice trailed off as a child peered around a door. Something hard lodged deep in his belly.

"I said get out here," she snapped.

Slow realization crept over him. "You can't possibly mean...surely Evelyn didn't intend I take this… this…" He pointed in the general direction of the child. He inhaled a sharp breath and tried again. "This is her… *belonging?*" *You were planning to sell in two days?* He wanted to punch his fist through the nearest wall.

Vera sauntered to the kid, took up its arm, and jerked. He stumbled into the room. Leo could see now he was a boy. A small boy so thin it would take months to fatten him up.

"Technically, Jamie here was *your* little gift to Evelyn." A sharp cackle burst from her at her little joke. "I've taken care of him as long as I dare." She glanced down at the kid and back to Leo. "Frankly, he's getting in the way."

Leo felt the kid's flinch down deep. The air left his body. "But…we took precautions." What did he know about raising a child? Nothing. Absolutely nothing. "How old are you, son?"

He turned his face into the skirt of Vera's wrap. She pulled away and shoved him toward Leo. "He's six," she barked. "Get your things, Jamie."

"B-b-but…"

"Now."

He ran back to the room he'd appeared from.

Leo scrubbed a palm over his face. "Look. Vera. I don't know anything about raising kids."

"Neither did Evie." A minute later she shrugged. "Find Evie's mother. Last I heard she was somewhere in Dallas."

That made sense. Evelyn's accent for one. Remembering her soft Texas twang saddened him momentarily. On occasion, she'd mention how she missed the Texas heat during that harsh Boston winter she and he had spent trying to keep warm. God, it had been just before he'd left for Europe *seven years ago*. Jamie reappeared, holding a bag that had seen better days. Leo peered closely at him, noting the light hair, stubborn chin, *blue* eyes.

Vera's harsh laughter filled the room. "Either you take him or like I told you or he goes to the highest bidder. I figure you owe me about fifty bucks for taking care of him since Evelyn's demise."

He wasn't sure what kind of care she alluded to considering his thinness and the state of his dirty clothes. His face and hands could stand a good soak in the tub as well. "What happened to Evelyn? Was she living here? With you?" He pulled a wad of bills from his pocket and tossed them on the table.

"She was murdered. With a kitchen knife." Her eyes were on the cash. "The cops believe the Sound End Slayer did her in."

"I-I'm r-r-read-d-dy," the kid whispered.

"Jamie stutters something terrible. Always under foot. Ain't nothing but a pest."

Leo stared at her, stunned, as words escaped him. He glanced back at Jamie and blinked. A scrawny mutt that looked as if it hadn't seen a meal in a month stood next to him. A kid *and* a dog? "The dog stays," Leo growled.

The boy dropped the bag and scooped up the dog. Both dog and boy lifted their chins. "I-I w-w-on't g-go. N-not if Willie c-c-can't."

"The dog goes too," Vera said. Her voice cracked, giving away the façade of her tough-gal.

Leo gave the surroundings another quick survey. He couldn't possibly leave the boy in these conditions.

And whether or not Leo had fathered him, finding a better home for the boy shouldn't be too much of a hardship, because no way Leo was prepared to raise a child.

He dug another twenty from his other pocket and tossed it on the table too. "Jamie, is it?" He snatched up the worn bag and opened the door. "Let's go."

Chapter Three

Four days later, May 10

Audra stepped through the doors at Club 501
Boston with a quick glance at her watch. Satisfaction
filled her. 4:13 p.m. Right on schedule. The club's
normal rush wouldn't peak until after nine that evening,
usually going strong until well after midnight. Audra
considered herself a morning person, but that didn't
mean one or two a.m. She needed her eight hours of
sleep which normally began to hit around the time Club
501's patrons were just getting started. Another little
difference between her and Lady Margaret.

Admittedly, Audra loved the club in this quiet time
of day. It allowed her time in assisting her father with
quick errands while still allowing her to make her shift
at the soup kitchen. Her heels clipped against the wood
surfaces near the empty orchestra pit and ample dance
floor. Behind a bartop of dark marble, Pauley was
putting the finishing polish on stemmed glassware, then
sliding them into the hanging rack above. Notably
missing was Leo Frisk. *For the fourth day in a row.*

It was a relief, Audra told herself. Leo's constant
presence underfoot was the bane of her existence. His
hair was too light, his shoulders too wide, his jaw too
stern. If he was anywhere within the vicinity, she
couldn't seem to breathe. He took up too much oxygen.
And yet there was still tomorrow night's dinner to get

through, where she would be forced to suffer not only him but her mother as well.

"Afternoon, Miss Dempsey," Pauley called out.

"Hello, Pauley." She stopped short of asking after Leo. Things like that went straight back to Daddy, and she couldn't stomach questions she had no answers for. Besides, however curious she might be on Leo's absence, she just couldn't bring herself to voice her curiosity. Like, why Leo hadn't married. Not that she had any intention of marrying anyone, and certainly not Leo. Ha! She could just see the headlines: LADY MARGARET'S DAUGHTER MARRIES LONG-TIME AGENT; AGENT MURDERED BY CLUB 501 BOSTON OWNER. A fit of unfamiliar giggles threatened to let loose. Or AGENT MARRIES LADY MARGARET'S ONLY DAUGHTER: KEEPING IT ALL IN THE FAMILY. Bitter contempt replaced the mirth. Audra shuddered, disgusted.

She reached her father's office and knocked sharply. After a short pause, she peered inside. Empty. Unusual, but she'd take the reprieve, so few they were. She spun about and aimed for the back exit, escape in sight, hand on the door with an opportunity to get to South End early. She hadn't seen Jamie or Willie since Monday. That left her uneasy with all the hoopla going on about the South End Slayer. She needed time to inquire after them. Someone had to know something.

"Audra." Daddy's words were sharp.

Her shoulders slumped. *So close.* She let go of the door, turned, and dropped a kiss on his cheek. "Hi, Daddy."

"Don't forget dinner tomorrow night."

As if that were possible. "I won't forget."

"I'll be late getting home tonight. Why don't you come by the club on your way back from the soup kitchen?"

She peered at him closely, noting the dark circles under his eyes, the strain about his mouth. He knew she wasn't the night owl he and her mother were, so he didn't ask often. Could she help it if her insides caved? Of course, she might not be worth a damn at dinner the next night, but what the heck? Could be a good thing. "Sure. I'll be here around nine-thirty or so."

He pulled her into a quick, tight hug. "Be careful. I'll see you tonight."

Tears pricked the backs of her eyes. She loved him so much. Nodding, she slipped out into the late afternoon sun and snapped up the first cab on the corner before he could see her swipe at the tears.

****

"We have to do something about that dog," Leo muttered.

The kid stiffened and clung tighter to the mangy mutt, were that even possible, eyeing Leo warily. "I'll run away."

Leo rubbed his chin, thinking. "No one's going anywhere. I just meant he needs a bath. And more food. He's too skinny. And, incidentally, so are you."

"A-are you really a w-war h-h-hero? My m-ma showed me p-p-pictures from the p-paper, but they were b-blurry."

Leo eyed the boy, his return stare loaded with questions. It had taken Leo two days to convince Jamie to get into the tub. Only after allowing Willie to remain in the bathroom with him did the kid finally comply. "I was in the Special Forces. I have a certain fighting skill the army found particularly useful." Leo considered Jamie's slight frame. "You might find it useful too." What the hell was he saying? As soon as Leo found Evelyn's family, Jamie would be gone. He'd already set Joe Scully on a mission to find the elusive grandmother. It had been almost a week now. Surely, one woman couldn't be so difficult to find.

Wide eyes stared back, unblinking. "F-fight?"

"Learning to fight smart builds confidence." Leo cracked a short laugh. "Never mind. Are you in school?"

"Of course not. I'm s-sitting right h-h-here. You can s-s-see me, can't you?"

Leo bit back a smile, thrilled at the kid's sudden cheekiness. Leo didn't know much about children, but Jamie's constant sullenness couldn't be normal. Could it? He shook his head. It didn't matter. "What I meant was, have you ever been to school before?"

Jamie laid his head against Willie's neck, hiding his eyes from Leo. "No." His mumble was muffled, but Leo heard it all the same. Why hadn't Evelyn told him about Jamie? And why hadn't she put him in school?

"Do you want to go to school?"

"I can't leave Willie. He would be lost if I wasn't here." That was probably true enough.

Leo surveyed his once pristine living area. Paw prints graced the carpet near the door, and surprisingly the sight didn't rankle Leo as much as it should have. Jamie wasn't so bad as a housemate.

The thought caught Leo by surprise.

The kid had an unusual habit of refusing to sleep on the bed in the spare bedroom. Leo peeked in night after night to see him curled up on a blanket in the corner, arm wrapped tightly around the dog. And the dog, almost eerily, would smile up at Leo. Unnerving.

Each morning after breakfast Leo would glance back in the room and find the blanket had been meticulously folded and placed in the closet out of sight. Right next to the bag Jamie would repack after Leo's assurances no one would disturb his belongings in the dresser drawers provided.

Curiosity licked at Leo. "Do you miss your mother?"

Jamie didn't raise his head, but Leo thought he nodded. He shuddered to think what sort of things the kid had witnessed in his young years. *Six years. Not so long.*

Willie stood and moved to face Jamie, flicked out a pink tongue, which elicited small childlike giggles. Jamie shot to sitting and hugged his dog, eyeing Leo with a wariness Leo found himself wanting desperately to dispel. "I miss Miss Dempsey more, though."

Leo started, heart pounding. "Miss Dempsey? As in Audra?"

Jamie shrugged. "I don't know her first name."

"You eat at the soup kitchen then?"

"E-every d-day." His head fell forward again. "Least I u-s-sed t-to. She sneaked f-food out to W-w-willie. *He* really misses her."

Of course, Jamie would see Audra. The constriction banding Leo's chest the last four days loosened so abruptly he felt a little dizzy. Like a plant under a splash of rain after a long drought as something blossomed within. It started small, morphing into the surge of a waterfall that pounded through his veins, rushing his ears. *Audra.*

Reality set in. Hell. She would never forgive Leo for Jamie. He was six years old, and though Leo hadn't known anything about him, he'd still deserted the kid's mother, and in turn Jamie. The blood in his veins congealed. Why couldn't anything be simple?

Leo's hands landed on the arms of his chair, and he rose. "Come on, kid. Let's fix something to eat for Willie. You can help."

Jamie scrambled to his feet, Willie fast on their heels, both jumping with excitement and anticipation.

Leo dragged himself to the kitchen, wishing he had the energy to jump with excitement and anticipation too. Telling Audra Faye was not going to be easy.

Chapter Four

Saturday evening, May 10

Donald was a merchant. Part of what gave him the nickname of Diamond Donnie. A businessman who dealt in products that were both a *service* to him and the interested party handing over his well-earned cash. He chuckled. Hell, back in the Roman days his products were considered necessary goods for the buying public. Nowadays, however, one had to conduct such transactions under the cover of darkness or down back alleys by the railroad tracks where a scream was lost in the roar of a locomotive or the conductor's whistle. *Nowadays* meant seizing one's opportunities to keep products available and fresh. *Nowadays* meant more money than he could count. He chuckled again. Him. The one his old man said would never amount to nothing.

Donnie had risen through the ranks in South End the same as many of his cronies. Giving the knocks as good—no—better than those he'd been given. Sure, he'd nursed a few broken noses, suffered a few indignities from one or two bastards growing up. But when the third one, a brute by the name of Cactus, grabbed him by the hair and bit his neck, whispered against his ear the atrocities he planned—well, suffice to say, Cactus never touched no one ever again. Donnie'd been fourteen that last time. He'd wet his pants, and uncaring, ran home, terrified. Wanted, needed the comfort of Ma's arms.

He'd burst through the door, shaking. An instant later finding his head slammed against the wall, knocking a hole in it. He'd blacked out. He didn't remember much but Ma's screaming at him to get out. Then hauled up by the collar, her nude body hidden behind a big hairy man whose boner was shrinking faster than a piece of ice in hundred-degree heat, he was tossed out on the street like stinking refuse. He'd never seen his mother again.

Donnie shook away the memories. He considered himself his people's protector. Course, he tried out the goods on all of 'em. Male or female. Didn't matter none to him. That way he could figure which particular *service* each one was good for.

The diversity of services Donnie offered were innumerable. Some men liked girls who resisted; some wanted total compliance. Others didn't mind a little whupping up on. Some liked young men, some liked young women. He never gave up no virgins though, he took care of the innocents himself. Hell, he deserved something for his trouble, didn't he? And he treated 'em gentle-like. A little ethanol never hurt nobody. A couple of times whilst out cold and said recruits were good to go. Yes, recruits. Such an apt term.

Killing was nothing he minded doing for his underlings. As their protector, it was his duty. But if they betrayed him? A measure of regret touched him over that last conversation with Evie. She'd always been one of his favorites. He'd discovered her a year or so after she'd had the kid. He had plans that entailed keeping Jamie from being so much underfoot. Those blue eyes would not only bring in a shitload of dough, but he was much too observant. It was getting long past time to initiate the kid into the life he was destined for. Donnie stepped behind a dumpster and whacked off to get hold of his control.

"Walk with me," he said. She'd had time. Plenty of time with the kid. Evie knew the score.

His gaze followed hers around the quiet neighborhood. A crescent moon creased the night sky along with a slight, cool breeze that mingled with a dog's distant bark. She glanced back at him. She looked tired, wary.

He brought his hand up. "Evie." But she didn't say nothing, just ducked away from his touch and fell into step beside him. It was a practiced move that heightened his aggravation to near fury.

Donnie tamped back the surge and led them east, toward the river. The closer they got, the chillier the air, but spring was just around the corner. From the corner of his eye, he noted the dark roots of Evie's platinum blonde hair, the deepening creases about her eyes and mouth. He let out a sigh. Damned broad was burned out, or near so. It happened. A sad fact of life. The stupid kid didn't help. She had a lot of talent left in her, but she spent too much time worrying over that brat of hers. An unnecessary concern if she'd just let Donnie handle him.

The wind kicked up, stirring the dirt around the boxcars, and she shivered. He held out his lit cigarette. She put it to her full lips and drew in deep. A pang squeezed his lungs, but he shut it out. Sentimentality didn't do no one no good.

He lit another cigarette, surprised to see his hands tremble. He strengthened his resolve. "It's time."

Her gaze jerked to his. "No. He's only six."

He clenched his jaw. "It won't kill him. We can't be feeding someone who don't do his share, Evie." He looked out at the night sky. "Don't worry," he said, careful to keep his voice all business. "I'll teach him myself. Bring him in slow. Slow as molasses." He stopped and looked at her. Her skin appeared almost luminous in the silvered moonlight. He cupped her jaw, brushed away a stray tear with his thumb. "Gentle like. In five or six sessions. Most boys only take two."

She snapped her head back as if he'd slapped her. "If you touch him, I'll kill you."

Donnie wasn't known for his patience. His hand flew out, landing soundly against her face. He grabbed her by the upper arm, but she was quick, sharp. He knew that about her. What a dumb jerk he was getting caught up in the fantasy that she might care for him, and after all he'd done for her, too.

But that slight hesitation caught him off guard. Again. Her other hand flew up. The cigarette clenched between her fingers—jammed right on his face.

He stood there, shocked, a full minute before registering she'd taken off. Back down Tufts. It was lucky his shoes were more conducive to running than those impractical heels she wore. He was on her in five steps. He snatched her by the hair. She cried out, and he pulled harder.

He hissed against her ear. "Shut it, bitch."

"Don't. Don't hurt him." Her voice shook in a husky beg.

Goddamn if her pleas didn't turn him on. His other hand caressed her throat. "I told you I'd be gentle with him." He squeezed, just a little.

"It's r-rape, you bastard."

He squeezed harder. The temptation to squeeze the life from her stole over him. He forced himself to calm. The South End Slayer didn't kill his victims by strangulation, did he? Even in a fit of passion. Donnie covered her mouth with his hand, let go of her hair with the other, and pulled the knife from his pocket. "Now, we'll take it real quiet-like, back down the street. One peep, and it's all over, my dear, dear Evie. If you don't, you can go to your grave knowing your baby boy didn't get it gentle-like. You understand?"

She was a marble statue against his chest.

He jerked her head, touched the knife to her neck, pricking that lovely skin until a drop of blood showed black in the silver-lit sky. "I said, you understand?"

Tears ran over his fingers, and he felt her faint nod. With a quick survey of the area, he turned the two of them back toward the rail yard.

Donnie tossed his cigarette down and ground it out with his heel. He sauntered to the end of Tufts where it met East Street. He was pissed at having missed Vera's last trick four nights ago. Not to mention the fast one she'd pulled in handing over the kid to the smooth-talking bastard that had been right under his own nose.

One thing Donnie could smell was money. The kid was a goldmine, and Jamie was the perfect age for expanding the boys' operation. Hell, Donnie had only gone down the street to check on Rip. But by the time he returned, that blighter was getting in a taxi four blocks away with Evie's kid, clinging to that damn mutt.

Ah, well. There were always the runaways and the less observant. *Opportunities.* It was all about opportunities. Still, his fury burned. Burned deep.

＊＊＊＊

Audra's and Iris's footsteps clicked over the uneven pavers of South End. "Well, why are you volunteering if you hate it?" Audra glanced at her friend as she slipped her jacket on and buttoned it up. The wind seemed a tad brisker than when they'd arrived at the soup kitchen for the dinner shift. It was Saturday, and she had that stupid dinner her father was lording over her to get home and changed for.

Iris sniffed. "I suppose I don't *hate* it. I just don't like it much. I can't let you come down here all alone. Besides, I need to do *some* kind of volunteer work." She glanced around and lowered her voice. "The South Side Slayer murdered a woman who visited the soup kitchen almost every day. I spoke with her shortly before she was killed. And all the articles in the *Chronicle*..." Audra felt her shiver from where she stood. "...I don't like your being down here without anyone." She rubbed her hands up and down her arms. "Mercy me, Audra. This is *not* the place for proper young ladies. Especially late at night."

Audra rolled her eyes as they set a faster clip down the street. "You sound like my father."

"Aren't you the least bit afraid?" Iris shivered, her eyes darting side to side. "Even after what I told you about that poor dead girl?"

She let out a frustrated breath. "I'm careful."

144

Iris pulled an abrupt stop. "Damn!" Her hand flew over her mouth. "Um, sorry. Pretend I didn't say that."

Audra pulled up beside her. "What is it?"

"I left my bag. We'll have to run back."

"You go. I'll grab us a taxi. I have that dinner with *Lady* Margaret tonight."

Iris snorted. "Don't you think its past time being so angry with Aunt Meggie? She didn't leave your father and you all those years ago." Iris grabbed her hand and squeezed. "Honey, she came right back."

Audra's back went up. Iris didn't know everything. "I'll wait here. My feet are killing me."

"I wish you'd refrain from using certain phrases at this particular moment," Iris muttered, her gaze moving over the area uncertainly.

Audra followed her gaze, and noting the dark alley right behind, strolled to the corner, dragging her friend by the hand. She took Iris by the shoulders and spun her back in the direction of the soup kitchen. "Go. I'll be right here, cab in hand by the time you return."

Iris opened her mouth, but Audra threw up her hand. "Hurry. It's getting late. I told Daddy I would make time to change my clothes."

After a slight hesitation, Iris relented. "Fine." She took off in a run.

Audra glanced at her watch in the waning light, grimacing. She would be cutting it supremely close. She squinted toward the old elm. The last place she'd spoken to Jamie. He hadn't been back to the soup kitchen since Monday, and she was concerned. No. She was *frightened.* Out of her mind. She'd never felt more helpless. The Chronicle's headlines from her nightmares glared through her. SOUTH END SLAYER

SLAYS AGAIN. That was Tuesday night. She swallowed. Wednesday's followed with FIRST WOMEN NOW CHILDREN, NOT EVEN YOUR DOG IS SAFE. After Thursday's, MANGLED BODY FOUND WITH MANGY DOG, she gave up on sleep at all. And now she had this stupid supper party.

"Well, aren't you a pretty thing?" The raspy voice had her jumping a foot off the ground. He reached out and ran a roughened hand over the sleeve of her coat. She jerked away. "Could always use a girl like you. All sweet and innocent lookin'." He tipped his head in the direction of the soup kitchen. "You working for ole Luther, are you?"

Audra backed away, didn't dare take her eyes from him. Slipping her hand in the pocket of her coat, she clutched her keys just as Mommy told her to do all those years ago. "Come any closer and you're liable to lose an eye." Only the tiniest tremor in her voice snuck through. She held his gaze.

He chuckled, shaking his head. "You'll make me a fucking fortune, chickadee."

She flinched at the crude language just as his hand snaked out and latched onto her free arm. But Audra was no victim. Her strike caught him off guard, the key slicing him just under his right eye. He let out a pained squeal and she ran. In a half block toward the soup kitchen, Iris was there hugging her.

"Did he…did he hurt you? Are you okay?"

Panting, Audra strove to gather her bearings, unable to answer right away.

Iris shook her. "Audra, answer me."

She nodded. Chill seeped through her jacket, and she forced herself to breathe, slowly and less steady than she could help. It took several deep tries to level it to anything resembling normal.

Iris flagged down a cab with a piercing whistle and quickly bundled them both inside. To safety. "When Uncle Harry hears of this, he won't let you come back. I, for one, don't think that's such a bad thing. It's too dangerous. We must be out of our minds being down here after dark." Iris continued her tirade another ten minutes before the words finally registered.

"Stop. Iris, just stop. I can't stop working at the soup kitchen. I'm *needed* there. Don't you see? At the soup kitchen, I'm not Lady Margaret's daughter." She'd get a gun. Daddy had plenty. He'd never miss just one. Oh, God. Could she truly shoot someone? And how was she to keep such a secret from Daddy? *It's for protection,* she told herself. Daddy would be good with that, come push or shove. She was almost positive. "I'm my own person. Doing good for a decent cause. Please."

Iris gaped at her as if she'd lost her mind. "You cannot be serious."

"Think about it. Your mom. She wants…wants certain things for you, right?"

Iris's chest caved with the depletion of her exhale.

Audra pounced. "Promise me you won't tell anyone what happened. Swear it, Iris."

"But…but what if he'd…he'd kidnapped you?"

Audra lifted her chin, clearly aware that her hands still shook violently. "He didn't though, did he?"

Iris's head swung back and forth. "Audra," she demanded. "It's much too dangerous. Doesn't that mean anything to you? Coming to South End makes me nervous."

"Then don't come," she said stubbornly. She let out a stream of air. Getting a gun would not be a problem, remembering how Daddy kept the one stashed in his desk at the club.

"I…" Iris stopped, inhaling deep. "Fine, I won't say a word. But if it happens again, I'm going straight to Uncle Harry. I'm promising you that too, Audra Faye Dempsey."

Audra threw her arms around her friend, hugged her tightly. "Thank you. Thank you. It will be fine. I'll admit, I let my thoughts distract me—" *To an alarming degree.* "—but it won't happen again."

"And from now on we take a cab every time we come down here."

Audra couldn't think of a single argument to that pronouncement. She'd been scared out of her wits. "Deal." She couldn't possibly walk in the house and convince anyone nothing overt had happened. "One more thing."

Iris gaze turned wary. "What?"

"Can I take a quick shower at your place? Daddy will take one look at me and lock me in my room for a month. Or a year."

Iris clutched her hand. "Of course."

Chapter Five

Desire pulsed the front of Donnie's trousers as he watched Vera stroll to the cheap coffee table. She took up a cigarette and put it to her lips, struck a match, and drew in deep. Once her mouth closed around the fag that stopped the tripe spilling from them, she looked pretty sexy.

"The way I see it," she said, smoke filing out with each word. "I saved you—" She pointed her cigarette at him. "—a lot of money and one hell of a headache."

Each word pricked at him like an annoying splinter under a fingernail, effectively killing his desire. Nothing good ever lasted, he thought. Ah, well. He could hardly wait to hear this; he took a drag from his own cigarette. "How do you figure?"

His question obviously took her by surprise. She blinked. "The kid, um, well, he won't be depleting the food stash…" she said haltingly. Then after some sort of internal debate, she narrowed her eyes on him.

"Suppose that's true enough."

Vera paced the small living space, keeping notably out of reach. She stopped, glanced at him. "Evie's last wish was…" Her words trailed off.

"Evelyn's dead, though, ain't she? South End Slayer did her in."

"Yes, but—"

Donnie curled one hand and studied his stubby nails, wondering where he might get him one of them

Asian girls to soften up the calluses. He hated getting his hands dirty. Bad business, that. He nailed her with a sharp look. "The thing is, sugar. She'd promised the kid to me." He almost bust a gut at the surprise covering her face.

"You!?"

"That's right," he said softly, deadly. Evie had learned that tone too late to do her any good. Didn't matter none. He had new blood in his sights. Petite, waif-like girls with short, curly brown hair and big blue eyes. He might even start a whole new service, one that catered to the whimsical fantasies. Brassy blondes were so overdone. This was the late forties.

Vera's head tipped to one side. "What am I missing?"

Her wrapper fell, exposing one shoulder. And, just like that, desire flooded his veins in a feral rush.

Vera's expression turned incredulous, then vicious. "I see," she said slowly. "Well, it seems as though I saved little Jamie a lifetime of hell."

"So it would. Just know, I'll be taking his cut from that nice round ass of yours."

She laughed. A deep, guttural sound that ground salt into an open wound. Fury seared the edge of his vision with blood-red hate. "Perhaps." She sauntered to his chair, placed a hand on each arm he had rested there. She leaned forward, bringing her almost nose to nose with him. Her perfume shoved away the anger, and his dick twitched again, throbbing against his zipper. "I think we can come to some kind of agreement."

Staring into her calculated gaze, the red roared back.

"I have information on you that could see you in the joint for a very long time. All I want in return is a little cash and my freedom."

She was brave, his Vera. But a bit too stupid for her own good if she thought she could blackmail Diamond Donnie and lived to tell the tale. He was King in these parts. A small fact she seemed to have forgotten. His hands snaked out and manacled each wrist. Feminine, delicate wrists. He squeezed until her eyes widened and her fear registered. Only then did he loosen his grip. "You were saying?"

She jerked her hands from his hold, rubbing them. "You bastard. Don't you get it? You were seen."

He frowned, and the pit of his stomach fell. "Seen?"

All polished gloss fell from her aging face, replaced with a sneer that showcased her true feelings where he was concerned—hate and fear. "You think you can just get away with murdering Evie like that."

Donnie focused on her fear. It fed a divine craving deep within him, mingling with an apprehension that raised the hair on his arms. Donnie reached into his memory, though nothing stood out from that night Evelyn had met her justifiable end. A sliver of moon in the inky black sky. Evelyn's fear, a dog's distant bark—

"Damn. It was the kid." He shot from the chair and pounced, grabbing Vera by the throat with one hand. "The kid saw, didn't he?" Blood rushed his head so quickly he thought he might pass out. He fought for his spiraling control. "Didn't he?" he demanded, shocked by how calm he sounded when rage all but blinded him.

Her eyes bulged out, and he reveled in her terror. He'd survive this. He was Diamond Donnie, and he'd survived less. Survival was his middle name. He smiled down at her.

"Please," she begged. "You don't have to give me anything. I'll stay. Just forget I said anything." Her voice was a choked whisper.

Donnie guided her to the tiny kitchen, their steps so in tune he felt a certain kinship with Fred Astaire swagger through him. He quelled an urge to spin. "Do you like dancing, Ginger?"

Confusion filled her eyes.

But the time for playing had seized, and he squeezed her neck a little harder because it felt *good*. He swiped a knife from the cluttered countertop and put it to her jugular. "So, the kid saw his own ma's demise, huh? What a shame."

The alarm in her eyes teased him. He wanted to play a bit more, but it was too risky. "Where is he?" He loosened his grip. Only a little, enough to let her speak.

"I-I don't k-know."

He squeezed again. "Where?" He let up.

She coughed. "I sent a note…to his father…he's gonna send him to Evie's mother."

"Give me a name," he growled.

"Frisk. Leo Frisk."

The war hero? He removed the knife from her throat. She sagged, her relief palpable. But he was out of patience and rammed the serrated blade in her ribs. He drove it up and twisted then stepped back. She fell to her knees, gasping.

With a swift kick to her mid-section, he said. "I don't play fair, sweetcakes. You should know that by now."

She was dead before she hit the floor.

Donnie surveyed the cluttered countertop. Seconds later he plucked up a soiled envelope addressed to Evelyn from a Florence Payne. Well, well, well. That should prove helpful.

****

"Been traveling, huh?" Harry strolled up, holding out a gin and tonic.

Leo accepted it, took a long hard swig. "Traveling?"

"Figured you were out of town all week."

Out of his mind, more like, as the image of the sullen boy situated cross-legged on his living room floor, mutt planted firmly on his lap, staring down his housekeeper's confusion went through his mind. All because the ornery little cuss refused to sit on a sofa designed specifically for comfort. Leo almost laughed. "Mm. Hectic." He glanced around the large parlor-type room, and after a smaller sip said, "Lady Margaret made it home from Europe, I take it."

"Of course. Anything differently would have set the newspapers afire as you well know."

Leo grunted a short laugh and looked around again. "Where's Audra? I thought she was supposed to be here." Leo hadn't seen her since Monday. He rubbed a palm over his chest. Had she missed *him* at all? He quickly turned that question away, fearing the answer would sting.

Harry glanced at his wristwatch, his mouth tightening. "She's late."

Unease slithered down Leo's spine. Just then the double doors swung back, and Lady Margaret glided in. Her soft blue evening gown molded curves that hadn't changed much in the years since Leo had taken over her career after his father's death. Meggie worked her magic around the room like the professional persona she was, speaking softly to each guest, her gentle laughter tinkling the air.

Leo glanced down at his own watch. Nine-fifteen. He raised his gaze, meeting Harry's. The man was worried. Which did nothing to level Leo's unease. "I'll find her," he said quietly to Harry. Leo handed off his tumbler to a passing tray, set to make an escape, but Lady Margaret swept up at that moment and snatched both of his hands in hers.

"Darling. How are you? Did you hear? The tour was a fabulous success. All thanks to you!" Her hand flitted out to a couple of others across the room, their star-struck gazes on their famous hostess. A broad grin covered her face and she leaned in conspiratorially, kissing his one cheek then the other. "I've brought you more business, you rogue."

"You are the gem client, my dear," Leo returned, smiling. She truly was a pleasure. Nothing like some of the other women he represented. Most of whom were vain and demanding. Difficult didn't describe some of them, but their business paid the bills. Meggie was just Meggie, delightful and generous. The hair at Leo's nape rose. His gaze shot to the door where Audra stood rigidly inside, piercing him with her light Icelandic-blue eyes. Yes, the color matched her mother's to their exact shade. The difference lay in the degree of their temperature. Where Meggie's were warm and inviting,

Audra's could freeze a man in place. Still, the sudden respite in seeing her home safe caught Leo by surprise. As did the sudden emotion gripping him inside out.

Audra stared straight at him, the air fairly crackling around her. Leo glanced at Harry. His features had slackened with relief.

Meggie dropped his hands and whooped with delight. "Oh, my darling girl. How I've missed you. Terribly so." She coasted across the room and pulled Audra into a hug so tight Audra flinched. Audra's gown of soft pink chiffon was gathered at the neck in both the front and back, leaving her delicate shoulders bared. The pretty dress was drawn in at the waist with a jeweled belt and smoothed over her slim hips. He almost groaned at the one long slit up the side, teasing him with a glimpse of her leg from mid-thigh down. Her short, dark hair was slicked back from her heart-shaped face that appeared paler than usual.

Leo snagged two glasses of champagne and sauntered over. Audra was not close to her mother, and he knew this was the one area Audra Faye would appreciate his assistance in. He took in her glacial, piercing gaze. *Or maybe not.*

****

Audra closed her eyes against Daddy's pain and tried…really tried to hug her mother back. But seeing her making a fool over herself? With Leo? It was too much. She just couldn't stomach seeing the two of them together. And *Leo.* How *dare* he flaunt his fixation on her mother right in front of Daddy. It was abominable. God, how she hated that man. How could Daddy stand him?

The confidence Leo portrayed walking toward her with those two glasses infuriated her. He probably believed no one could see through that slick veneer of his. She could, however. Her hatred of him consumed her, rose another notch with each step he drew closer. She would *never* be his friend. There was nothing he could do or say to change her mind. He should just crawl back under the rock he came from.

Had his step hesitated? She wasn't sure. He tossed back the contents of one glass, his eyes never moving from her. His look hardened even as he snatched up another flute and continued in her direction. The move was fluid and predatory. She turned her back on him and observed her mother spreading her phony magic among the other guests.

Audra forced herself to inhale and exhale slowly and steadily, until she'd managed to master her fury—a futile attempt when Leo's spicy scent soon battered her overdrawn senses. How much more was one expected to endure in a single day? Shoulders tense, she turned her head and managed to keep herself from jumping back at his invasion of her personal space. He stood much too close. She seized one of the glasses from him and sipped. Calm, cool, collected, all the while moving back so as not to draw attention. Things that normally came easy to her—just not around him!

Wrath colored her reason, and Leo had escaped censure for far too long. "Truly, Leo? In front of God, Daddy, the *guests*?" she murmured from behind her flute.

Astonishment flickered across his face but disappeared just as quickly. Any other time she might have howled with laughter if not for the hurt that squeezed the air from her chest.

His eyes narrowed on his drink then cut to hers. They brimmed with fury. "Let me make certain I understand you, Audra Faye," he said behind his own glass. "You think…your *mother*…and…*me*…"

"Don't sound so surprised. I've known the truth for years." Her voice came out a hiss, so furious, her previous caution of others fled. She threw back the contents of her own glass and jammed it in his hand.

"Where in hell did you get such a ludicrous idea?"

Her eyes glittered with fury. "Of course, *you* would deny it." Fighting off a sputtering cough, she stalked away. She was halfway across the room when his booming laugh erupted. It struck her as somewhat bitter. Of what, she couldn't begin to imagine. Her mother's feelings regarding Leo were as clear as day to anyone observant enough. Audra couldn't stomach another encounter with either of them. Audra picked up her pace, aiming for the safety of her father.

"Where have you been, young lady?" His growl was the last straw.

The tears sprung. "Please don't yell at me, Daddy. Not tonight." Her mother was the actress. Not she.

****

Leo was rooted to the floor, his glass halfway to his mouth. He snapped it shut as her words swirled through his murky brain. Good God. *Him* and Lady Margaret. Leo had never heard anything remotely ridiculous or insulting. Even in his twenties, he'd never fantasized bedding Lady Margaret. Audra was out of her mind. Where on earth had she dreamed up such a notion? His eyes followed her slight form tearing across the room where she stopped in front of her father.

Well, one thing was for certain. If she believed him capable of having an affair with her mother under her father's nose, for heaven's sake, that didn't leave much in the way of asking her help regarding Jamie, did it?

He could feel the tremble he saw in her shoulders. Jesus. Harry was about to read her the riot act. Audra Faye's day was not faring well, and while she might think the absolute worst of Leo, no way would Leo allow Harry to rail her for doing something she believed in. Jamie and Willie were proof enough to Leo in that regard.

Leo set the empty flutes aside and meandered over, fairly certain his presence would keep things civil to some degree. Harry wouldn't purposely do anything to embarrass his wife. Audra was a different matter. He was overprotective to the nth degree. Audra's back was to the center of the room, and as Leo edged closer, he realized she was crying.

"Audra, sweetheart. You know this supper is important to your mother."

Leo cringed. *Those aren't the words to help the situation, Harry.* Not now that he realized Audra's inner turmoil. Audra threw back her shoulders, all signs pointing to one hell of a scene on Meggie's first night home. Audra abhorred the spotlight, and with the reporter from *Look* standing next to a young Errol Flynn doppelganger, Audra would be jumping feet first right into the flames of her own living hell. She would hate herself, and despite her low opinion of Leo, he would give her a much needed out.

"All you think of is her—"

"Audra Faye," Leo interrupted taking her arm. Harry shot him a grateful glance which Leo ignored.

Audra's eyes drilled him. They glittered with unshed tears but her anger with him would serve her well enough. It worked every damn time up to now, he'd wager.

Leo pressed his lips together, drawing the handkerchief from his pocket, and handing it to her. "You have something in your eye."

She snatched it from him. "Thank you," she muffled in the starched white square.

"I've got this, Harry. Lady Margaret was asking for you. It appears Audra and I have a little issue to clear up," he said, eyes never wavering from Audra. He drew her to the terrace doors. "I could use some air. How about you?"

Resentment radiated from her but to his relief, she complied. "Yes. Yes. That's exactly what I need."

Once outdoors, Leo removed his jacket and slipped it about her shoulders. He could see her temptation to refuse, but the night air was cool. Her "Lady Margaret" upbringing kept her from being outright rude, at least at this moment, murmuring a small "thank you" instead.

"Audra, about your mother—"

Her hand flew up, palm out. "Don't. I refuse to discuss it." She moved back to the terrace doors.

He had to stop her. "Wait. Don't go. Not yet."

"Give me one good reason," she bit out.

"Don't let Harry get to you. Don't let him give you a hard time for being late. You're an adult, and he should respect that."

Her shoulders fell, and she changed direction, heading to the terrace wall instead. She set her elbows atop, resting her chin on her fists, looking out at the clear, star-filled sky. "I wasn't *that* late," she said softly.

"He just worries for you."

She glanced over at him. "I know." The silence grew between them, and for once it wasn't the awkward uncomfortable one they usually shared.

"At the risk of sounding like your father," he said gently. "Those articles regarding the South End Slayer are worrisome."

A small smile touched her lips, and it warmed his soul. "The minute 'damn it, Audra' leaves your lips…"

Unable to resist, with the tip of his finger, Leo brushed that lip. A lip as full and as soft as his dreams had promised. He couldn't pull his eyes from them. She turned her head fully facing him. He dragged his gaze from her mouth to her eyes. "Why?" he asked.

"Why what?" She sounded confused by the question.

His eyes fell to her lips again, and the urge to take her mouth ripped through him. He was barely able to rein in the compulsion, leaning forward, until he felt her breath touch his chin. "Why do you go to the soup kitchen every day?"

Her voice fell into a husky tone that sent a shot of desire straight south. "There are people without homes, without food. Hungry children. I'm useful there…I'm …Audra."

He blinked and lifted his gaze to hers, the spell broken at her incongruous statement. "Audra? Of course, you're Audra."

She looked back out to the night sky and let out a sigh. "Never mind. It's complicated. Sometimes, even I don't understand."

Understanding hit him in the solar plexus. "Ah. You're Audra Dempsey, not Lady Margaret's unmarried daughter."

Her shocked gaze shot to his. He'd nailed it on the head.

The curtain whipped aside, and the Dempsey's butler poked his gray head out. "Dinner is served. Miss Dempsey, Mr. Frisk."

"Thank you, Martim." And just like that, the companionable moment was recharged with tension, along with Audra's voice once more back to its normal efficiency. "We'll be right in." She spoke to Martim, but her eyes remained on him, her gaze thoughtful.

Leo was suspended, hovering between universes. No words forthcoming. Despite the urge to take her into his arms, kiss away the doubts he saw in her eyes, he stood immobile.

"I owe you a thanks, I suppose. I, uh, rarely lose my temper. But I guess you know that. It has been a particularly trying day."

He nodded, a silent self-chastising moment, realizing he'd mucked up the only opportunity he'd ever been granted with Audra Dempsey, not Lady Margaret's daughter. Something struck him. He wouldn't call himself clairvoyant by any stretch, but there was something. "I thought so. Did something happen at the soup kitchen?"

"No," she said quickly. *Too* quickly. He'd ponder that later. God knew, his nights were free enough. A second later, she turned a calm smile on him, her cool demeanor sternly intact. "No. I, uh, appreciate your interest."

But Leo knew her too well. He'd seen the deep breath she drew attempting to mask...fear? To steady herself. He wanted to demand the truth. But Audra Faye had always kept her cards close to her chest. Her mother's public persona had done well in creating her sense of self-preservation.

A frown crossed her features, and she narrowed her eyes on him. "Unless you are asking for my father."

Leo's head snapped back, fury surging through him. All their previous rapport completely decimated. "I'm not your daddy's spy, little girl," he bit out.

"Little girl?" Moonlight revealed the quick spark of anger glittering in her eyes, the white of her all-teeth smile that turned sickeningly sweet.

He swallowed a groan. He should have been prepared.

"Of course, you aren't Daddy's spy. I'm quite aware that Lady Margaret is more to your taste."

He stood there, stunned. On many levels: her cheap shot glaring between them; her silky bared arms bathed in the moonlit sky as she slipped his jacket from her shoulders; and the fact that he'd been inches away from devouring her mouth.

She tossed his jacket. His hand darted out instinctively, snatching it up before it hit the ground. "Please don't worry that I'll make a scene any longer, Mr. Frisk. My emotions are back under strict control. Enjoy the rest of your evening."

****

Audra disappeared inside. How could Leo's heart thunder with such fury and longing simultaneously?

162

Shit. Him and Meggie? Audra seriously needed her head examined. As angry as he was though, he picked up on something else beneath Audra's complicated surface. Something had happened before she'd arrived tonight, and it had shaken her up good. The question was what? He let out a frustrated sigh. God knew, he'd never learn anything from Audra. He was the last person she'd confide in. His desire for her put everything out of kilter. He had the most insane urge to drag her home and lock her in his room. Never let her out. Leo swallowed a groan. His chin burned from the heat of her breath. That small burst of passion. Was it passion? He could have dreamt it. Letting his thoughts plunge in that direction was asking for disaster. He pinched himself hard.

Jesus. That hurt. The night cooled his ardor, cleared his head. He needed a plan. A way to keep Audra free from danger yet didn't impugn her independence. He'd known Audra a long time, knew she valued independence above her own safety. He sure as hell couldn't ask Harry if something was up. One word from her father would do nothing for her protection because she was just stubborn enough to rebel and sneak away.

Like a pool of honey on a slight incline of wood—thicker than blood, slower than molasses, clinging to every fiber of his being, a flicker of joy spread through him. Jamie *liked* her and Willie "*really* missed her." The very thought gave Leo the thread of hope he'd been searching for. Now, he just needed a way to get her to open up. How else was he to move past this limbo his life had become?

A burst of wind pierced Leo. He moved through the terrace doors to outside the dining room doors, pausing with his hand on the knob. Listening as silver clinked against delicate china and the low hum of chatter. First on his list of priorities was the need to clear up Audra's misgivings regarding him and her mother. There was no way he could eat with Audra's accusations ringing his ears. He and Lady Margaret were due for a little tête-à-tête.

Fuck, dinner. He turned to Martim. "Could I trouble you for note paper, please."

Martim complied. Leo scribbled a quick note and handed it to Martim. "See that Lady Margaret receives this. It's urgent. I'll be foregoing dinner tonight. Have her telephone, no matter the hour."

****

Where the devil was Leo? He should been into dinner by now. Guilt pierced Audra, but she pushed it off. The relationship between her mother and Leo was as strong as ever. She'd seen the evidence with her own eyes. It sickened her.

"How absolutely thrilling to be the daughter of the great Lady Margaret."

Audra tugged her gaze from the closed dining room doors to the young lady to her left. She was an up-and-coming starlet. Audra couldn't recall her name but remembered meeting her at an afterparty in last year's production of *Yours is my Heart* on Broadway. "Yes, it is," she murmured. What else was she supposed to say?

Chapter Six

Sunday, May 11

"Knock, knock." The door creaked back.

What the devil. Today was Sunday, wasn't it? Her one day of leisure? Plans that later included lunch and the cinema with her friends. It would be the first time in ages she, Sophie, Iris, and Maddie were all four together. With Maddie's residence in London, overseas travel had been near impossible the last few years due to the war. She was just thankful her friend had survived such perilous conditions.

Audra squinted at the clock and groaned. Daddy would never wake her so early, most especially at seven-thirty in the morning after a late supper part—

"Oh, splendid. You're awake."

Too late to pretend she'd slept through the racket. "Hello, Mother. You couldn't sleep?"

"Don't be so prickly, darling. I've fresh scones and tea." Sure enough Lady Margaret pushed her way through the door, laden down with a tray of steaming crockery and sporting a plate of "fresh from the oven" scones. The fragrance filled the room, and Audra's stomach growled.

Going back to sleep was out of the question now. Audra scooted to the far side of the bed and piled the surrounding pillows against the headboard and leaned back. "Why didn't you just have Jilly send the tray up instead of carting that load? You might have dropped it."

Despite her mother having reached the untenable age of—well, Audra wasn't quite certain how old her mother was since she'd refused to discuss such a "revolting" topic for as long as Audra could remember—Lady Margaret was still breathtakingly beautiful. Something the cameras and grainy newsprints inevitably failed in truly portraying. And at seven-thirty in the morning, Audra found it all the more irritating.

The infamous "Lady Margaret pout" touched her lips. "I didn't wish to give you the opportunity in putting me off. Again. We've hardly spoken in the two months I've been abroad." Her expression shifted to an impish grin. "Besides, Jilly did fetch the tray. How else do you suppose I managed the door?" Meggie set her burden on the bed, climbed atop, then poured out two cups of Oolong tea.

Audra picked up a scone sprinkled with cinnamon and breathed it in. She took a bite and moaned. "This is delicious. Is Aunt Charli in town?"

"Not for another couple of days. But somehow Jilly procured one of her prize recipes. Takes me back some twen—" She cleared her throat and selected one of the smaller biscuits. Silence, not uncompanionable, filled the air while her mother nibbled the edge. The sight surprised Audra. Meggie was notoriously conscious of her slender image on film. "Mm. Heaven." As expected, she set it back on the tray half-eaten.

Audra braced herself. Mother and daughter mornings had ended over a decade ago. Not that her mother hadn't put forth an effort. That blame lay squarely on Audra's shoulders.

"At the risk of igniting your ire, your father is concerned with the amount of time you're spending at the soup kitchen."

The whoosh of air left Audra's lungs along with her appetite, and she dropped her scone back on the tray as well. "Moth—"

Meggie threw up a palm. "Don't get so contrary, darling. I set the man straight." She smiled like the cat who'd found the hidden cream. "Men are simple creatures," she confided, then laughed, a gay sound that set Audra's teeth on edge. She tipped her head conspiratorially toward Audra. "I have a way with them, you know."

The image of Leo's hands cupping her mother's shoulders, each whispering in the other's ear only God knew what blinded Audra momentarily with rage. *Rage.* The vehemence of its depth stunned her. Then again, why should she care if Lady Margaret and Leo— the words refused to form, even in her head. Why? Because it was her *mother...and Leo.*

For years now, Daddy had chosen to overlook the obvious. She didn't understand why he pretended. It hurt and repulsed Audra's own standards that were set as high as the cliffs of their home on Martha's Vineyard in Edgartown. Was Leo Meggie's only lover, or were there others? Her throat closed, choked with tears. Truly, how could she sit here and make-believe her own mother didn't roam the globe handing out her favors to any Joe Blow with light hair, broad shoulders, and firm lips. *Oh, God.*

"Darling, I spoke with Leo late last night." Meggie's voice severed her thoughts. She took Audra's hand. "I don't know where you got your notions, or we'd have straightened out this silly fuss."

"Silly fuss?" Audra blinked, and her mother's expression floated into view. One that portrayed concern. Such was the actress. "I—"

Audra, filled with outrage, jerked her hand away from Meggie's and edged off the bed. She flinched from her mother's outstretched hand. "Silly fuss? Is that what you call it?" Her voice was a hiss of fury. Her heart pounded. Her pulse roared in her ears.

"Audra. How could you possibly believe—that Leo and I—" Meggie's voice fell into a hurt whisper. "I would *never* do anything to hurt your father. Or you, darling. Please, you must talk to me. Is that what the distance between us has been over all these years? I simply abhor it."

Panic banded the air in Audra's lungs. She couldn't breathe. Lady Margaret's artistic skills were so convincing, Audra felt herself being sucked down in a swirling pool of emotion. Her near nomination for one of the first Tony awards for her performance in *Finnian's Rainbow* was notorious. Shockingly, the nomination was a rumor, but Audra had witnessed her mother's acting skills for years and knew her to be a phenomenal talent.

There was no way Audra had been wrong all these years. Her head seemed to move side to side of its own volition as she backed away. "Mother…please. I-I don't, can't talk about this," she whispered.

"We *will* talk about it, Audra Faye. Leo is my agent. *My agent. Period.*" If Meggie had been standing, Audra was certain she'd have stomped her foot.

Anger rushed through Audra. Perhaps it *was* time to clear the air. "What is there to talk about? Your career was always more important to you. Daddy *never* left me."

Confusion colored her mother's features though her mouth remained set. "Darling. Your father and I rarely disagree, but marriages are inevitably built by two individuals. Of course, my career was important to me. It still is, darling. But when have I not been there for you? Answer me that."

Audra felt a little dizzy, twelve years falling away in a mountain of pain. "You said you wouldn't move from New York."

"Are you speaking of that little discussion on our move to Boston? Darling, that was years ago." Meggie moved from her corner of the bed, letting out a huff of frustration, pacing the spacious room. "Moving to Boston *was* a difficult transition for me, Audra, but things have worked out nicely since. Don't you think?" Her hand covered Audra's. "I wasn't about to desert you *or* your father. I admit there were adjustments to be had. And yes, some of my travel became a bit more complicated from Boston versus New York, but my goodness, Audra—" Her mother paused and pierced her blue eyes on Audra, the same blue Audra faced each morning in the mirror.

Audra shifted under her scrutiny. "But, you...you called him..." *darling.* She couldn't say the word aloud. But she called Audra that too. Audra's mind scrambled for something. Anything. "But Leo lied. He said you were expecting him. But you weren't. You said..." Her voice fell away, and she glanced around her room, trapped by the past. Her father's cold voice telling

169

Mommy he wouldn't be leaving Audra behind. The scene played through her head like a film reel, only the colors were vivid and detailed. Her pink dress with its pretty flowers, her shiny Mary Jane's, the etched steel in Daddy's tone. Her mother's white face, then rush of fury.

"Audra. Your father is a proud man. It stung his pride fiercely when I balked at him opening the club. My life, *our* life was in New York. *At the time.*" She stopped, then spoke hesitantly. "There was something else, darling. His mother. Your father's mother. I never learned all of the ins and outs, but I think she quite resented Harry's father for ruining her stage career." Meggie shrugged. "That was many years ago."

"But you left that summer."

"Yes, darling. Leo was just beginning to assist his father in the business. He'd inadvertently lined up…oh, I can't remember what now…but it was too late for me to back out." She moved forward, grabbed Audra's hand, and squeezed. "The fact of the matter is, Audra, I love my career. And I wouldn't change a thing. No matter what anyone says, and," she said gently, "I don't believe your father would either."

The thoughts snarled like tiny, tangled, intricate chains through her head. Too knotted up to set to rights properly. *She'd been wrong? For twelve years?* Audra's stomach curled and churned. "You—" Bile pinched the inside of her cheek. She swallowed it back. "You and Daddy aren't just together for…for appearances?"

"Is that what you've believed all this time?" The shock in Meggie's voice ricocheted through every limb of Audra's body. She wanted to curl up and die. But her mother wasn't finished driving the nail in Audra's psyche-coffin. "There's never been anyone for me but your father." Meggie's eyes narrowed on Audra. "Tell me, daughter. How on earth did you come up with such a theory?"

"I-I heard you fighting. You thought he was leaving, but he said he would never leave me." She shook her head back and forth, the tears forming a river down her cheeks. "Then you…you left." Could she, in all honesty, trust that her mother was speaking the truth? How could Audra have gotten things so twisted?

Audra backed away unable to comprehend all the words thrown at her. At the foot of the bed, she made a break for the bathroom, slammed and locked the door.

Her mother pounded, then rattled the knob. "Audra Faye! Open this door. Right this moment, young lady." Stern words that trembled with emotion.

The problem lay in identifying the emotion. Was it hurt? Anger? Brilliant acting? Audra couldn't tell. Another picture stole through her memory—Leo's astonishment when she'd accused him of mauling Meggie in front of Daddy, their guests, the reporter from *Look* Magazine. But he'd been furious too. If it wasn't true, then why hadn't he defended himself? *Because you never give anyone the last word. You're a spoiled brat.* Her subconscious berated her.

Was it possible she owed her mother an apology? Leo?

Audra dashed across the lavish bath and twisted the faucets on the large tub to drown out Meggie's hurt and her own fears, doubts, and confusion. Audra had been angry as long as she could remember, but never in her life had she outright hated herself. Not like she did in this instant. She sank down to the floor and allowed the rage of tears to collide with the rushing water.

****

Leo bolted upright, startled out of the depths of a hard sleep. Scrubbing a palm over his face, he searched his mind thinking he'd had a nightmare. His dampened forehead and heart slamming against his ribs were reminiscent to the early days of his return from the war. That was the last he'd been prone to bad dreams. While his head pounded from too much champagne at Lady Margaret's supper party the evening before, nothing should have startled him from a solid sleep unless someone was breaking in. Perhaps it was too much Audra Faye. Maybe. Probably. All right, definitely. Every minute detail came roaring back.

Most prominent? That almost kiss he should have seized. God, he wanted Audra so badly he ached.

Every encounter ended with her glowering, him bumbling, her furious, him lashing out, and—now, after her mortifying charges—flat out stunned. Designs on Meggie? Laughable. It had always been Audra. She was the burr under the blanket on the horse. And that made for one very testy animal. Yep, that about summed it up. He was a testy animal with no outlet for his pent-up frustration. Who the devil was he supposed to talk to? Harry? James? *Willie?*

He barked out a laugh that echoed throughout the silent house.

Silent. House.

Leo cocked his head to one side. The townhouse was quiet. Too quiet. "Jamie!" Leo stumbled from the bed and snatched up his trousers. "Jamie," he yelled again, almost falling on his face, ramming one leg in then the other. No answer. No four-legged paw's nails, tapping against the tiled floor, as was the case every other morning of the past week.

Apprehension speared him. Each threshold he crossed into another empty room, his stomach clenched tighter. "Damn it, Jamie!" *He ran away.* Please, God. Not South End. Dashing back to the bedroom, Leo grabbed his shirt and jammed his arms in the sleeves. He was back down the hall when the front door opened then closed.

Leo flew down the hall, followed the tapping nails to the kitchen, his heart pounding like a sledgehammer against a brick wall. "What the hell do you think you're doing?" Fear turned his tone harsh.

Jamie flinched, fear etching his childish features. He stood at the sink, Willie's water bowl in hand, water sloshing over the sides. "I-I t-t-took W-willie…" His stutter was so pronounced he couldn't finish his sentence.

Leo felt like a heel. He pushed a hand through his hair. "I'm sorry, kid. I woke up and…" Leo went to the sink, took up the bowl, filled it, and handed it back to Jamie. "Look, let me know when you step out. Will you do that?"

Jamie set the bowl on the floor and nodded without looking at Leo, making Leo feel worse. "I'm sorry. I don't know what came over me. I woke up and…look. Let me make it up to you. How about we catch a Sox game today."

Jamie turned around, his expression cautious. "Y-you m-mean a real b-base-b-ball g-game? In p-p-person?"

Leo ruffled his hair and smiled. "Yeah, kid. The Yankees are in town."

"The Yankees!" His shrill could probably be heard across the river all the way to Club 501.

"You think you can stand to leave Willie alone for a few hours?"

"I don't think he would like all those p-people." He leaned down and hugged his dog. "W-willie thinks the Sox will t-take it all the w-way this year."

Now that Leo's heart had slowed to a relatively normal beat, relief flowed through him, noting Jamie's speech impairment improved with his excitement. "That's the hope, kid. All right. Come on then." The phone blared. "Get cleaned up, and we'll make a day of it," he said, hurrying down the hall to his home office. He grabbed the receiver. "Leo Frisk."

"Hey, Frisk. It's Scully. I got some info for you."

"Give it to me."

"Her name's Florence. Florence Payne. Lives in Dallas just like you thought."

Leo picked up a pen and scribbled down the address and phone number. "Thanks, Scully. Send me a bill." He clicked for a new connection and made the call.

****

The thought of being cooped up on the bus nauseated Audra. Not after the morning she'd had. She needed air. Smoothing her hands over the navy, polka dot, silk skirt of her dress, she donned her white gloves and chose the thirty-minute walk through the Public Garden to the Plaza. Surely, that would calm her frazzled nerves. She glanced down at the navy suede, Cuban-heeled pumps and sighed. Fine. If the walk became too much, she'd catch a cab. Swiping up the matching cartwheel sunhat, she faced the mirror and adjusted it to a slight angle, grabbed her clutch, and set out. Despite her melancholy, she couldn't wait to see the girls, Maddie in particular. It had been an age.

Audra strode into the Park Plaza's upscale grill, hoping to at least beat her friends to the table. The hostess greeted her. "Good morning, Miss Dempsey. Your party has already been seated. The usual table, of course."

"Thank you," she murmured. She hurried over, excitement trilling through her. The other girls hadn't sat down yet. Maddie caught sight of her first.

"Audra." Maddie rushed over and threw her arms around her. "I can't believe we are all finally together."

"You look terrific, Mad." Audra was hit with an onslaught of emotion and hugged her back tightly.

"How did dinner go last night?" Iris said.

Audra accepted the pulled-out chair by the server and used her hat to shield her face. "Um, fine. I was only a couple of minutes late. Daddy almost caused a scene."

A small giggle erupted from Iris. "And with a reporter there from *Look.*"

"*Look!*" Sophie was beside herself. She had grandiose notions of being featured herself someday. To be fair, Sophie had a good shot. She was a superb artist. "Uncle Harry is a hothead for sure. How did you get him to stop?"

Heat crawled up Audra's face.

Iris laid her hand over hers. "Oh, Honey, you look terrible. What's wrong?"

Good heavens. "What makes you think something is wrong?" Audra said, adjusting her skirt, tugging the gloves from her hands, placing them in her purse, setting her purse aside. Anything to avoid the all-too-seeing eyes of her closest friends in the whole world.

"Your eyes are puffy. You've been crying."

Unable to evade her friends any longer, Audra glanced up. "I'm fine, really." To her utter disgust, her voice shook, and she found herself blinking back another onslaught of tears.

Iris's hand covered hers. "Did Uncle Harry—"

She snatched her hand back and pierced Iris with a sharp look. "No. It's…it's my mother. She waylaid me this morning—with tea. And *scones*."

"But that's wonderful," Sophie said. "Things are better then."

Maddie stuffed a tissue in Audra's hand, and she dabbed her eyes. "I-I don't know what to think."

Maddie glanced around the table. "I don't understand," she said.

Iris gave Audra a pitying look then turned to the others. "Audra still believes Aunt Meggie and Uncle Harry are only together for appearance's sake."

Was it really necessary for Iris to blurt things out so…so *plainly?*

Maddie's brows rose. "Still? After all these years?"

Audra bristled, utterly mortified by Iris's bluntness. There was nothing to do now but grab the bull by the horns. Truly, what choice did she have? "It goes a bit deeper than that," she said, defensively. Audra inhaled deeply and surveyed the concern in her friends faces. "The thing is…my mother…and Leo—I mean Mr. Frisk, they've—" She dropped her eyes. Oh, lord.

Could she even say the words out loud? "Well, they are really close, and I think—*thought*—that they—"

"What—" Sophie said.

"Sophie, please." Audra's gaze shot around the surrounding area. "Keep your voice down."

Sophie's mouth curled into a cheeky grin. "—You don't want to admit that Mr. Frisk is mad for Aunt Meggie?"

Audra was ashamed. Just hearing the actual words made her realize how utterly ridiculous they sounded.

Sophie glanced about the dining room and lowered her voice, though it was filled with laughter. "Leo Frisk is besotted all right, Audra, but it's not with Aunt Meggie."

Giggles erupted from Iris, and Maddie smiled, but Audra's emotions were too ingrained, too raw. How could she trust something so out of tune with everything she'd believed since she was ten years old? Besides, she'd never seen Leo with anyone. "Fine. I can admit—" (sort of) "—their relationship isn't what I've always believed—" (possibly). "But Leo—Mr. Frisk— he...he *loves* her."

Sophie picked up her menu and perused it. "Everyone loves your mother, Audra. She's Lady Margaret."

The other girls nodded. "That's true, Audra," Iris said. "You've got to let go of your resentment toward Aunt Meggie. It's killing you. And sad to watch."

Audra blinked back more tears knowing they were right and touched by their frankness. That's what true friendship was about.

"Can we talk about something else now?" Sophie demanded.

Audra could live with that. She never wanted to touch on the subject again as long as she lived. Unfortunately, it appeared she owed her mother and Leo a huge apology. Audra forced a smile, heart heavy for a different reason now. One of guilt and time lost. "Of course."

"My graduation party is Saturday, you know. And we still have not decided on tonight's movie at the cinema. I think something dark and thrilling like *Boomerang* would be fabulous."

Maddie and Iris's groans coincided with Audra's. "No murders. Not with all that South End Slayer business hitting the papers," Iris said.

"Spencer Tracy and Katherine Hepburn are in *The Sea of Grass*," Maddie threw out.

"I'm in." Iris.

"I'm in." Audra.

"Fine." Sophie.

Chapter Seven

Fenway Park

"Can I have another cola?"

Leo laughed and ruffled Jamie's hair for the third or fourth time that day. He'd lost count. "Your stomach doesn't ache yet? After three franks, cotton candy, and two cokes."

"I only ate two franks." Jamie shoved his hand in his pocket and pulled out a bundle. "I saved this one for Willie cuz he couldn't come." A frown creased his brow. "We're gonna win, aren't we? We haven't scored in a while."

Leo glanced over the field, trying to put away the sight of Willie's hot dog in Jamie's pocket. "I can't promise anything, but we're at the top of the eighth and still ahead by three."

The crowd roared with boos, and just like that, the Yankees gained another run on them. Leo hoped the Sox could pull it out. If only for Jamie's sake. Another round of groans saturated the air. Hell. Lindell just hit a single.

"Hey, kid. How would you like to meet a few of the players after the game?" Maybe Jamie wouldn't care how the game turned out once Leo whisked him to the locker room after the game and introduced him to Doerr, DiMaggio, and York.

Jamie's expression was priceless. Leo's chest tightened. "C-could I?"

"Come on. Let's make our way down to the locker room."

****

Audra barely managed to sit still through the entire movie. *The Sea of Grass* was not one of Hepburn and Tracy's better efforts. It didn't help that Leo's eyes, glittering with fury, kept edging the picture on the screen from her mind. And she absolutely refused to dwell on the tingling teasing her lips from that almost kiss. She not only truly owed him an apology, she wanted to apologize. Maybe even test herself with the taste of his lips.

If this movie ever ended, she was heading straight to his house, she vowed. No. Daddy would kill her. Besides, how was she supposed to get away from the other girls? An odd flutter tickled deep in her abdomen at the thought of seeing him. Audra pressed the tip of her finger over her lips, taking advantage of the darkened theater to revel in the memory of his feathered fingers touching her. Her eyes drifted shut as she imagined his lips whispering across hers, hot breath singeing her skin. Chilled bumps prickling her skin, pulse battering her insides—

"Are you ill?"

Audra's eyes shot open. The lights were up, and three concerned faces bore down on her…studying her. She cleared her throat. "Ill?"

Maddie laid the back of her hand against Audra's forehead. "Your face is flush. Are you coming down with something?"

"Coming down with—oh. I-I, uh, think I might be."

Worry creased Sophie's usually cheerful face. "You can't get sick. You can't miss my graduation."

Audra clasped Sophie's hand. "There is no possible way I would ever miss your graduation or the party."

A bright smile lit up her friend's face. "Good. I shall hold you to it." Sophie glanced at the others. "I don't feel much like the country club tonight. There's just too much to do before next weekend. Not to mention my parents storming town on Tuesday." A sharp gasp escaped her. "Oh, Lord. I don't have a dress."

"Well, there's nothing open now. It's Sunday for one thing," Iris said. "Hey, why don't we take the train into the city tomorrow? We'll make a day of it."

Maddie smoothed her hands over her sadly outdated taffeta skirts. "New York sounds divine. I'm in. I haven't had anything new in an age."

Iris and Sophie's burst of laughter left a hollow in Audra's chest. She smiled, and it was weak at best. She needed a dress too, but a whole day without knowing where Jamie had disappeared would kill her. On the other hand, a day away from Daddy certainly couldn't hurt.

Sophie nudged her. "What do you say, Audra? It's been forever."

Audra held back a dejected sigh at the hope and excitement in Sophie's eyes. "Of course. I think it's an excellent plan. I'll call Mr. Ruthers and let him know Iris and I will be unavailable to help out at the soup kitchen."

As the four worked their way past the theater exit to the street, excitement filled the air, people whooping and hollering.

"What the devil?" Sophie said.

"Sox beat the Yankees 8-7," a man called out. Cheers went up from the surrounding crowd gathered just outside the movie house.

The news tugged Audra from her somber mood momentarily. "Maybe we really can take it all the way this year," she said.

Maddie let out a delicate snort. "Good heavens. What is all the fuss about?" she said in her clipped British accent.

Sometimes it slipped Audra's mind that Maddie lived in England with Aunt Jessica's sister, Lulu. "The Red Sox lost in the championship game last year. It was heartbreaking."

"Devastating," Iris said.

"Frustrating," Sophie finished in a grim tone. "I spent all winter creating an unflattering series of caricatures of the players."

"Cricket?"

Audra, Iris, and Sophie stopped and turned to her. "Baseball," they said in unison.

Audra shook her head. "See you in the morning, girls?" Plans were nailed down and hugs given.

"It's too early to turn in. The Reds won. We need to celebrate," Sophie said.

Iris chimed in. "I agree!"

All Audra wanted to do was wave down a cab, but Maddie was in town for the first time in years, and Audra hated to be the Debbie-Downer.

"We don't have to stay late," Maddie said.

There was nothing to say to that. The four caught a cab to Club 501. Maybe Daddy had taken the night off.

Audra dropped her coat with the coat check and followed her friends into the boisterous atmosphere of Boston's Club 501. Her father's pride and joy. The orchestra played a lively tune she didn't recognize, but then she was not devoted to music like her mother. She tried to keep from wincing as the horn section hit their stride. Pauley, the bartender, caught sight of them and waved them over.

"What a pleasant surprise seeing my four favorite girls."

Audra stood back and watched him hug each of her friends with genuine enthusiasm while the urge to flee choked her. Audra had never thought herself claustrophobic before, but her fear for Jamie and his dog suffocated her. Audra ordered a club soda from Pauley.

Nerves battered her stomach. She couldn't stand the bright lights, the loud music, the raucous chatter. Every sound bruised her skull from the inside out. She leaned in and whispered to Iris, "I'm not feeling well. I have to go. Would you tell the others for me?"

Iris hugged her. "Of course."

She hadn't seen her father, but it was a sure bet that he was there somewhere. Keeping an eye out for him, she made her way to the coat check.

Once outside Audra felt able to breathe again. Perhaps she should stop at the soup kitchen first. She glanced at her watch. It was only seven. She ordered a cab from the valet. "South End, please. Utica, near Memorial Park." She unclasped her purse and took out her gloves. The cab didn't move; she looked up, meeting the driver's shocked expression in the rearview mirror. "Is there a problem, sir?"

"Beggin' yer pardon, miss. Are you sure?"

"Quite sure. I need to look in at the soup kitchen."

"Dressed like that—"

Outrage struck first, but she glanced down at the sweetheart neckline of her silk dress, the expensive clutch between her fingers, and the soft white gloves. "Oh, yes. I see what you mean. Right, then, um—" Well. She let out a long-winded sigh. *Home, it is.* Fleetingly, she had the idea of going to Leo's to hand over her apology, but seeing him after that scene on the terrace the night before—well, she might as well face facts—she was a coward. "I guess I could change then head there. Take me to 16 Marlborough St. and then just wait."

The cab shot forward, knocking her back against the seat. Ten minutes later, Audra tugged on the door handle to let herself out. "I'll only be a moment." She slammed the door and ran up the shallow steps and into the house.

A radio blared somewhere. Audra dashed past her father's study and took the stairs two by two.

Meggie stepped into the hall from her parents' bedroom, smiling. "Hello, darling. You're home early."

"Hi, Mother. I'm just changing clothes and dashing out again."

"Oh." Disappointment marred her expression. "Perhaps we could go shopping tomorrow?"

Audra stopped, guilt pricking her. "The girls... they, uh, want to take the train into the city. We still need dresses for Sophie's graduation party on Friday. I-I'm sorry. I told them I would go..." Her voice trailed into a whisper. She hated to disappoint her friends, but she had to make things up with Meggie. "Of course, Mother. Sure." Her escape that morning was not one of Audra's prouder moments.

Meggie gave her a bright smile, though hurt poured from her. "Don't be ridiculous. You go with your friends, darling. Suppose I give Bergdorf-Goodman's a call. Will Iris and Maddie be going as well?"

Tears threatening, Audra nodded.

"All settled then." Meggie dipped forward and wrapped her in a warm hug. "I'll let Edwin know to expect you then. You should take the early train."

Audra was overcome with emotion. As her mother withdrew, a surge of panic rushed Audra's veins, and she threw her arms around back around Meggie. "Oh, Mother. I'm such a fool. How could I have thought something so horrid about you? Ever."

Meggie's hold tightened. "Not another word, darling. We shall talk when you get home." She drew back, cupped Audra's face, and wiped her tears away. It felt as if all the heavy black in her heart shattered and floated away with a good cleanse.

Audra smiled seeing the tears flow down her mother's cheeks too.

Meggie straightened, yet her lips curved, her eyes shining. She turned Audra toward her room. "Now, go. But know this! I refuse to have more silly misunderstandings."

Audra could only nod. She reached her bedroom door and clasped the knob. She glanced over her shoulder. Her mother stood there looking at her. "I-I love you, Mother." She ducked into the room and tossed her hat on the bed, shaking inside out. She kicked off her pumps then peeled away her dress and pulled on the black "Hepburn" trousers and a dark blouse, glancing back to the door. It was dark. Perhaps she should wait…but that meant two more days before she could ask about Jamie. Snatching up a black trench coat to complete the ensemble, Audra grabbed her clutch and darted out, her heart a hundred times, no! a million times lighter. She skipped down the stairs, unable to stem a grin that made her cheeks ache. How could she have thought something so hideous about her mother and Leo?

Because he's an attractive man. And you wanted to kiss him. No! She didn't want to…to kiss Leo. She stopped at the bottom step stunned. Because that was exactly what she desired. To kiss Leo Frisk.

The front door slammed, jerking her attention. Daddy blocked the door, his lips compressed, eyes flashing a ferocious rage.

Audra's gaze followed the taxi's shrinking taillights flickering through lace coverings on a side window to the right of the French doors.

"Just where do you think you're off to at this time of night?" His voice had that deadly tremor. The one he used when some drunkard got too friendly toward her at the club.

While Audra might appreciate his protection on occasion, her own ire spiked. "What are you doing here? I thought you were at the Club."

"Your mother's home. I took the night off." His gaze narrowed. "Answer my question. Where do you think you're off to at this time of night?"

Never was she allowed to defend her *own* honor. Well, he'd played the heavy hand once too often. She lifted her chin. "I have things to check on." *Drat it.* Her voice trembled like she was still in nursery school.

"Is that so?" He moved like a cat in her direction, stopping just short of touching his nose to hers. "The cab driver believes you were headed to South End."

She took a step back. "People in South End still have to eat, Daddy."

He looked at his watch, leveled her with a steel gaze. "Not only is it almost eight at night, Sundays are your days off, are they not?"

She stomped her foot. "Quit! Quit treating me as if I haven't graduated from college. As if I can't take care of myself. How am I supposed to garner a husband? A family of my own if my father is still dictating my life?" Each word grew shriller than the next until she was yelling at the top of her lungs with her heart pounding and hands shaking.

Hurt flittered across his face but for the breath of a millisecond. "*You* live in *my* house, Audra Faye. That makes me in charge."

She spun on her heel and stomped up the stairs, the thick carpet frustratingly muting her steps. Two could play that game. She glared at him over her shoulder. "Not for long. I'm moving out." Taking the last two steps to the landing, her gaze landed on her mother's pained expression. "I-I can't do this anymore," she whispered and ran for the safety of her room.

****

Leo steered the sedan through the crawling game traffic along Storrow. He shot a glance to his passenger who'd consumed so much sugar, Leo didn't know whether it would keep the kid awake half the night or if they'd make it home before the kid passed out altogether.

"How'd you know all them players, Leo? Did you see Rudy York field those balls? I thought they was gonna lose, but man-oh-man."

Leo chuckled as Jamie rattled question after question, never slowing long enough for Leo to answer.

"When can we go again? You better step on it. Willie's gonna be hungry. I have his food in my pocket still."

"We'll be there soon." Leo settled back against the seat, listening to Jamie's excitement fill the car with chatter, hardly pausing for a breath, all the way to Bunker Hill. He really wasn't bad for a little kid. They made good time, twenty minutes. Even crossing the bridge.

Leo parallel-parked and finally interrupted Jamie to tell him poor Willie might starve by the time they got through the door.

"Oh, Willie. Hurry, Leo." Jamie dashed up the steps to the stoop, hopping from foot to foot while Leo fumbled with the lock. Jamie shoved the door back and fell to his knees, hugging his furry friend. "See, Willie. I told you we'd be back. Look, I brought you some food."

"Uh, let's take it in the kitchen, kid."

Jamie jumped up. Willie was now caught up in the excitement as the two made for the kitchen.

"And let him out the garden door," Leo called out, a second later cringing as the door crashed back against the wall then banged shut. Grinning, Leo shook his head and closed the front door then leaned back against it. Sure would be nice to confide in Audra. But he knew in his mind he already had.

Just her name whispering through his head sent a rush of longing over him. Why hadn't he kissed her last night? He'd been so close. The scent of her kept him awake at night. The mornings left him hard and desperate. All he wanted was a taste, a small taste to carry him through for the rest of his life. Because once she learned he'd deserted his son she would never give him the time of day…

Yep, Audra was Harry's daughter. Stubborn. Proud. Righteous.

Not that he didn't like and respect Harry. But the man was a reckoning force with only one daughter. A daughter he was mightily protective of. What a dismal thought. Leo pushed away from the door and plodded his way to the kitchen, pulled a tumbler from the cabinet, and poured himself a couple of fingers of Jack.

He lifted the glass but paused midway. The upside was that Audra was Meggie's daughter too. Sweet—to her friends, at least. Kind to those less fortunate. But what of him? Sure, he'd almost kissed Audra. The problem with that was the "almost" part.

"Almost" allowed her to keep Leo at a safe distance.

"Almost" let her reinforce the walls she had erected and hid so well behind.

Wary. Prim. *Polite.* It was her polite demeanor that drove him mad. He wanted the fiery Audra he knew existed beneath the prudish, polished, well-mannered Audra. The wildcat she tried hiding within when those blue eyes flashed was just an illusion. He'd witnessed the aura of blazing fire on those occasions she stood up to Harry. Occasions Leo relished most.

Even better? The sharp contrast of cool night air to her hot breath touching his lips. Yes, wildcat was the perfect description for her. Lithe and graceful like a cheetah wary of its predators while waiting patiently and ready to pounce herself.

Leo tossed back the whiskey as the garden door smashed back. Jamie flew in the kitchen, Willie close on his heels. "Hey, Leo? I'm hungry."

Chapter Eight

Monday, May 12

Leo stood in the arch of Harry's office arms crossed. There was only so much a grown man could confide in a son he'd only known for two weeks. Hence, the reason Leo stood there. Well, that, and to prod Meggie into keeping quiet about their discussion on Audra's long-held beliefs of his and Lady Margaret's supposed affair of the heart. The words still stung to a shocking degree.

"Hey, Leo. Come on in. Whoa—" Harry pointed to the mangy beast next to his legs. "What the hell is that?"

Leo's gaze dropped to the dog and back up. "Yeah. This is Willie."

"What I mean is, why is he in my club? Don't you feed him? He looks scrawny."

"I feed him. *And* he's had a bath. Where's Meggie?"

"Goodness." Her British lilt reached him from behind. "Who have we here?"

"That's Willie," Harry said. "He's a dog."

"You don't look like a dog to me."

Leo turned around where Meggie had crouched down and was face-to-face with one curious six-year-old. "This is Jamie. Willie belongs to him. Pretty much, where one goes the other follows."

Harry rose from his perch behind the desk. "There's another one? Leo, the health department is going to shut me down, damn it."

"That's enough, Harry." Meggie rose and addressed Jamie. "How do you know Leo, darling?"

"He's my dad."

Leo cringed. That wasn't quite how he pictured breaking the news.

Harry turned a sharp gaze on him. "Is he, now?"

"Just give me a minute, and I'll explain everything." He glanced at Meggie. "Jamie is thirsty."

"No, I'm not."

"Yes, you are," he said pointedly.

Lot of good it did, based on Jamie's mutinous expression.

Thankfully Lady Margaret's instincts had kicked in. "Pauley's behind the bar, Jamie. Why don't we see if he has refreshments fit for a prince and his mighty hound?"

Harry dropped into his chair. "You might as well sit and explain those two." He motioned to the empty doorway.

He scrubbed a palm over his face. "Yeah, well. There's no easy way to say this." He met Harry's stern look. "Jamie's mother's dead."

"That doesn't explain why the kid believes you are his father." Cutting to the chase was Harry's specialty.

"I, uh, suppose not." Leo explained how he'd been seeing Evelyn just before he was called to serve in the war, finishing up with Vera's note.

Harry's narrowed gaze pierced him. "You gonna claim him?"

Irritation flickered through Leo, though he rubbed a sudden ache in his chest. It seemed to help in holding back the defensive retort he longed to blast Harry with. "Of course I am." Leo refrained from mentioning the conditions he'd found Jamie in. "He's a good kid. Smart, really smart," he said gruffly. But memories from the day before had a grin splitting his face. "He's a big Sox fan. Knows his shit. He can't be all bad."

Harry responded with a grunt. "Is that why you were absent all last week?"

"Pretty much."

Meggie strolled in and took up the matching chair facing the desk. "I suppose you've an explanation?"

"Harry can fill you in, Meggie. I wanted to talk to you about Audra. She doesn't need to know—"

"Dear lord. That girl! Harry, had you any idea your daughter had the unconscionable notion Leo and I were lovers?"

"What!"

Her chuckle sounded a bit awkward to Leo's ears. "Don't worry. I cleared up any misunderstandings." She shook her head. "I just can't imagine what made her believe such a thing."

Leo cringed for the second time, feeling the "almost" kiss from Saturday night fizzle and dissipate in an invisible poof of air above his head. *Great.* "And, of course, you mentioned that I'd talked to you." He was sunk.

"What the devil was I supposed to do, darling? Let her believe that nonsense? Why, I—" She stopped. It was a long and thoughtful hesitation before she turned her soft smile on Harry. "She wanted reassurance that our marriage wasn't for appearances only."

193

A spark of hope ignited through Leo.

"Hell." Harry pushed a hand through his hair. "Where on earth could she have gotten an idea like that? We've always been so careful—" He shot Leo a chagrined look. "—disagreeing in front of her."

Leo listened to the exchange, both slightly entertained and embarrassed beyond words.

Meggie didn't seem to notice. "She mentioned us 'talking' about the move to Boston," she said. She looked at Harry, brows furrowed. "She must have overheard us. Good heavens, that must have been fifteen years ago," she said, looking somewhat stunned.

"Twelve." The words fell from Leo in instant clarity. Both Meggie and Harry turned thoughtful eyes on him. He was certain they could see the heat infusing his neck, his face.

Meggie tapped a perfectly tapered nail on her chin. "She said you lied to her."

That set Leo aback. "How could *I* have lied to her? I'd only just met her. If you remember, my father had to handle a crisis for Alyce Kutcher and sent me to Martha's Vineyard in his place."

"Yes, yes. I know all that. But Audra wouldn't have known or understood. She was a ten-year-old child consumed with the excitement of everyone being together." Meggie's hand fluttered out. "Regardless, I seem to have gained my daughter back in the blink of an eye. So, I cannot say I'm sorry for speaking out." She turned a brilliant smile on Leo. "And for that, I am *truly* grateful."

"Twelve years, huh?" A smile curved Harry's mouth. "Anything else come to mind from that day?"

194

"She stomped on my foot when she ducked out the door past me."

They grinned at him.

Leo dropped his head in his hands and groaned. He had it bad.

****

Audra faced the mirror so Maddie could zip up the fourth dress she'd tried on. "My father is driving me mad." She'd barely spoken on the train ride in from Boston, pretending sleep and shocked that she hadn't with all the tossing and turning from the night before. But guilt was a horrid sleep aid. She lowered her voice. "We had the worst fight ever last night. I told him I-I was moving out."

Maddie's fingers froze halfway up her back. "Oh, Audra. You didn't."

Audra grimaced, meeting her friend's widened gaze in the glass. "I did."

Silence filled the dressing room except for the buzz of the rest of the zipper going up. "There," her friend said smoothing a hand over the sheer black lace covering her shoulder. "You look beautiful. This cut is perfect for you. What are you going to do about Uncle Harry?"

Frustrated and a little terrified, Audra fingered the neckline on the bodice that hugged her bosom. She eyed the expanse of skin beneath the sheer lace. It *was* fetching. "I-I don't know." She frowned. "But something has to give soon, or one of us will end up saying something unforgivable. I love him, but he has to let go." Audra moved back from the mirror for a better view. She turned around. The full skirt, in soft black, fell just above her ankles in an adorable tea-length. She did a small spin. The skirt flared and fell in a soft swoosh. She stopped, observing the back. A small fabric-covered button clasped the top back of the lacy portion left an engaging slit to the solid material at her waist. She'd need shoes. "On the upside, Mother and I, well…" She blinked back an unexpected surge of tears, spreading her hands over the skirt to avoid her friend's eyes.

"What?"

"I-I misjudged her." Her voice broke. She covered her face unable to stem the tears. *"For twelve years."*

Maddie wrapped her in a hug. "Oh, Audra. I'm so sorry. But thrilled for you and Aunt Meggie just the same." Maddie stood back and grasped her by her upper arms. "Look. Why don't you come to London for a bit? Stay with me? It would give you some time away from Uncle Harry, and frankly, I would love the company." Each word that tumbled out, Maddie's voice grew with a fervored excitement. "Oh, it's a brilliant idea. I'll have a sporting time taking you about."

A pound on the door startled them both into smiling. "Hey, what's going on in there?" Iris demanded. "We want to see your dress, Audra. Sophie's is lovely."

Audra smiled a watery smile. "Thanks, Mad. I might just take you up on that." And that wasn't the half of it. To be so wrong about her mother…it was then a certainty she owed Leo an apology. A groveling one.

****

"The MET! Do we really have time for The MET?" Iris dropped her napkin on her plate and pushed it away.

Audra wasn't wild about the idea either. She was anxious to return and learn if there was any word on Jamie and Willie.

"Oh. Please," Sophie begged. "We're only two blocks away. There is a Nicolas Poussin exhibit I simply must see." Her exuberance spelled trouble, and likely they would not get out of a trip to the museum. "The works just arrived last month. We have to go."

"But the train—" Iris said.

Sophie was already signaling for their checks. "There's a later train."

Audra caught Maddie's amusement from the corner of her eye. They were stuck. "I suppose it wouldn't hurt. It's not as if we come to the City all that often," Audra relented. She clasped Sophie's hand. "Fine. We'll go and have a most informative visit. A *short* informative visit."

"Short it is." Sophie hugged her. "Thanks, Audra."

They paid their tab, and all four meandered their way down 5th Avenue. All except Sophie. She marched all the way to the Ruskinian Gothic structure that loomed ahead on either side of the museum's entrance.

After dropping their shopping bags from Bergdorf's at the coat check, Audra breathed in the history as she made her way to the Impressionisms on the second level. She truly loved this museum. The art was fascinating, her favorite being Renoir's *Hills Around the Bay*. She stared at the soft clouds and fancied herself at the top of the world surrounded by that field of flowers looking over the Moulin Huet Bay at Guernsey. There was just something so calming about an art museum's atmosphere, something so private. So personal. Renoir handed out that specialty with a vibrancy that made one want to crawl into his work and stay there.

The others seemed to feel the same, Audra thought as she wandered the rooms in companionable silence. Sophie, of course, had disappeared. When Audra stood before a magnificent piece such as the *Hills Around the Bay*, it was hard to fathom life feeling so complicated. Or believe bad things could happen.

But bad things did happen, didn't they? The alarming number of murders appearing almost daily in the newspapers gave testament to that fact. So many in such a short amount of time. *Please, God. Don't let anything happen to Jamie or Willie.*

That man accosting her the other night had terrified her. Jamie was a child, more vulnerable than her. Audra's stomach clenched. There must be something she could do to find him. To protect him. And then it hit her. Daddy's gun.

She'd borrow Daddy's gun. Only until she found Jamie and Willie and got them out of South End, then she'd return it. If luck was with her, her father would never even realize she'd taken it. She willed her palpitating pulse to slow and glanced about, impatience rippling through her. Maddie was studying the *Corneille de Lyon's* and Iris had moved to the *Frans Hals*.

Iris caught her eye and sauntered over. "We shall have to go soon," she said in a hushed whisper. "It will take us twenty minutes to convince Sophie."

Audra nodded just as Maddie walked up. In all, it took only fifteen minutes to locate Sophie. She was sitting on a leather sofa in the ladies' lounge, tension radiating from her. "We need to go, Sophie, if we are going to make the train at Penn Station."

Sophie jumped up, her agitation so prominent it took up two of her. "Yes. Yes, of course."

Maddie went over and wrapped an arm around her shoulders. "Is something amiss?"

Sophie shook her off. "No. Um, I'm ready. Let's go."

Clearly, *something* was wrong. They gathered their packages and dashed down the street just in time to catch the bus to Penn Station.

The train ride home was somber. Why, Audra couldn't say. Perhaps they were all just weary from rising so early. Audra didn't think that was the problem, not after observing Sophie's clenched fingers about the pamphlet she held. "What is that you have, Sophie?"

Sophie pulled her gaze from the window and looked down at her hand. She seemed surprised, a wry smile touching her lips. She loosened her fist and smoothed the paper out over her lap. "It's the brochure on Poussin's rendition of *The Rape of the Sabine Women.*" She offered it to Audra. "It's fascinating, though the title might leave some a little uncomfortable."

Audra took the leaflet and watched Sophie turn her attention back to the passing landscape. Audra glanced at Iris, who shrugged. Really, Sophie shouldn't be so upset that they had to leave. The train schedule was out of their control. Audra shook her head and set to reading through the brochure. Anything to keep her mind from dwelling on the worst possible scenario regarding Jamie's fate.

Chapter Nine

Saturday, May 17

Audra snuck a glance at her watch. 2:30. How long were graduation commencements supposed to last? Surely, hers hadn't been this drawn out. If they didn't wrap things up soon, she wouldn't have time to sneak down to South End before Sophie's graduation party at Daddy's club. Audra's subtle inquiries every day since Tuesday hadn't turned up a thing on Jamie's whereabouts. No scraggly mutt trotting after a tow-haired child. Not a single word. It wasn't possible to disappear into thin air—not like one could in a body of water—

Stop it, Audra Faye! God. Could she be any more morbid? Of course she could as another Chronicle headline popped through her head: ONE LESS MOUTH TO FEED. She started to drop her head in her hands, barely remembering at the last moment where she was and who she was with. She quickly dropped her hands to her lap. Errg, negative thoughts were not the least bit helpful.

"Audra, darling, what is it? You are white as a sheet."

She blinked, bringing her mother's worried face into focus. Audra did a mental shake and mouthed "sorry." Making out President Jordon's speech with the jumbled mess going on in her head proved impossible.

Her foot tapped with nervous energy until her father's hand landed on her knee. Her leg stilled, and she glanced up quickly only to meet another set of concerned eyes. Her father's.

What a horrid friend she was. She'd promised Sophie she would be there for her graduation, and physically she was, but…God, Jamie's big eyes filled her vision, blurring it with tears of him hugging his dog. Every day, every hour, every passing moment, her worry grew more frantic.

She took another look at her watch. 2:40 P.M. Jeeps, her own ceremony had not taken this long. She was certain of it. *I'm sorry, Sophie*. Her leg started the nervous jig again; again, her father's hand landed on her knee.

She'd find a way to finagle her way to South End. Somehow. Daddy would have a conniption fit if he had any inkling of her wanting to sneak away before tonight's grand celebration. And there was the sticky matter of changing into her party dress and making it to the club with no one the wiser. What choice did she have? She'd try to at least let Iris know.

The sun burned her eyes from lack of sleep. She couldn't remember the last night she'd slept all the way through.

"Sophia Noble." Her friend's name echoed across the lawn, jerking Audra's attention.

Iris and Maddie jumped up, screaming wildly. Aunt Charli, Aunt Jess, and her mother wiped away tears. Uncle Felix too, Audra would swear. Audra was right there with them, truly happy for her friend. But, jeeps, it was 3:30 already.

Time crawled by as everyone gathered around Sophie, hugging, kissing, and congratulating her.

When Audra finally had her chance to wish Sophie well, Audra was struck by the poignancy of the moment. "Gosh, Soph. We're all growing up. Someday, we might all be married...*with children*. Where has the time gone?"

Sophie sniffed into a tissue. "I know. I-I can't believe it."

It was close to four before the congratulations wound down with Maddie and Iris walking just ahead of Audra while Sophie, her parents and grandmother, angled for the opposite direction. All without giving Audra the opportunity to let Iris know her plans.

Daddy held out his hand, smiling. "Are you ready to go, daughter?" It was the sweetest smile Audra could remember seeing from him in forever. Guilt racked her, but she had to check for Jamie. She'd never get through the evening otherwise. She took his hand and squeezed.

"Oh." Glancing at her friends in front of her, she put her free hand at her lower back and crossed her finger, asked for a silent forgiveness. "Um. I'm going to ride with Iris and Maddie." His disappointment was like a knife in her eye. "If...if that's okay with you."

Her father pulled up and turned to her. After a long searching moment, he leaned down and kissed her cheek. "Sure, baby. Have a good time. I'll see you tonight."

She threw her arms around his neck, hugged him tight, wishing she was still that ten-year-old girl with all the trust and faith in the world she'd had then. "Oh, Daddy. I love you so much." Then took off in a run before he saw her tears breaking free.

Once she found Jamie, she would confess everything. Her need for going to the soup kitchen every day. She finally realized why. But telling her father? It was like she didn't trust herself. If she shared her fears for Jamie, Daddy would pat her on the head, tell her not to worry, tell her to sit tight and that he would take care of everything. That was the crux of it all. Daddy couldn't take care of this for her. Jamie trusted *her*.

And she meant to follow through. Not run to Daddy. She patted the outside of her purse holding the gun she'd confiscated from his desk. She could take care of herself and Jamie.

****

Audra stepped out of the taxi at Kneeland and Utica a little after six clutching her purse to her chest. "Wait here, please." The party was due to start in less than an hour and she had yet to change clothes. There was no getting past the fact she'd be late, but she'd worry about that when the time came.

Regulars lined up outside the soup kitchen doors. And, no surprise, no Jamie or Willie. There was no way around it, she would have to flat out ask someone. The closest person she recognized, tall, lanky, and hunched over, was Mr. Stone. "Excuse me, Mr. Stone. How are you doing? Getting enough to eat these days?"

He shuffled around slowly, turning to face her. With the sun at her back, his bushy brows drew together as he squinted against a bright sun, low in the sky.

"It's Audra Dem—"

"My, my, Miss Dempsey. Aren't you a sight for sore eyes? That's a might pretty dress you're wearing.

Yes, sireee, mighty pretty. Best watch yerself 'round these parts. You alone, darlin'?"

"Mr. Stone, I-I'm concerned about a small boy. He hasn't been seen in a couple of weeks. Always had his dog with him?"

Mr. Stone rubbed a gnarly, spotted hand over his chin. "Yep. Boy like that's bound to get took up. His ma was in the trade, ye know. 'Magin' he's followin' in her footsteps."

It took a full minute for Audra to find her voice. "—but he's a-a child."

"'Fraid that's the way of these parts, missy."

Head shaking, Audra backed away, stumbling off the curb, breaking the heel of her ankle-tie shoes. She was lucky it hadn't been her ankle or her neck.

Surprise registered on the old man's wrinkled features. He shuffled over and reached out, helping her to her feet. "You all right, Miss Dempsey. I din't mean to startle you none. I sometimes fergit myself. You bein' a lady and all."

"Th-thank you, Mr. Stone." She doubted he even heard her whisper. Her stomach roiled. She was terrified she would throw up, right there on the street. She swallowed back the bile and managed to clear her throat. "Wh-where would I f-find—"

"I'm sorry, Miss Dempsey. If they's got him, chances are you ain't never gonna find him. The good news is, ain't been hide nor hare heard of that dog of his either."

She stopped as his words penetrated. They instantly soothed something deep within. Gave her a spark of hope. "Yes. Yes, that's right, isn't it, Mr. Stone. Thank you." She grasped his hand. "Thank you."

Audra darted in the cab and glanced down at her watch. And groaned. 6:25.

****

Audra had the fastest shower ever of her Audra Faye Dempsey-slash-Lady Margaret-daughter life, applying minimal make-up that would leave mother appalled. She dabbed gloss across her lips, then slid her feet into the new black satin sling-backs. Mother had the most wonderful connections, thinking of Mr. Goodman as she snatched up her jewel-trimmed clutch. The party was scheduled for seven, and it was only 7:45. Sophie might well kill her. No. Not Sophie. Sophie would be too busy to notice how late she was. Daddy, on the other hand…

It was impossible to keep her mind on Sophie or her father as Mr. Stone's matter-of-fact words hovered like buzzards over a dead carcass washed up on the beach at Edgartown: "Boy like that's bound to get took up." *Dear God. Child prostitution.* Everyone knew things were bad in South End, but *children.* It was horrid. Just horrid. The more the words circled, the closer the bile edged up, until Audra thought she would choke.

Audra tripped out of the cab at Club 501, nerves fluttering. She ducked inside and ran for the lounge, managing to avoid looking anyone in the eye. Thankfully, due to the early hour, the plush room was empty. Palms flat against the mirror, she leaned in and stared at her too pale cheeks. Her eyes seemed too large for her face, her fear stark and staring straight back. With a deep breath, she fumbled with her clutch. She hadn't taken the time to toss in any blush. And her fingers absolutely refused to work. She dug out a tube of lipstick and dabbed some on her finger and worked it along each cheekbone. It wasn't much, but it was better than nothing.

Giving up any further effort, she patted cool water over her face and forced herself to inhale, counting to four then slowly exhaling by the same measure. She needed to talk to someone. But, who? *Leo.* Yet what purpose would that serve? She shoved his name and his image from her mind. She hadn't seen him in almost two weeks. Something intangible stole over her, gossamer, too light and delicate to grasp. Why...she almost...*missed* him. It was a shocking thought.

She rallied her breath in deeply through her nose. It was way past time to make an appearance. Two more inhalations and she hit the door, edged her way past reporters and friends to the bar where she spotted Iris standing next her mother. Definitely her best option. Audra pushed her way out of the throng of Sophie's well-wishers and pulled up—

Drat it. Daddy stood beside them, his hand entwined with her mother's. His eyes met Audra's with an unreadable glint. Lifting her chin, she forced her feet forward. The orchestra finished off its lively number just as she reached them. Iris hadn't yet spotted Audra and was touching trembling fingertips to her lips. Audra's stomach took a nosedive.

Absolute fury emanated from her father. Audra froze. As the music leveled and trailed to background noise, Iris's voice carried over the humming chatter. "I-I'm just frightened it may have happened again, Uncle Harry."

Oh no. No. No. No. Audra's muscles constricted and froze as if she'd looked straight into the damming eyes of Medusa herself. What was she saying? "Iris?"

Her mother's long fingers wrapped Daddy's arm, her blood-red nails glossy against the black sheen of his tuxedo. She thought she heard her mother. "Harry." But couldn't be sure over the rush pounding her ears.

But Harry Dempsey was never one to give a fig what the press thought. Not if he was angry. And he looked beyond angry. He was fuming. "Audra Faye? You mind telling me where you've been?" The low hum in the club stilled to dead silence.

Humiliation blazed through Audra's veins, flamed over her skin like a fevered rash. The world slowed to a snail's pace. In some small part of her brain, she registered the faces around her: shock, pity, curiosity, discomfort.

Audra's gaze found Iris's. Tears couldn't hide the guilt or fear in her friend's eyes. She hurried over, grabbing Audra's hands. "I'm sorry, Audra," she whispered. "I was so worried. You should have been here an hour ago. And, after the last time…" Her voice trailed.

A roar of violent rage ripped through Audra; hazed her vision in crimson rivaling a crime scene she envisioned worthy of the South End Slayer.

There was nothing left to say. If Audra didn't make her escape now, she'd never know another moment's independence—not for the rest of her natural life. She spun on her new heels and ran for the door, ignoring her father's shout. Let the papers have their field day. Her mother could weather anything. She was Lady Margaret. And Daddy? Well, he would as well.

England didn't seem far enough.

Chapter Ten

Well. Leo took in the domestic scene before him.
Jamie on his stomach, lay on the floor, one arm about
his permanent sidekick, both their attention on the black
and white tube where *Doorway to Fame*, a talent show
played on the DuMont Television Network. Currently,
there were only two networks—DMN and the National
Broadcasting System. In Leo's line of work as a talent
agent, he had high hopes for the little box going bigger
than radio. Rumors were flying through the
entertainment industry of Columbia Broadcasting
scheduled to come out sometime in '48. If Leo was
right, he stood to gain a lot of money with his
investments. Time would tell, however.

His plan for making the Noble girl's celebration at
Club 501 was a bust. He'd hoped to attend as the only
place he'd seen Audra in the last two weeks was his
dreams. Sharp blue eyes in her heart-shaped face, her
pert nose wrinkled in irritation when he tugged her into
his arms and planted his mouth over hers. Yeah, the
recurring dream haunted him nightly.

Jamie's shout of laughter over something Leo had
clearly missed startled Willie into a sharp bark.

Leo, barely able to summon a smile, fell back into
his musings. Sure. He'd never managed to get past
Audra's impenetrable walls of solid marble outside of
those dreams, but on most occasions he took great

pleasure in trying. Getting her back up day after day used to be the highlight of his day.

Two weeks. It left him both irritated and amused.

He let out a sigh. The "graduation" season was apparently in full swing, as his housekeeper's daughter was finishing high school and hadn't been able to sit with the kid. Hell, his housekeeper sported a more social calendar than Leo did.

It shouldn't matter since Leo's only motive in attending would have been to see Audra. A thought which only served up more frustration. Leo rose and left the office where he kept the television and went into the living room. He unlocked his front door and stepped outside for a much-needed breath of air, Jamie and Willie fast on his heels. The kid looked up at him, eyes shining. "That's swell television, Leo. I've never seen one before."

Leo wondered if Jamie might ever see fit in calling him dad then shook his head. Where the hell had *that* thought popped out from? "Let Willie out, would you?" he said gruffly.

Leo went to push the door shut and paused as a cab slowed on the street below, then stopped at the bottom of the walk. His walk. His insides stilled.

Alarm, or shock, held him spellbound, watching Audra's heel-clad feet hit the pavement. His pulse tripled.

The driver unfolded his lanky frame from the car and moved to the trunk and pulled out a large travel bag. Once he'd settled it on the walk, Audra shoved some bills in his hand. Her eyes followed the taxi roaring off into the night. Her purse snapped shut loudly in the quiet street. Her shoulders heaved.

Leo blinked, not quite certain he wasn't imagining things. She pivoted slowly and lifted her eyes, meeting his. No hat covered her short, ruffled curls. A long moment passed before she smoothed gloved hands over a formal dark full skirt that didn't reach the ground. A view of trim ankles sent his imagination soaring. She hadn't even worn a coat.

She lifted her chin and started the long uphill walk to his porch, each step igniting the fire deep within his belly.

His fingers itched to touch her, and he flexed his hands. He opted for the wiser course, draping himself with a calm that was all show. It did nothing to subdue the shiver of want that encased him, galvanized him. Yet, despite his crazed yearnings for her, her accusations gnawed him, and damn if he didn't grasp them with every molecule of his being, donned them with the intensity of medieval chain mail just before the life-and-death joust. It was his only advantage.

Leo waited and watched. Wondered what the hell had her crossing the bridge to Bunker Hill with no warning. Dressed to the nines, and on a night of celebration for one of her best childhood friends. With a suitcase. Trouble was in the air, walking up the steps. The only question left was how brutally Harry was going to murder him.

Paused on the walk at the base of the steps, Audra took a deep breath, seeming to gather some of her inner pluck. "Hello, Leo."

He steeled himself against her soft pleading tone. This was no ordinary visit. Her eyes shimmered with unshed tears, but her chin angled at her stubborn tilt. That reassured him. He shifted his attention to the bag at her feet. This was not an overnight sized bag. Curious.

As he moved his gaze slowly up her body, he lingered on a bodice that hugged her small, luscious breasts. Followed the curves up the sheer black fabric at her chest that teased him unmercifully—he was a glutton, craving such dire punishment—finally resting on her plump lips and tearstained cheeks. He hardened himself against the picture before him, squelched his urge to allow her presumptions to go unchallenged. He deserved better. He just hoped he could outlast the challenge he'd set up for himself.

Leo folded his arms over his chest, planting his feet wide. "Hello, Audra Faye. Planning on staying a while?"

Her lips tightened at his address, and he relaxed a bit. This was an Audra with which he was familiar.

"Isn't this the night of Miss Noble's big to-do?"

The comment seemed to surprise her. "It is, but—" Her chin raised another fraction. "Please. Might I come in? I won't stay long. I-I need to talk to you," she said, sending a thrill of anticipation surging on the crested wave he'd never be able to denounce. He'd waited too long to hear such words from her. He was definitely sunk. It was only a matter of time. In seconds, not minutes, he'd wager.

Leo sauntered down the steps and tipped his head at the suitcase. "Shall I leave that there?"

"Um. Of, course. I'm sure it will be fine." It was a stupid thing for her to agree to.

He shook his head and jerked it up with one hand, indicated she should precede him. Of course, the gardenia scent about knocked him to his knees. "You and Harry finally come to blows?"

"You could say that. The whole town, if not the country, can read about it in tomorrow's Chronicle, Post, Globe, and Times."

Great. "I see." He followed her inside and closed the door on the inky cool night. "You headed somewhere else, then?"

Her gaze moved about, surveying his humble home. "Oh. Um, yes," she murmured. Her eyes landed back on him. He set her luggage next to the door, trying to remember his hopes were not hers, and that he had standards. He had pride.

Her eyes dropped to her twisting hands, and his resolve melted. "Audra—"

"I-I owe you an apology," she interrupted quickly. "I was a fool accusing you...you and my...my mother of..." Her cheeks pinked.

Right then, he decided he wanted more, wanted her to say the words out loud. It was the only way for her to realize their absurdity.

"Audra. I love your mother."

Her eyes shot to his.

"*Everyone* loves your mother. She's Lady Margaret. The whole country, the whole damned world *loves* your mother." A small burst of laughter erupted from him. "Frankly, I'm not sure whether I'm flattered or insulted." He took her hand. "Harry would kill anyone who went near her without proper intentions. Or looked at her the wrong way."

Audra's bottom lip poked out. Desire raged through him. He wanted to ravish it. Lick it. Revel in it. "Yes. I can't believe that didn't occur to me." She gazed up at him, a lopsided smile curving her lips. "It's just that…well, I overheard them argue, and she left. It was a long time ago, but I've never forgotten." Her eyes fell again. "She left with you." This was whispered.

"With me?" He edged closer and took a chance on touching her—lifting her chin. "I'm her agent, Audra. Her friend. Harry's friend. Your—"

"—my?" Her eyes fell to his mouth and his stomach tensed, desire a coiling knot ready to spring.

"Don't kid yourself, Audra. I'm *not* your friend." His voice was a harsh growl. "That's never been my aim."

Audra jerked her hurt expression away, moving quickly from his reach. "I should go." Her eyes darted to her bag.

"Damn it, that's not what I meant."

The garden door crashed back, and doggie toenails tapped the tile. *Shit.* Jamie. He needed to tell her about Jamie. Willie, instead, did the honors with a little yelp of recognition and a mad dash. His front paws landed on her skirt, snagging an intricate outer layer of lace on what would likely set Leo back several hundred bucks to repair or replace.

****

Startled, Audra stumbled back. "I didn't know you had a dog," she said. There was a lot she didn't know about Leo, which was strange since he'd been a part of her life since that fateful day in '37. She put a hand to her head, feeling a little light-headed. What an odd thing to think, she thought as her system went into some sort of psychogenic shock. Her mind couldn't seem to comprehend what she was seeing. This animal …this dog…she *knew* him. "Willie?" It couldn't be. His fur, clean, combed out? She stripped off a glove. Too soft. Jamie! "Dear God," she whispered. *He was dead.* Her vision teetered, blacked at the edges. Her arm flailed, reaching for something, anything to hold on to. Molten heat grasped her upper arm, and in an instant she landed on the sofa, blinded by a monsoon. She couldn't breathe. "He would never abandon his dog."

"Audra."

Leo was shaking her as the tears coursed down her cheeks. "He wouldn't. Leo, he wouldn't. He wouldn't." The words came out shriller and shriller, pilfering her every breath.

"Audra." Why was his voice coming from that long tunnel? The black in her vision tingled with spots. One minute, her limbs were giving way, the next she was folded over, her full skirt suffocating her with her head shoved between her knees.

"Smaller inhales, Audra." It wasn't a tunnel, it came from farther away—a distant valley, through a cavern that echoed against cold stone walls. A warm hand smoothed over her back, her shoulders. "Slower, darling. You're hyperventilating."

She followed his voice. His instructions to a "T". She'd been an excellent student in all her classes. Graduated at the very top. Two years before her fellow classmates.

"That's it, darling, you're doing fine," he said. "Again. Steady now."

The spots ebbed away. He helped her straighten, and she met his eyes. Concern etched his forehead and deep lines creased the sides of his frown. "Jamie is—"

"Miss Dempsey?"

That small voice, she would it recognize anywhere. Audra's gaze spun. A second later, her back colliding against the sofa's cushions, thin arms wrapping her neck, Willie's cold nose tickling her knees. "Oh, dear God. Jamie. You're safe. But how?"

"Whoa there, boys. Where are our manners?"

Her fingers curled around Jamie's hair. Clean, shiny hair. She glanced at Leo, confused.

Resignation tinged with chagrin met her eyes. "Would you care for a drink, Miss Dempsey?" He rose quickly, heading out of the room.

Her eyes moved from the top of Jamie's head to Leo's back. "Yes. Yes. I believe I would." He left, and Audra took Jamie by his small shoulders. She set him away so she could look at him, unable to let him go. Assured herself she wasn't dreaming. "I've—" She cleared her throat. "I've been horribly worried about you." She tried for a light tone, but it cracked. She quelled the instinct to shake him from the intense relief flooding her, instead hugging him tightly to her chest. "I don't understand. How…how—"

"Leo found me and brought me and Willie here." Jamie's eyes blinked quickly. "Willie missed you somethin' fierce, Miss Dempsey. On account of you savin' him food and all."

At the sound of his name, Willie's tail whipped fiercely, his whole body a fervid ball of innate happiness.

Somehow, she managed to swallow tears past a constricted throat but couldn't keep the tremors from her voice. "I couldn't possibly let him starve, now could I?" She wrapped Jamie in another fierce hug, squeezing her eyes tight. So many questions swamped her, but right now she just wanted to revel in what she was seeing. Her most fervent prayers answered. "Oh, Jamie, I'm so happy you are all right."

Leo strolled back in, wine glass in one hand and a tumbler of something stronger in the other. "What do you say you and Willie get ready for bed, kid?"

Something hitched in his voice, drawing Audra's consideration. She studied him closely. He was clearly uncomfortable. She'd never seen the stern war hero so uncertain. It was…sweet. Iron banded her chest, and she inhaled a slow, shallow breath.

Jamie nodded and stopped. "You won't leave will you, Miss Dempsey?"

Unable to utter a word at the emotion choking her, Audra shook her head.

He started down a dark hallway but turned and ran back, throwing his arms around her, muffling in her neck. "I-I m-missed you t-too, Miss D-demps-sey."

****

Deep trouble, that's what Leo found himself in. His special detail overseas seemed less complicated. At least when a person was dealing with war, things were understood. It simply came down to life or death. Wondering if Audra would despise him for life was pure torture. Not a single detail would slip by this girl. He strived for control of the situation. Now. "Okay, Jamie. You can speak with Miss Dempsey in a bit. She and I need to talk."

"Yes, sir." Jamie made it all the way down the hallway a *second* time before he again stopped. "Will you b-be here in the m-morning?"

Pink tinged her cheeks. "I—"

"You could have breakfast with us." He turned to Leo. "Can't she, Leo?"

Leo almost laughed at her mortified expression. "Of course. But we'd best leave that up to Miss Dempsey."

"Will you, Miss Dempsey?" His stutter had all but dissipated.

"I'll speak with Leo about it," she said faintly.

"You'll come say good-night, won't you?"

Her smile softened. "You couldn't tear me away."

A grin split his face and, finally, his steps tore down the hall. "Come on, Willie."

Her tears shimmered but didn't fall. Leo couldn't take his gaze from her watching the kid and the scraggly mutt scramble out of sight. After a minute, she tugged off her second glove. A maneuver that saved her from meeting his gaze. Only for a moment, he promised.

"Drink this. I think you need it," Leo said gruffly, handing her the wine. Then to lighten the mood, and just because he couldn't help himself, he gave her a playful leer. "So. You want to stay the night? Of course, my murder and your father's eventual imprisonment will be on *your* head."

She accepted the glass and took a large gulp, saying nothing, still avoiding his eyes.

This was completely out of her character. Letting out a sigh, he rested his gaze on her luggage. "And just where *were* you off to this evening?"

"A hotel, then Lond—" Her eyes snapped to his, flashing fire. "Don't even think about turning the subject, Leo Frisk."

"Right." Resigned, Leo dropped beside her.

She shook her head and leaned back, her shoulder grazing his. "How did you learn about Jamie?" She shot forward, her body shimmering with sudden fury. "It was Iris, wasn't it? That girl never could keep a secret."

Iris? Her bitterness surprised him. "What do you mean?"

Audra did some internal shake before an irritated huff erupted from her. "Never mind about all that." Her eyes took on a shiny glint again. "I've been sick with worry." She drew in a deep, slow breath. "I might as well tell you. It won't be secret for long. After Sophie's graduation today, I went to South End. I was late getting back. By the time I'd showered and dressed, well, I...I didn't arrive at the party until almost eight. Needless to say—"

"—Daddy was furious," Leo finished for her. He had to stifle a surge of his own anger and chastisement picturing her traipsing down to South End alone. It was beyond stupid. He cleared his throat. He refrained. "What happened?"

"He yelled at me in front of everyone. My friends, his and Mother's friends. Even the band had quit playing." She picked at the snag on her skirt Willie had gifted her. "The press was in attendance. I mean, how could they not be? Lady Margaret had just returned home. With Aunt Jess and her 'princely' husband in tow." Audra's voice dipped low. "That's not all."

Trepidation knotted his insides, and he braced himself.

"One of the soup kitchen's regulars—a Mr. Stone—I asked him if he'd seen Jamie." A shudder racked her slender frame. "He said—" She swallowed hard. "He told me a boy like Jamie was bound to get taken up. It makes me ill to think of it." She covered her face with one hand, her wine dangling from the other. "When I saw Willie, I thought…I thought…" Her wrenching sob filled the room. "I thought Jamie must be…dead," she whispered.

Leo snatched her glass, set both drinks on the floor, and pulled her against his chest. It was almost funny, how perfectly she molded against him, two parts of one whole. But he didn't feel like laughing. He should be railing at her. *That neighborhood is thriving with crime. Already three confirmed dead by the South End Slayer. Who knows how many more?* He ran his fingers through her soft, short curls. Fixated on her warm body in his arms for the first time, her heart beating in sync with his. His dream come to life.

A long moment passed before she eased away and peered up at him. Red-rimmed eyes bordered by spiked lashes, and she was still the most beautiful woman he'd ever laid eyes on. One blink set free a lone tear that slid down her dewy cheek. His hands framed her jaw, his fingers curving at the nape of her neck.

"Oh, Leo. I'm so thankful to see Jamie and Willie safe."

His eyes fell to her mouth, and a luscious temptation set his lips tingling, aching, yearning for a touch, a taste. "I'm so sorry, Audra Faye."

"For what?" Her lips parted on her words, and he was officially lost.

Chapter Eleven

Leo's mouth moved over hers. No warning. Just his tongue sweeping in, shocking her. Ensnaring her. Warming her. His lips firm and soft. Each brush of his tongue sent her spiraling in a vortex of sensation. She grasped his shoulders to keep from hurtling headlong into a world without gravity. He angled his head, and his kiss penetrated her soul. Stroke after stroke pulverized her well-constructed barricades until each wall she'd erected crumbled, leaving her with nothing to sway against except him. Until she was nothing but malleable wax under the heat of a scorching summer sun. Liquefied in the most delicious way a woman—

Cool air feathered her lips as he pulled away. Her fingers dug into his shoulders, and slowly she pried them loose. She'd never been kissed like that. So thoroughly, so possessively. Mortified and unable to face him, her eyes remained shut. *Oh, God. She was kissing Leo. Leo Frisk. Her mother's long-time agent—* her eyes opened and flew to his.

His body shimmered with challenge. "Don't even think it, Audra Faye."

Her hands fell away, and she fumbled with her clutch, swiped her gloves from the sofa with trembling fingers.

His large hand covered hers, and she stilled. "Don't." His whisper caressed her. "Don't run away like a scared child. You are anything but."

Indignation poured through her. She threw back her shoulders and jerked around. After a long moment, she rose and stepped back. "I-I'd best say my good-nights to Jamie." She spun on her heel and followed the path Jamie had disappeared down earlier. That familiar sear on her back between her shoulder blades burned as if the comic Superman had come to life and scorched her with his x-ray vision. It was a ridiculous notion. She increased her pace.

Just down the hall, she found a door slightly ajar. She poked her head through. Enough light from the hall spilled in to illuminate an empty made-up bed. She frowned. "Jamie?"

"I'm here, Miss Dempsey."

Her eyes followed his voice to a corner in the room. His small form was swallowed up by a large blanket spread on the floor, Willie's head rested on a lump that must be Jamie's hip. The mutt's tail thumped uncertainly.

Audra moved into the room and slipped off her shoes. Dropping to her knees, she peered at him. "Why are you sleeping on the floor? I'm pretty sure Mr. Frisk wouldn't mind you messing up the bed."

"Willie is scared to sleep alone." His voice was soft and barely audible. "And what if Leo m-makes us leave and we d-don't have time to pack our s-stuff?"

Her heart broke for him. Audra scooted onto the makeshift bed and lay next to him with her knees drawn up. "How did you come to be with Leo?"

"He's my father."

Rendered speechless, Audra froze. Questions pummeled her mangled thoughts. *How old are you? Where is your mother? Why were you eating at the*

Soup Kitchen? Yet not a single one was appropriate to ask a six-year-old child. After a long moment, when she'd steadied her breath, she cleared her throat. "If Leo brought you here in the first place, what...what makes you think he would make you leave?"

Jamie wrapped his arm around Willie. "He wanted me to leave my dog. I wouldn't. I won't ever leave Willie. I'll run away." His voice tensed with stress.

She hurried to reassure him. "No one's going to take Willie away from you, darling. Least of all, Leo." *She hoped.*

"Will you stay with me? For a little while?" His voice was so small, yet so precious.

Her heart stuck in her throat. "Of course. But just until you fall asleep." After all, she had a hotel to find. Taking Maddie up on her offer had its own complications. She would need all her wits in planning the next phase of her life.

"That's swell, Miss Dempsey. Willie is real happy about that, aren't you boy?"

The room grew quiet with their companionable silence. Just the sound of Jamie and Willie's soft breathing. Only Audra's chaotic thoughts kept her from succumbing to anything restful. How was she supposed to get to England? People flew across the Atlantic now, of course. That sounded unnecessarily dangerous though. She didn't know the first thing about planning an overseas voyage. Jeeps, she didn't even know when Maddie was due to go back.

More importantly, how could she possibly desert Jamie right now? She couldn't. Not for even a little bit. And Leo?

She swallowed her groan. That was a whole other complication.

Chapter Twelve

Leo paced the living room, his stomach jumping in knots. Every ten seconds he glanced down the hall, starting at every small murmur. The murmurs would quiet then started up again in oddly spaced intervals. He should have told her, he berated himself. He entered the kitchen, picked up his gin, but set it back down. Getting soused wouldn't help anyone. It would only lower his inhibitions…his defenses. And he needed every arsenal in his pack. He was a celebrated war hero, for god's sake. He was a talent agent that represented a multitude of famous screen stars and athletes. How did a slip of a woman and a runt of a child and his scrawny dog turn such a man to mush?

He glanced at a clock on the stove. After ten. He'd waited long enough. He dumped the contents down the sink, noting how all had once again quietened. He dipped his glass under the running water her words just hitting him. *Hotel? Lond*—surely, she wasn't about to say London. Long Island, perhaps? No. Gut instinct was his forte and said she was planning a visit to England. That must have been some blow out with Harry. *Hell.*

Well, Leo could talk her out of that. He paced the kitchen. She'd want to be near Jamie. Yes. More gut instinct told him that. What if she stayed here? With him? She could stay in his room. He'd sleep on the couch. That elicited a groan. Yeah, and that would fly with her father.

Leo charged back to the cabinet and jerked out another glass, filling this one with water, and downed it. Back in the living room, he forced himself to settle into a chair and pushed his fingers through his hair. Maybe he should check on them.

From the arch of Jamie's bedroom door, Leo spotted two of his three guests soundly sleeping. The third thumped his tail, only his eyes rising to meet Leo's. Quietly, he made his way in and stood there contemplating the situation. Then turned down the bed and lifted Audra and tucking her in. He didn't bother with Jamie. The kid was terrified Leo would be angry if Willie got on the bed. He moved back to the door studying the scene as the war continued its wage through his brain.

This was the family he wanted. Audra, Jamie, even Willie, permanent fixtures in his life. On silent steps he went back to the living room and settled back into a chair. No one was leaving without his knowing about it.

He would only change one thing in the entire situation.

Audra's sleeping arrangements.

****

Sunday, May 18

"Leo…Leo. Why are you sleeping out here?"

Leo shook off an annoying nudge on his shoulder and attempted to roll over, but the nudge refused to abate. His tongue felt heavy and fuzzy, and the first effort in prying open his eyes failed. He managed one but squinted against an unforgiving bright eastern sun streaming through a crease in the sheer linings on the windows. He'd forgotten to draw the drapes.

True to form, Jamie didn't wait for an answer. "I gotta take Willie out."

He groaned. *Why did little kids wake up so early?*

With Willie jumping up and down, Jamie ran to the front door. "Don't forget. You were gonna make breakfast for Miss Dempsey," he said. The door slammed behind him.

Audra. Leo bolted straight up. He rushed down the hall to Jamie's room and peered in. Jamie's pallet was nowhere in sight, presumably folded neatly and stashed in the closet next to his packed bag. Audra lay on the normally unused bed curled to one side, fist beneath her chin, lashes sooty against pink cheeks, lips plump and pouty. His own tingled at their memory. How he'd managed to stay away from her all night was a mystery not worth exploring. He doubted he'd manage a second night.

She looked sweet, genteel…very un-Audra like. Her shoes were stacked on the dresser next to her clutch and gloves. The formal black dress with its full skirt had ridden halfway up her thigh and looked uncomfortable to boot. A sight that did nothing to quell the shot of blood racing to an already healthy—bordering painful—erection.

He should leave. Quit staring before she woke and—

"Leo?" Her eyes fluttered, and her mouth turned down in a puzzled frown. "What are you doing—" She gasped and glanced around. "Where is Jamie?"

"He took Willie out." His mouth twisted. "A dog has needs."

227

She sat up, smoothing a hand over her short, unruly hair. "Oh. Of course." Her eyes moved from his wrinkled shirt to the front of his trousers. She blinked and quickly looked away as a delicate flush spread up her neck to her cheeks.

"Um, I'll put on coffee." He turned and moved down the hall and called out over his shoulder. "There are fresh towels in the adjoining bath." Sanity had deserted him, and when Harry learned where his daughter had spent the night, Leo would be at the top of his hit list.

Yeah, he'd heard the stories. Straight from Lady Margaret who'd dressed up as a bootlegger one night. It was somewhat of a tall tale Leo wasn't certain he believed—except for the part where Harry had shot *and hit* Legs Diamond, the gangster, some twenty-something years ago.

Leo paused in the hallway, weighing this information. Hmph. Harry's wrath was worth any price if it meant saving Audra from disaster. He couldn't possibly have let her get a hotel at that time of night. Alone. Harry would likely be grateful to him.

Once Leo heard the water in the bathroom turn on, he went to the kitchen and began putting the basics for a hot breakfast together.

The front door crashed back, and Willie's nails tapped happily to the kitchen.

Willie plunked back on his hind haunches and smiled, tongue hanging out. All set for his patient wait. It had become a daily ritual. "Where's Jamie?" he asked the non-compliant dog.

As usual, Willie had nothing to say. Not until the bacon sizzled in the iron skillet and permeated the air.

His tail thumped against the floor, and his small begging whimper escaped.

"Where *is* Jamie?" Audra's soft question startled Leo, and he fumbled the spatula. It hit the floor, and Willie was on it.

"Shit." He swiped it from the dog and turned on the faucet.

Audra went to the coffee and poured out a cup, then planted herself at the table. "So. You want to tell me how you and Jamie found one another?"

Leo busied himself washing the spatula to collect his thoughts. After a moment he turned around and leaned back against the sink. "His mother—hell. You might as well see it for yourself." He went down the hall to his home office and jerked open the top drawer. The note from Vera was right where he'd stuffed it. He handed it over to Audra with a mixture of dread and relief.

He moved back to the stove and flipped the bacon, watching her from the corner of his eye. He flipped the oven on broil and buttered some bread, beat a couple of eggs, and slammed the bread on a cookie sheet and tossed it in the oven.

Her brows creased adorably. "Who is this Vera—" Outrage quickly replace confusion. "She was going to *sell* him?"

Something shifted inside him. Pride. Hope. "I don't know if she would have actually gone through with it. I got the feeling she cared more for him than she let on. But, based on what you said the old man told you, she might have been getting him out of there as fast as she could."

Audra's hand settled over her heart, her face pale. "Thank God she contacted you." She lowered her voice, held out the note. "Leo, Jamie can never know about this letter. Ever."

He retrieved the paper. Then nudged the skillet aside and set the corner over the open flame. A minute later he dropped it in the sink where it safely burned to ash. "He'll never learn it from me."

"What are you going to do with him?"

That was the rub. He liked the kid. Hell, even the dog was growing on him. "I've been trying to locate his grandmother."

"Are you...are you really his father?"

"The resemblance is there, and the timing fits. But even if I'm not, I could hardly leave him with Vera. That's no life for a kid."

"What do you mean?"

He hesitated. Audra was a proper young lady, and this conversation was not suited for—Audra's work at the soup kitchen was something she cherished. Who was he to keep her out of the conversation? "She's a prostitute. A productive one at that."

"And Jamie's mother? Did you, um, love her?"

"No, I—" Leo cleared his throat. "No. I met her just before I left for Europe." He glanced at her then turned back to the bacon. "No. I didn't love her."

"Was she..."

Leo had a feeling he knew what she wanted to ask. But he waited just the same.

"When you knew her, was she selling—"

Leo let her off the hook. "She was older than me. Not by much, I guess, and certainly more experienced.

But no, I don't think she was in the trade seven years ago."

Silence reigned while he set the bacon on a towel, drained the grease off in a container, and poured the beaten eggs in the skillet before she spoke again. "But you feel guilty."

Hell, yeah. "She wrote me a couple letters when I was overseas. I never answered. We knew it wasn't going anywhere when I left. But she never mentioned Jamie."

"Oh, Leo." Audra rose from the table and was suddenly next to him. In her stocking feet, she came barely to his shoulders. Those light blue eyes, large and luminous, met his. She touched his arm. "I'm so sorry."

He clenched his jaw and the spatula he held to keep himself from smothering her in an embrace and never letting her go. He wanted to take her back to bed, but this time with him. He leaned over and breathed in the scent of his shampoo in her hair.

"Have you located his grandmother?" Her voice trembled. "Do you think she'll let him keep Willie? They have to stay together, Leo. Willie is Jamie's lifeline." Her tone was husky, intimate.

A distant ring touched his ears. He ignored it. Ignored everything except her lips. Plump lips he was desperate for. God, how he wanted her. She was here. In his home. Right where she should be. Her eyes drifted shut, he leaned down—

"Hey. The phone's ringing, and what's that burning smell?"

Audra jumped at Jamie's high pitch.

Leo's heart thumped wildly as he peered over at the kid. He stood in the arch, his hair damp and slicked back. There was toothpaste residue dried on his little pointy chin. *What just happened?* "I'll get the eggs. You get the phone," Leo said to Audra. His voice was downright husky. "Down the hall past Jamie's room." *Hell.* Smoke was filling the kitchen. He flicked off the fire. "Jamie. Get the garden door."

Chaos abounded. Jamie ran for the door, Willie jumped up and down on his hind legs with excitement as Audra darted around the corner and out of sight.

"Hello." Audra's soft voice held reluctance. Leo didn't blame her. For all she knew he had a string of lovers from Los Angeles to New York City. "Hi, Daddy."

Leo groaned. *Oh, geez. They forgot to call Harry.*

****

"Audra?" She jerked the phone away certain Leo could hear her father's fury all the way in the kitchen and not on the phone, but across the river. "I. Want. You. Home."

Just like that, her temper ignited in a hot rush of fire under a broiling sun and high winds. "That's enough, Daddy," Audra said. "I'm not coming—"

He cut her off. "—I've been sick with worry."

"I'm sorry you were worried, but you need to stop." Embarrassment crawled up her neck. She glanced over her shoulder. "I am twenty-two, Daddy, not twelve!"

"I'll pick you up. I'm leaving now. I'll fucking kill Leo—"

Her mother mumbled something Audra couldn't make out. But she must have snatched the phone from his grip. "Audra, darling. Take all the time you need. *I'll* handle your father." Her voice fell away, and Audra could practically see the scowl her mother directed at her father through the line though her voice remained calm. "That's enough, Harry. Leave it be." Her stern tone surprised Audra. There was a long pause, then Meggie's voice came back, softly and clearly speaking to Audra. "He just worries over you, my sweet. Don't be too angry with him."

Don't be angry with him? That was rich. "Thank you, Mother."

"We'll see you when you get home, darling."

"I-I'm not coming home, Mother. I-I can't. I'm a grown woman. It's time he treated me so." She blinked back an unexpected flurry of tears.

In the bout of silence, Audra could practically hear the wheels grinding in her mother's head. "Not coming home?"

"Give me that. You get home right this minute, young lady. I'm on my way—"

"I'm sorry, Daddy. I can't," she whispered, then slowly replaced the receiver with trembling fingers. She fell into the chair in front of the desk and dropped her face in her palms, trying desperately to steady her breath. She'd never stood up to him so. The whole ordeal scattered her wits.

"Audra?" Leo pulled her hands from her face. He was crouched before her, his eyes wary but level with hers. "I should have called Harry first thing this morning. Last night even, but I fell asleep...I'm sorry—"

She squeezed his hands. "Leo, don't. I'm an adult, and he needs to realize it." She turned her head, looking out the single window in the room. "It's crazy, you know. My mother crossed an ocean when she was my age. I can't even go to brunch and the cinema without him monitoring my every step."

He stood and pulled her to her feet. Touched his lips in a quick caress against hers. "It's funny in a not so funny way."

Her lips tingled. "What do you mean?" She was thrilled with her normal tone. She took it as a private victory.

"Yesterday, I woke up and couldn't find Jamie anywhere in the house. I—" He gave her a sheepish smile. "I panicked. He was out of my sight for a few minutes, and my common sense was seized by aliens." He tugged her to the door. "Come on. Willie is liable to get all the bacon if we don't stake our claim."

In the kitchen, her gaze slid to Jamie. Leo cleared his throat and gestured to a chair. "Let's eat."

Nodding, Audra accepted the seat across from Jamie and watched Leo scrape the unburnt portion of the eggs into a bowl and set it on the table. He pulled the toast from the oven, and the scent filled the kitchen. Audra was stunned at the intimacy that enveloped her in the cozy atmosphere.

"All is not completely lost," Leo said.

Silence ensued while they filled their plates. All except for the small, whimpering begs from Willie, who was perched between Leo and Jamie.

Leo broke the quiet. "How bad was it?"

"Oh. Well—" Audra swallowed, mortified in crushing his efforts. "They aren't scorched too horribly…"

Leo's lips curved slightly. "I, uh, meant Harry."

"Oh, right," she said trying to will back the fire in her cheeks. Quite unsuccessfully. "I can't believe you didn't hear him." Her eyes narrowed on him. "Mother said she'd handle him. She seems to do that well."

He grinned. "That she does."

"By the way, he threatened to—" She stopped and peered at Jamie. "Never mind," she murmured.

"Is your pa mad?" Jamie spoke around a healthy amount of burnt eggs.

"Kid, it's not polite to talk with your mouth full," Leo said.

"Sorry."

Audra bit back a grin as Leo's eyes rolled to the ceiling. "He didn't know where I was last night and was worried. Just as I'm sure your mother fretted over you," she said to Jamie.

"Oh, my ma never worried about me on account of Willie."

Audra frowned. "Of course she worried about you. All parents worry over their children."

"No, she didn't. Sometimes if I came home too early, her and Vera would lock the door and make me wait in the hall."

Audra dropped her head, took a bite of eggs, knowing she would likely choke, and not because they weren't edible. Words weren't possible. She couldn't cry. Not with Jamie and Leo sitting right there across from her, staring at her.

"That's all changed now, hasn't it, Jamie?" Leo's deep voice grounded her. Calmed her.

"Is that why you yelled at me yesterday morning? When all I did was take Willie out? He had to go real bad."

Audra schooled her features and looked up. An odd quiet had fallen over the room. Eggs from Leo's fork toppled, falling back onto his plate, though his hand seemed to have turned to stone. Jamie seemed to be holding his breath, his gaze pinning Leo, both cautious and hopeful.

Leo was the first to move. He blinked, shoveling the eggs back on his fork. "Yes." The word came out gruffly, as if he were surprised to have admitted it. "Yes. Like I told you yesterday, I want to know exactly when you walk out that door. Where you are going and when to expect you back. Even if you have to wake me up."

The beaming smile that lit Jamie's face squeezed Audra's heart, Jamie's hero-worship worth millions. "Yes, sir."

Was this how her father felt? Terrified for her when she was nowhere he could reach her? She'd been beside herself when she couldn't find Jamie. Looking through that tiny peephole revealed how self-centered and indifferent she'd behaved toward her father. Showcased the chances she'd taken in searching for Jamie with no thought to how her parents would suffer if something happened to her. Keeping things from Daddy when he only wanted her safe. And there was a difference. She was a grown woman, graduated from college, and Jamie was just a child.

How ironic to realize in insisting that she was grown to her father just emphasized how great her immaturity. The air left her body in a rush of grim cognizance. Her actions had spoken volumes.

"Jamie, why don't you get cleaned up and presentable, and we'll run Miss Dempsey home."

"But I had a shower already." Leo lifted one brow. "Okay, but can Willie go?"

"No," Leo said.

Audra looked up. "I can't go home."

"And where exactly *are* you going then?"

"A hotel."

"No," Leo said.

Truly? This again? "I couldn't possibly intrude on your hospitality."

"Yes, you can. Leo won't mind. Right, Leo?" The excitement in Jamie's eyes broke Audra's heart.

"You want me to stay *here*?" There? With...*him?* "With you?" She looked from Leo to Jamie to Willie. Perhaps a couple of days wouldn't hurt. One thing was certain, she needed distance from her father. Things could not keep on their current path.

Leo pierced her with one of those gazes she couldn't decipher and said, "Your father will kill me."

Her gaze moved back to Leo. "Um, yes. He said as much."

****

"Will you, Miss Dempsey? We could be a family. A real family. You could sleep in my room," Jamie went on. Willie jumped up and down as if he understood every word.

Or mine, Leo wanted to shout. Of course, he remained quiet, not a whisper of breath escaping him.

Apparently, he hadn't punished himself enough as thoughts of waking up beside Audra filled his vision, her dark curls mussed and stark against the white pillowcase, in his bed. The knot at her throat moved, her swallow audible.

Red infused Audra's cheeks. The pulse in her slender throat palpitated erratically. He feared her blood pressure would blow. He half rose from his chair, but she threw her hand up, stopping him.

Leo decided to put her out of her misery. "You'll take the spare room, Jamie and Willie will stay with me." Yep. He was a dead man.

The phone blared from the other room.

"If that's my father—" she said faintly.

Suppressing a wince, Leo cut the rest of Audra's sentence by jumping up, his chair scraping across the wood floor. God, he couldn't help it, but he relished the opportunity of having her near. It was worth taking his chances with Harry. He snatched up the receiver. "Frisk." He turned around and found the entire household had followed him.

"Mr. Frisk? This is Florence Payne." The voice was thin and feminine. He had trouble placing the name, but a frisson of unease inched up his spine. "Evie's momma."

"Evie?"

"Evelyn Payne, Mr. Frisk, was my daughter."

Leo's reflexes jerked, and his eyes met Audra's. Her mouth turned down, and her arm wrapped Jamie's small torso from behind. "Uh, yes. Mrs. Payne. First, please let me extend my sincerest condolences."

A short, awkward silence ensued. "Er, thank you. Mr. Frisk, I understand my grandson is living with you."

"Yes." His eyes fell to Jamie's anxious expression. "You'll be thrilled to learn my son is doing admirably in his new dwelling," he returned.

A bright light lit Jamie's eyes, creating a manacle across Leo's chest. He winked at Jamie and turned his back to his audience.

"Praise the Lord." Her cries crashed through the receiver loud enough to jerk his head back, holding out the receiver. Cautiously, he set it back to his ear. "That just warms my heart, Mr. Frisk. But if it's all the same to you, I'd appreciate seeing Evie's boy."

He glanced over his shoulder. Audra's one hand was squeezed into a fist at her side, knuckles white. Willie sat at their feet still as a statue for once.

"Of course, Mrs. Payne."

"I ain't seen my boy since he was a babe swaddled in cloth."

Her fear pressed through the phone, and Leo hastened to reassure her. "I'm certain we can work out something, Mrs. Payne. You understand I want only what's best for Jamie?"

Palpable relief reached through the phone. "Thank you, Mr. Frisk. Thank you. If it's all the same to you, I'd like to see him today."

****

Audra stood at the window in a den area where she could observe the front of the house. A cab pulled up, and a woman in an unfashionable grayish dress made her way awkwardly out in front of Leo's home.

Audra glanced down at her twisting hands and forced them to still, linked them tightly together at her lower back.

"S-she's here, Miss D-d-dempsey." Jamie spoke from the arch of the door. "She won't m-make me s-stay with her, w-will she?"

Audra turned around. "Come here." She went down on her knees, bringing her face-to-face with him, Willie right at his side. "You want to stay with Leo?"

"Willie really l-likes it here. He ain't b-been hungry once," he said softly.

"What about you? Do you like it here?"

He nodded. "Will you b-be here when I g-get b-back?"

She pulled him into a tight hug. "Of course."

He squeezed her neck. "You p-promise?"

"I do."

They both flinched at the soft knock on the door from the living room. It wasn't Audra's place to interfere, no matter how much as she longed to rail at Leo not to let Jamie go.

Big tears filled his eyes. "Leo said W-willie can't g-go."

"Perhaps Willie can stay here with me?"

"He'd l-like that." Jamie leaned down and hugged his dog., "Willie, you s-stay here with M-miss Dempsey. I'll b-b-be back soon, it's just lunch…and d-d-dinner." It struck Audra Jamie's level of stress related directly to his stuttering. Willie lay on the floor, his head on his front legs, soulful, sad eyes begging Jamie to change his mind. But Jamie was the bravest little boy Audra had ever known.

"Jamie, you ready?" Leo appeared in the doorframe.

Audra scratched Willie's head. "I'll look after you, Willie."

She gave Jamie an encouraging smile. Jamie left without a backward look, breaking her heart. Audra moved quickly to the window, one hand on her heart. She had a notion her tears were mirrored in his eyes.

She turned her gaze to Leo as he spoke to the woman. The wool hat that covered her hair blocked her eyes. She was thin, seeming more youthful than one pictured a grandmother. But then Jamie was only six. If his mother had him at age eighteen, or even younger, and her mother the same, the grandmother could be as young as her mid-thirties, perhaps younger. A small shudder skidded up Audra's spine. Audra was all of twenty-two.

What a difficult and tragic way to live. Audra's blessings were many even if she hadn't realized so at the time. She'd been raised by a father who loved her beyond reason. Stiflingly so. Her mother's career had given her privileges few others enjoyed: travel, access to an excellent education, wonderful friends she loved as sisters. Independence.

Looking back at that day all those years ago, seeing her mother poke her father in the chest. *Don't you dare think to intimidate me, Harry Dempsey. I had enough of that from my toplofty mother my entire life. They still telephone weekly, only to let me know what a disgrace I am to the family, the title I abandoned—no—should have married. I refuse to fall victim to yours or anyone's threats.* Or words to that effect. Most importantly…her independence. Laying out the advantages she'd received humbled her.

She feasted her eye on Leo. His shoulders were broad enough to hoist the world. He might not believe it, but he would be a wonderful father to Jamie. And she…she would be there to see it. Them. Her heart thumped loudly against her ribs. She could see herself ensconced in their lives, kissing Jamie goodnight, kissing Leo—

Clearly, her thinking had skewed to something that belonged in Hugo Gernsback's *Modern Electrics*. She knew little of Leo's time in the war, only that he'd been welcomed home a hero. And not just some ordinary Joe. She remembered whisperings of his work, mostly behind enemy lines. She could well believe it, she thought, watching him accompany Mrs. Payne down the steps to the street. She'd never met anyone so aware of his surroundings. The way he was able to sneak up on Audra was a testament to his panther-like demeanor.

His lightish-chestnut hair, disheveled from running his fingers through it, lifted in the soft breeze. A small smile touched her. He truly was one of the most attractive men she'd ever met. And she'd met plenty, her mother being in the business and all.

Body language was a curious thing, and Leo's was tightly coiled. He didn't want Jamie out of his sight, just like he'd said at breakfast. The thought warmed Audra through and sent the awareness of her father's sensitivity to her well-being blossoming. Leo's hand rested on Jamie's shoulder.

The phone trilled from the other room. Audra tore herself from the scene before her and hurried down the hall, wondering who Mrs. Payne reminded her of. The obvious was Jamie's mother from the soup kitchen. Audra must have seen her on the rare occasion.

Audra grabbed the phone as it occurred to her how quickly she found herself at home in Leo's bachelor abode. "Hello?"

"Audra?"

"I've told you, Mother, I'm not ready to come home. I'm sor—"

Lady Margaret was not one to back away from a challenge, and for the second time that day Audra could hear the wheels grinding in her mother's head. "Lunch then, darling? One o'clock, the Lenox. I won't take no for an answer."

The instinct to fight fled as suddenly as it had flared. Audra *wanted* her mother back in her life. She'd been a fool shunning her under the misconceived notions of that ten-year-old child from a world that had blown up in her face so long ago.

It was time to let go, just like her friends had told her. "I... I would love to."

****

Leo studied Florence Payne as she came up the steps. A stone the size of a boulder lodged itself in the pit of his stomach. Every day with Jamie gave him a new understanding of Harry's predicament despite Audra being a grown woman. The thought of either Jamie or Audra being out of his sight for even a minute was as intolerable as it was impractical. The woman was his grandmother. It was downright unreasonable.

Mrs. Payne's unfashionable dress was faded but clean and comforted Leo to a degree. Her hat hid a good portion of her face, and Leo eyed the older woman warily. He brought his gaze back to Jamie. "You sure about this, Buddy? You don't have to go."

Trusting eyes met his. "I won't go if you don't want me to," he said.

That wasn't exactly what Leo meant. He swallowed his groan. "She's your grandmother, son." He looked up at Florence. With a short wave, her steps quickened. "Have you ever met her before?"

His small body pressed into Leo's thigh, but his voice was sturdy. "Nah. Just Aunt Vera and Uncle Donnie. Is that her? My momma's momma?"

Uncle Donnie? Leo filed away that tidbit to explore later. Evelyn's mother, from this distance, appeared young, but Evelyn's life had been hard. He wondered if Florence's had as well. He fought the urge to snatch Jamie up, dart back in the house, and bar the door in her face. "I believe so," he said, unsure if he was reassuring Jamie or himself.

She ran up the last of the steps to the porch and pulled Jamie in an embrace that threatened to suffocate the poor kid. "Dear Lord. You look just like your mama. And now, to have you in my arms… well, it just gladdens my heart." She set him on his feet but didn't relinquish her hold. "Your mama did a fine job raising you, she did." Leo listened to her southern twang slightly mollified.

Jamie scrubbed his nose. "You smell like cigarettes."

Her hacker's laugh filled the air. "Those things'll kill you. You ready for lunch?" She started away, her hand tightly clasped to Jamie's.

Leo felt a surge of panic. "Hold on there, Mrs. Payne." Her nervousness set him on edge. "I believe I'll accompany you."

Her head dropped in instant contrition. "Of course, Mr. Frisk. Whatever you think is best."

Beneath Leo's hand, Jamie's shoulders relaxed, a telling sign.

But Florence Payne kneeled, looking Jamie in the eye. "Is that what *you* want, Jamie? We'll do whatever *you* want."

The long interval startled Leo. Hurt his feelings some, truth be told.

"Mr. Frisk is welcome to come, Jamie. I just want to visit a bit." She cut her eyes to Leo. "We'll just have a burger and malt. I reckon we'll be back by five."

Jamie turned his soulful gaze on Leo. "D-don't worry, Leo. I'll b-b-be okay," Jamie said. "Miss D-dempsey might need your h-help with Willie." This concession was monumental, and Leo took it as such. Jamie was trusting Leo and Audra with his most prized and precious possession.

Leo gently squeezed his shoulder. "Of course, Jamie. We'll take good care of him until you return."

Mrs. Payne stood and gentled her tone. "Mr. Frisk. We shall take the taxi to the local drug store. We'll be right as rain and back before you know it."

The local drug store was only six blocks away. He'd let them go and follow a few minutes later with neither of them any the wiser. He gave a sharp nod, knowing Audra would be happy looking after Willie. Leo assisted them into the taxi. Then fighting the urge to follow, watched them disappear around the corner three blocks down.

A fierce urge to see Audra roared through him. He needed to touch her. Kiss her. Have her reassurance that letting Jamie go with Evelyn's mother had been the right thing to do.

Leo scooped up the Chronicle from the porch and pushed back the door. Willie's whimper tore through him, and he snatched the dog's collar before he could slip past. Guess he wasn't alone in his misgivings. "Whoa there, boy. He'll be back."

Leo shut the door and went on the hunt for Audra, realizing for the first time in his memory he was alone with her.

Alone.

With Audra. And she wasn't angry with him.

It was a delicious sensation. Dog nails clipped the wood floors. Ah. He smiled. *Almost* alone then.

She stepped from his home office, bottom lip enticingly puffed out, like she'd been biting it. A little habit he intended to incorporate as one of his own—biting her bottom lip. All his blood rushed south. He turned from her to hide her affect, not sure whom he was protecting from embarrassment. "Everything okay?"

Her brows furrowed. "Why wouldn't it be?"

Leo moved forward, took her hands, and wrapped them around his waist. Leaned down and nuzzled her neck with his nose.

Her small, sharp gasp encouraged him. He nipped then licked. The side of her neck might not be her lips, but it was an excellent start.

Her shoulders slumped. "My mother wants to meet for lunch. You'll have to dog sit."

Chapter Thirteen

The Lenox was one of the most exclusive hotels in Boston. Its restaurant divine, crowded, yet not seemingly so. Audra would normally prickle at the special treatment afforded her mother, but uneasiness clung to her like an oil slick. While their secluded corner table overlooked a view where Exeter intersected Boylston through windows on both sides, Audra's gaze followed well-dressed pedestrians that combed this area of the city despite being Sunday. Her gaze, but not her thoughts. Her thoughts were with Leo and the delicious kisses he'd feathered over her neck, and Jamie along with her promise to be at Leo's when he and his grandmother returned. The grandmother from—

"Tea. Black." Lady Margaret bestowed one of her signature smiles on the young, impeccably dressed server who would likely pass out from heart palpitations once he disappeared to the kitchen.

Audra shook her head, hiding a smile behind a cup of coffee, laden with milk *and* sugar, the key to Leo's house burning a hole in her purse.

Meggie sipped her water, her brilliant blue eyes turned on Audra. Audra struggled against fidgeting under the intense scrutiny. After a long silence, Audra lost her patience. "What?"

"I said nothing, darling."

She squirmed. "You want to."

"I do indeed."

Meggie's tea arrived, saving Audra from an onslaught of forthcoming questions. How could her mother *not* have questions? Meggie sipped quietly, contentedly, then let out a satisfied sigh. "Your father is concerned, darling."

Of course he is. To him she was still a child. The heat in Audra's cheeks escalated. She forced herself to remember her fear when she'd believed Jamie missing and modulated her voice. "I felt I owed Leo an apology. I went by last night and…and Jamie." His image with his grandmother floated before her.

"Ah, his son. He's quite precocious."

Surprised, Audra said, "You've met Jamie?"

"Leo brought him and his cute little pooch by the club last week."

Referring to Willie as a "pooch" made Audra smile. She took a deep breath and looked her mother directly in the eye. "Jamie frequented the soup kitchen, Mother. He'd disappeared, and I was sick with worry. *Jamie* was the reason I couldn't stop going to South End. Every day I didn't see him, every day another murderous headline appearing in the newspaper…I had to look for him. He's so young. His concern for Willie in not getting enough to eat—"

"—you, of course, made certain he did."

"Well…"

Meggie smiled. She looked…proud.

Audra swallowed a lump. "I…yes. How could I not?" she said softly.

A small smile curved her mother's lips. "I understand, darling. Truly, I do. It's clear you want something more in life than to be known as just Lady Margaret's daughter."

Audra stared down into her coffee. "Yes." There were no answers there, and she looked up again, meeting Meggie's eyes. "It's that obvious?"

"That, and the fact you're my daughter." Silence, not uncomfortable, reigned momentarily, her gaze assessing. "I once ran away too."

Cup poised, Audra stopped. "Yes. You've never talked much about that time. We girls—Iris, Sophie, Maddie, and I—only know that each of our mothers and Maddie's Aunt Jessie ran away. On a ship," she said pointedly. "Across an ocean." Audra sipped her coffee.

"We were bent on being careful, I suppose. It feels different when your own child asserts her independence. The point is, I should be devastated if you took a boat and ran away from your father and me," she said softly.

Audra found her expression difficult to read. But Audra's self-centered behavior struck another chord through her. "Do you suppose Grandmother was devastated?"

Meggie didn't answer for a long while. "One would hope," she said finally.

An interesting response.

After a long moment, her mother seemed to shake off an invisible sadness, and her hand flitted out. "My mother was of the old school. Determined to marry me off to, what she deemed, an 'acceptable' man." Her bitter laugh startled Audra. "A friend of my middle brother, who, as it turned out, preferred men."

"Mother!"

"She abhorred my love of performing." Meggie's grin returned full-fledged. "Something I delight in, each time I take the stage." She leaned in, speaking quietly. "Do you know my mother still calls weekly? Still expects me to return home? And, after twenty—er, some years."

Audra grinned at Meggie's almost slip. "Did you see her on this last tour?"

Meggie's nose wrinkled. "Of course I did, darling. But I'm most careful to keep my visits short."

The arrival of their lunch gave Audra a minute to mull this over. Audra dipped her spoon in her bowl of green turtle soup and stirred.

"Your father is more bark than bite, you know. He only wants what's best for you."

The short comradery dissipated like a puff of smoke. "Yes, well. What he doesn't seem to realize is that I am a grown woman." Audra winced. "Granted, perhaps an immature one, but definitely grown."

"Well." Her mother reached across the table and squeezed her hand. "Don't worry. We shall speak to him together when you return home."

"I'm not going home, Mother."

Her mother stilled. An entire restaurant stilled. No polite tings of utensils against china, no hum of conversation. Blocked by the blood pounding Audra's ears, drowning out all normal sounds.

"Not going home," Meggie said slowly. "And where…"

"I'll stay a few days at…er, Leo's while I decide what recourse I wish to take."

Fork poised, a small crease marred her mother's almost flawless forehead. "What of your friends? Iris or Sophie?"

Maddie's name, of course, didn't surface. She lived in England, and Audra refrained from mentioning Maddie's offer. She didn't wish to hurt her mother again, not unnecessarily. Too much time had passed. An offer like Maddie's was something Audra felt inclined to consider. And, right now, she just wasn't ready for that fight.

"Sophie lives in a boarding house, Mother. And Iris..." Her voice trailed, unable to explain the anger that plowed through her along with the memory of Iris's betrayal. Yes, Iris had been concerned, but Iris should have trusted Audra more. They were friends. The *best* of friends, or so Audra had believed.

A long sigh left her mother as she set down her fork loaded with red snapper and leaned back. "I see." Her eyes went to the saltshaker, though focused on something unseen, sending Audra's stomach into a twisted coil of knots.

Regret filled Audra. So much had been lost. Perhaps if Audra hadn't been too stubborn to trust her mother enough to ask, this wall of awkwardness would not be quite so high or quite so thick. There was so much she longed to ask, but suddenly felt she didn't have the right. Not after the accusations she'd tossed about like salad ingredients. What a fool she'd been. Audra's appetite deserted her. She set down her own fork. Of course, her parents loved one another. "Mother—"

"Audra—" Meggie's hand landed on hers. Audra waited. "Darling, I love you more than life itself. I only want the best for you."

Audra inhaled deeply. "But?" she asked cautiously.

"Are you certain about Leo?" Meggie shook her head. "Yes, yes. He has a lucrative business to be sure. But is *his* the life you desire?"

"Desire?" Audra was stunned. The touch of his lips against her lips, her skin, glided through her. His predatory watchfulness of Jamie and Wille, and perhaps, her. Oh, yes. She desired Leo Frisk.

Meggie's gaze turned shrewd, and then her laughter floated over the table. "Your father does not want you with *anyone*, darling. In his eyes, you are still age five." Meggie leaned in, squeezing Audra's hand again, lowering her voice. "Is Leo who *you* want, Audra Faye?"

"Yes," she whispered. The word escaped her without hesitation. Her heart leaped.

Meggie leaned back, simultaneously releasing a large whoosh of air. "Then we shall have to inform your father. The news, while opening his eyes, will likely devastate him. Harry loves you, and me. He wants us—you—to be happy. He just has a difficult time expressing the sentiment due to his paternal nature."

Audra's short snort escaped, but her mother appeared not to hear.

"It's different than what my mother wanted for me. England is all about the class sectors. She wished to see me married and settled for a name, property, prestige with that pasty-faced nob of my brother's." She shuddered. "But that's neither here nor there. The fact of the matter is, your father and I do want your happiness." Another small smile. "And you are correct. Harry does not see you as the esteemed young woman you've grown into. He still considers you—and will likely *always*—consider you the doting child you were. I'm afraid we're at the untenable position of cutting the apron strings. Men have a terrible time with such feats."

An exasperated huff erupted from Audra. "But what do we...I...do?"

"We shall just have to tell him." Her hand flew into the air, signaling the server. "We'll go straight away."

****

Audra paced the family study, shoring up her defenses, glancing at the wall clock every two minutes. It was already four, and she needed to get back before Jamie returned from his outing with his grandmother. She'd promised.

If only Leo were standing here with her. Her head fell into her hands. Oh, God, she was supposed to be this strong independent woman. Every thought felt traitorous. But in her heart she knew Leo would had she asked.

Stand there.

Beside her.

With her, she realized. Leo would respect her independence, her maturity. Her decisions. Even if he hated each and every characteristic.

Nerves fluttered deep in her abdomen. She squared her shoulders. The only way Daddy could force her to stay home was to physically lock her away, and surely Mother...

The door flew back, and Lady Margaret—*not* her mother—entered in with all the aplomb of an "Opening

Night." Saying nothing, Meggie lowered gracefully into a chair—though she did toss out a quick wink in Audra's direction. Audra was too keyed up to smile. Or sit.

Daddy burst in, right on her heels. "Audra!" He swept her off her feet in a fierce embrace. "Thank God."

An unexpected torrent of emotion rushed over her. She wrapped her arms around his neck and squeezed, unable to speak.

"Audra. Baby. I'm sorry. I know I shouldn't have berated you, and in front of all those people. But I've been so worried."

"I've grown up, Daddy. I'm not a child any longer." Her tears soaked his shirt. "I know you want what's best for me, but you can't keep me in a glass jar forever. I love you, but you have to let go."

"I never want to let go, baby. Never."

She gently pulled away, forcing him to set her on her feet. "I know. But...but you have to." Audra led him to the settee and sat down, still clasping his hand. "I know it's difficult, but—" She pulled but he resisted. "I have some things to tell you."

Finally, he lowered onto the space beside her. "I'm listening." His gruff tone was abraded with sentiment she knew he strove to restrain.

Tears pooled, blurring her vision, then slid down her face. "I-I don't quite know where to start. I've been a fool, Daddy. A silly, spoiled brat. I've wasted so much time. Time I'll never get back. I've missed out on so much because of my stubbornness and pride."

His large hand tightened on hers. "Baby—"

"No. Please. Let me finish." Her mind went back to that day her world shattered, truly making her feel ten years old again. "I overheard you and Mother arguing. You were angry. You told her you were leaving New York and taking me with you. You said she only thought about herself, *her* career. All these years—" Her eyes found her mother's. It was softness and encouragement that met her, gave her courage to go on. "I thought you were staying married for image purposes."

"New York," he said. He pushed a hand through his hair. "That must have been '35 or '36. Audra, all this time? How could you believe—"

"I-I don't know. I'd never heard you so much as bicker before. Let alone threaten. And Leo—"

"Leo!" He leaned forward, and his mouth tightened. *Oh, dear.*

Meggie cleared her throat. "As I recall, Harry, it was just a few years before Leo left for war. He was still at University and beginning to assist his father in their business."

Her mother's words had their intended effect. Daddy relaxed slightly again, this time leaning back.

"The thing is, I thought…well, I wanted to run as far away as possible. I ran to the front door, unwilling to hear another word between you and mother. There was Leo, all set to whisk Mother away, and—" Audra swallowed. "—and I thought Leo and…and—" She needed a fire extinguisher for the heat rushing her face. She snuck a look at her father from lowered lashes. The shock would have been stageworthy if the topic hadn't been so mortifying.

He glanced at her mother with an expression that didn't appear all that surprised and chuckled. A sight that didn't seem to sit too well with Meggie. "Leo was what? All of seventeen at the time."

Her nose lifted in the air. "I'll have you know, Harry Dempsey, such a situation is not so uncommon."

Audra narrowed her eyes on the two of them. "I get the feeling this isn't the first time an affair between Mother and Leo has been visited."

Red stained her father's cheeks. "Audra!" She didn't respond, just glared at him. "Er, uh, no. Leo spoke to your mother…"

Tension tightened her shoulders as she filed away that information.

Meggie huffed out her impatience. "Go on, Audra."

"Well, I suppose there isn't too much more to say. After I, um, accused Leo of…him and Mother…"

"Good God. I can't believe you said something so incredible to a strange man." Her father's incredulity raised the hair on her neck.

"Really, Daddy, a strange man, Leo?" She shook her head. That was a whole other discussion. "Besides, I believed it at the time," she shot back.

"And you don't now?"

"No. Last night when I left the party, I went to apologize to him. That's when I learned about Jamie." The rest of the explanation went more smoothly, though the more Audra spoke of Leo and Jamie, the greater her anxiety mounted. Another glance at the clock: four-fifteen. The urge to hurry ate at her.

Harry sat forward, elbows on his knees. "So, the whole reason you kept returning to the soup kitchen was to find Jamie?"

Audra nodded. "He went missing, and I was beside myself with worry. Every headline more sensational than the next set my imagination wild. I was terrified for him. His mother—" The lump lodged in her throat made the words difficult. "Leo thinks she was one of the Slayer's victims."

His face grew pale, his hands tightened into fists, his voice, however, remained steady. "So you aren't going back?"

"Of course, I'm going back. I can't desert Jamie now." *Or Leo.*

"The soup kitchen," he said impatiently. "Are you going back to the soup kitchen?"

Was she? So many people were in need. If Leo truly cared for her, perhaps she was needed elsewhere. With Jamie and Willie comfortably and permanently ensconced at Leo's. *Permanently?* A sudden image of the slim woman entered Audra's mind and the pieces locked neatly into place.

The woman dragged down the street, on too-tall shoes, limping on a turned an ankle. A prostitute. She wasn't Jamie's grandmother at all. She was a prostitute.

Audra jerked straight. She needed to call Leo.

"Audra?"

Her eyes bolted to her father's. She couldn't possibly tell her father. He'd never let her out of his sight. With tremendous effort, she steadied her voice. "I'm sorry, Daddy. I'm afraid I'm going to have to get back. I promised Jamie I would be there when he returned home after lunch with his…gr-grandmother."

"But you just got here."

She squeezed his hand. "I promised him, Daddy."

His nod was reluctant. Audra seized her advantage and rose. "I'll just give Leo a quick call to let him know I'm on my way." She leaned over and kissed her father on the cheek. "I love you, Daddy. Please don't worry for me. I know you still think of me as a child." A sharp bitter laugh escaped. "And half the time I've acted as one, and perhaps will on many occasions, but I'm growing up." She crossed her fingers at her lower back. "I'll be fine." She leaned in and cupped his jaw, kissed his weathered cheek. "The credit is all yours." Audra went to Meggie. "I'm so sorry, Mother. I love you too. I know I can never make up for the years of lost time, the hurt, the mistrust, but…"

Meggie stood up and pulled Audra in her arms. "We've years and years, darling. I'm so proud of you." Her words trailed in a husky cry.

Unable to speak, Audra hugged her back tightly then pulled away. "I'd best call Leo. It's getting late. I'll use the phone in the hall."

Minutes later Audra's lifted the phone, poised to dial—Leo's number. Oh, God. She didn't have Leo's number. Her father kept a small black book on his desk. She dashed down the hall and found it quickly. Her fingers shook so badly she could hardly dial. *Leo, please answer. Please be there.*

Busy signal. What now? Traipse to South End, to find Jamie? Every fiber in her being told her that woman would not be bringing Jamie home. For the briefest second, she considered asking her father's help. But he really would lock her away. It was a chance she couldn't take. She dialed again.

Still busy. She couldn't wait. She'd intercept Leo at the house.

Chapter Fourteen

"Goddammit, Scully. What do you mean Florence Payne is dead? You said you found her. In Dallas, just like we thought." Leo's blood pressure shot to something lethal. He'd been on his way out the door when the phone rang.

"Sorry, Mr. Frisk. She's dead. Appears it was a morphine overdose."

Shit. That meant one thing. Jamie had been kidnapped. Panic surged up his veins. A true anxiety attack. He couldn't breathe. He slammed the phone down, the same time a welcoming yap met his ears from the front room. Praying he wasn't too late, he dashed out the front door, barely catching Willie by the collar. "Whoa, boy. Hold up a minute. You need to stay here. I'll bring him back," he promised.

Leo shut his ears to Willie's whimpers and rushed down the steps. There wasn't a minute to lose.

****

Audra jumped out of the cab and dashed up the steps. It took three tries to stab the key in the lock of Leo's townhome while pounding the door. Breathless, the door opened, and she fell on her knees inside. "Leo. Leo." Willie met her in a fury of yaps and wet kisses. "Jamie. He's in danger—" She dashed through the house, looked in every room, until she realized she was speaking to an empty house except for the dog. "We have to get him," she panted aloud. She circled slowly, dazed and unsure. "What should I do?" She couldn't just stand there and do nothing.

Audra laid her hand on Willie's head, willing herself to calm. Heat from his busy little brain penetrated her fingers. It was the only comfort she was afforded.

The police. She should call the police.

Audra had a description of the woman. Closing her eyes, she raised her head and silently begged, *please let them find Jamie before...before it was too late.* She ran for Leo's office, Willie on her heels. Just as she reached Leo's cluttered desk the phone blared, startling her. She snatched up the receiver.

"Please. You gotta save him." The feminine voice on the other end was breathless, desperate. "Evie... Evie didn't want this for her baby."

"Jamie! Where's Jamie?" Panic pitched Audra's voice up two octaves into a shrill she didn't recognize.

"The tracks. He keeps a place for initiations. That's what he calls 'em. Meet me at the park. Near the soup kitchen. I'll take you to him. You must...hurry..."

"Wait. Where by the tracks, and who? What do you mean—initiations? Please, tell me your name."

The connection died on the woman's whispers. The dial tone echoed against Audra's ear. She dropped the phone, seeing nothing. Seeing everything. A curtain billowing softly from wind through a cracked window stirred Leo's sport coat and tie that had been tossed across a chair. Willie stared at her, alert and poised. A sickly wave of nausea swept Audra, shifting her panic to full-blown terror.

She glanced at the phone. She still hadn't called the police. What if something happened to her? She needed added precautions for every eventuality. She grabbed the phone and dialed the operator.

"Opera—"

"Please. Listen carefully," Audra interrupted. "My name is Miss Audra Dempsey. A small boy has been abducted. He's been taken to South End. Please, you have to notify the police."

"Where are you calling from, ma'am? You say your name is Audra Dempsey?"

"Mr. Leo Frisk's residence. In Bunker Hill. I need you to contact Harry Dempsey—"

"Harry Dempsey. Harry Dempsey. Why does that name sound familiar?"

Audra pulled the phone away from her ear, stared at it, stunned and furious. "Operator, did you hear me? A. Child. Has. Been. Abducted. Please call Mr. Harry Dempsey. At BO5-2951. Please hurry. I think the child is being held somewhere near the tracks."

"He, who, Miss Demp—oh!" she gasped. "Lady Margaret's daughter's name is Audra. Are you—"

Frustration tore through Audra, her temper fueled by fear snapped. "Operator! Please. Call my father, then the police." She slammed down the phone and ran down the hall. She snatched up her purse and ran out the door, tripping over Willie beating her out before she could hold him back. *Fine*. Willie's stake in Jamie's life equal to hers. She would take him. They dashed to the corner where she waved down a cab.

****

Leo's first stop at the drug store had been fruitless. What a fool he was. He'd make a horrible father. Jamie deserved much better than him. Unfortunately for the kid, Leo was all Jamie had. Leo located a place on the street a block from the soup kitchen and got out of the car. He stood a moment unsure where to begin his search. The soup kitchen was closed this time of day. He started walking and found himself on East Street near Tufts—and wasn't that ironic…or perhaps a sign? A crowd gathered ahead, and more disturbingly was the yellow crime tape blocking the entrance to the apartment building where Vera had shoved Jamie into his unwilling care at the time, changing the course of Leo's life. Forever.

The diverse crowd included beggars, prostitutes, thugs of varying ages and ethnicities. Leo made his way toward an old man on the perimeter. "What's going on?"

The old man's gaze never wavered from the cop monitoring the crowd. "Evie Payne's friend. She's been murdered. Ain't no one seen the boy or his dog for days. Now his mama and her friend…" he shook his head. "Both dead by the Slayer."

Leo's gaze jerked to him. "The Slayer. And no one's seen the kid?" Apprehension tingled. The back of his head *tingled*.

"A shame, that. That dog, neither. That nice Miss Dempsey was asking about 'em the other day. 'Fraid I upset the girl a bit." A sharp chuckle escaped the old man. "Imagine Evie and Vera's old man ain't too happy with the turn of events."

"Old man?"

"Their pimp. Diamond Donnie." His gray hair flittered in the breeze as he shot a look in both directions before turning his rheumy eyes on Leo. "You can't miss the bastard. He wears a large diamond on his pinky and his voice is raspy-like. He all but owns these parts." With a quick shudder, the old man shuffled away, head shaking.

Leo stared after him, the flash of that diamond searing his memory. The glowing tip of a cigarette. He felt sick and sure that Diamond Donnie had somehow kidnapped *his* son. Full-fledged fury won out. No one fucked with the people Leo cared about, and now the bastard would pay.

Chapter Fifteen

"Stop here."

The cab screeched to a stop. Audra threw open the door and scooted out, Willie tumbling out over her. Nerves shot, she fumbled with her purse, reassured by the small handled pistol within she'd forgotten to return to her father. She dug out a bill and tossed it to the driver, not even certain of the denomination.

The cab roared away, leaving her at the curb at Memorial Park. The soup kitchen was closed during the day. They weren't due to open for three more hours. Oddly, the entire area was deserted. Audra spun around. What a strange sight. At the least, one could usually count on seeing some of the soup kitchen regulars straggling down the street, towing all their worldly possessions.

Her stomach dropped, sickeningly, realizing what that meant. Her mysterious caller was also nowhere in sight. Willie darted off in the direction of the large elm where she'd frequently found Jamie. "Willie, wait. No. Stay." Of course, he didn't obey.

Audra took off after him, following him to the far side of the tree. She pulled up, dread crawling over her skin. "Oh. Oh, no." There on the ground lay the same woman who'd claimed Jamie as her grandson.

Even with a bloodied lip, blackened eye, and unconscious, Audra could see she couldn't be much more than thirty. Her faded print dress was ripped at the shoulder. Willie sniffed furiously at her hands. Audra took that as a good sign. The woman had been with Jamie, and maybe not so long ago.

"Well, well, well. I feel a little bad now for smacking poor Ginger so hard." That raspy voice. She recognized it from the night Iris had forgotten her purse. Cigarette smoke rent the air.

Audra lifted her gaze. The sun glittered off a diamond on the man's little finger along with a lethal jagged-edged blade he gripped. The hair on Willie's back raised, and his growl rustled the leaves. Willie leaped. "No," she whimpered.

He slashed out with the blade, catching Willie's front paw. Blood spurted, but that didn't stop the brave dog. His teeth clamped onto the man's ankle. The man's foot shot out violently, shaking Willie off. He landed a solid kick, and Willie dropped like lead. Audra jerked free of the man's hold and backed away.

He grinned, exposing tobacco-stained teeth. Her vision swam. She was too late. In two strides he had her wrist in a steel grip. "The only place you're going, sweets, is the initiation den. Where I can suck on those luscious tits of yours to my heart's content. I may not even put you up for sale for a couple of months."

His words ripped through Audra like a disease, and she swung, hitting his jaw, flinging his cigarette to the ground. His fleshy lips compressed, and his hold tightened. She was trapped. A scream started deep in her chest, gathering momentum as it choked past her throat. But in a quick maneuver, her back was against his chest, his hand clapped across her mouth, and the sharp end of his knife pricking her neck.

"Now, you don't want to go doing something stupid like that, do you? If I have to go and kill you, you might never see that little boy again, will you…Miss Dempsey?"

Audra froze, squeezed her eyes shut, forcing back the harsh sting of tears. A long moment passed, and she nodded. She clutched her purse with a death grip.

"Yes. I know who you are. You'll bring a mighty pretty price. Won't nobody in this neighborhood spill your true identity. Nah. They'll revel in the fact they got a piece of the legendary Lady Margaret's own daughter." His raspy laugh skittered like iced torture down her spine. "Now. We'll just mosey out the backside of the park. While the little ole murder investigation several blocks away is a big help in my cause, it won't last forever." He snatched the unconscious woman's hat off the ground and plopped it on Audra's head. Next came the woman's threadbare coat. "That fancy dress of yours is a dead giveaway." He chuckled, shaking his head. "Diamond Donnie is one lucky bastard."

With no other option but to follow, Audra stumbled forward. It wouldn't matter if an opportunity presented itself to escape. She had to find Jamie. And tell him… tell him…that Willie—she choked back a sob. "W-who is Diamond Donnie?" A painful jerk of her arm jarred her.

"Me, bitch." That raspy timbre would haunt her forever. "Quit dawdling."

Where was Leo? She needed Leo—

Audra stumbled, and Raspy Voice jerked her up. Numb to any pain, her mind flew. She forced herself to focus. She shifted her gaze about, attempted to memorize her surroundings. If she was lucky and was able to find Jamie, he might be unconscious. She would have to find her way—*their* way back.

Raspy Voice tugged her, not so gently, down a graveled road. Her balance was precarious in the impractical heels she wore. Dust blew through the air, leaving a haze of smog. Audra could detect the odor of the water. Up ahead, hundreds of railroad tracks, some empty, some with cars, their rusty exteriors in desperate need of paint, stood empty. Sparse copses of trees dotted the trodden area. Nowhere could she see anything remotely resembling a hideout.

"Where—" She cleared her throat. "Where are we going?"

"Someplace cozy. I'll make you comfortable. Don't you worry, sweetheart."

Her abductor's head shot around. Her gaze followed his, her heart sinking. Nary a soul dotted the landscape. She was in grave danger, the worst ever. He pulled her from the gravel road to a dirt path they followed on past an empty railcar. Trash littered the area. A myriad of Chronicle headlines cluttered Audra's head. LADY MARGARET'S DAUGHTER USED AND TOSSED LIKE YESTERDAY'S GARBAGE or HAS LADY MARGARET'S ONLY CHILD FINALLY FOUND HER OWN PROFESSIONAL VOCATION? LA! THE ANSWER HAS DIED WITH HER.

Audra swallowed and tried to pull her arm free. His hold bit into her skin.

"Enough," he growled. He spun around and tossed her over his shoulder like a sack of potatoes, sending the straw hat she wore sailing to the ground. Still, she clung to her bag, kicking out with every bit of strength she possessed. One foot landed a solid hit. He grunted though one arm remained folded across her lowered legs in an iron-clad grip. She wriggled, fought with her free fist. "Let me go, you...you bastard."

Spindly branches tore at her hair as his steps quickened. She was helpless against his strength. Still, she battled. Battled for her very life. All to no avail. He kicked out at something solid, and a door crashed against a wall and he stepped in. Darkness loomed.

He jerked her off his shoulder and threw her on a makeshift bed of rags covering straw. Her head bounced on the wall behind, sending a swath of swirling stars before her. The distinct sound of a zipper rent the air. Audra stilled, even as panic rushed her veins like raging rapids, hugging her bag to her chest as if it would protect her.

"Don't be scared, little girl. With my help, we'll have you ready for business in no time."

Ready for what? The words couldn't push past the constriction to voice. She shook her head, scooting back, but there was nowhere to escape. Her bag! Fingers fumbling with the catch, she grasped the small one-shot gun. Hands shaking, she pulled it out and aimed it in his general direction.

He stilled, his short pause filling the air. Seconds that felt like hours milled past before his loud guffaw bounded against the slated wood walls. And why shouldn't he, with her hands as steady as a percussionist's cymbal. She could do this. Swallowing, she lifted the gun, pointing it in his direction. "I-if you c-come any c-closer, I'll s-shoot."

"You couldn't hit the side of a house, doll."

Ducking her chin, Audra's fingers squeezed the trigger, her eyes mimicking the movement.

"Don't—"

The pop of the pistol deafened her momentarily.

She opened one eye. The shot flailed wide, and he jumped. "You bitch!"

A scrape sounded, followed by a small sharp gasp she couldn't pinpoint, but the noise came from somewhere outside the small, dark room she was trapped in. The vile man let out a terrifying hiss.

Desperate, she called out. "Jamie? Jamie, if that's you, get out. Run. Find Leo. *Run*. The park, Jamie. The park."

A thin rope appeared in the man's hand. She shook her head and dove forward, but he was too quick. He wrenched her arm, and she let out a cry. "No. No, please."

A sneer twisted his lips, and his beady eyes zeroed in on her. She flinched.

He snagged her left wrist, then the right, thrust them above her head, and looped the tie on some sort of hook she couldn't see. He grabbed her chin, forcing her to look at him. "Don't worry, sweetheart. You'll keep." He ground his mouth against hers in a horrific violation.

Again, she flung out her legs, this time making direct contact with his most sensitive area, felling him to his knees. The back of his hand flew out, landing against her jaw, flailing her head against the hard wood of the wall she was tethered to like a wild animal. But her head was no match, and she succumbed to an eddying vortex of black.

****

Leo worked his way through the throng of onlookers to the closest cop. Two more officers had since appeared to assist with the growing crowd. Knots wound deep in his gut. His anxiety spiked to Appalachian heights. With every passing moment, his skin switched from chilled bumps to a burning itch. He was living a nightmare worse than his ride up the Talavera River knowing the Japanese were set to take their pot shots the second they had him in their viewfinders. Leo's instincts had served him then, and they would now. Where the devil could a man stash a quick-moving kid like Jamie? There was no doubt in his mind that his son would give the bastard a fight. Unless he was—*don't even think it.*

He scrubbed a palm over his face, pulled in the Ranger Training that had saved his ass for his entire stint overseas. Where? he demanded, silently.

Just then the hair on the back of his neck lifted. Leo straightened, his gaze darting around. His eyes must be deceiving him. He darted through the crowd and took off at a run. "Jamie!"

But Jamie didn't appear to hear. The kid was fast. He ducked in and out of entryways, his focus sharp, his small body on the move. Leo slowed, trying to gauge what Jamie was looking out for. But Leo didn't see anything out of the ordinary and kept up a steady pace, determined not to lose him. They were heading east on East Street in the direction of the soup kitchen. But no, Jamie darted past the closed kitchen and raced across the street. Leo yelled out again. "Jamie!"

Pay dirt! This time Jamie stopped. "Leo." His direction changed, and within strides hurled his tiny body into Leo's arms.

"Thank God." Leo squeezed him against his chest. "Thank God. Are you all right?"

Jamie's small body quivered in terror.

"It's all right, son. You're safe now. No one will ever take you from me again." A sharp yelp reached his ears from a corner across the park. Leo's head snapped up. *Willie?* No. Willie was home. Safe and sound. There was no way he could have gotten out. Gotten to South End. Dread snaked through Leo's bloodstream like a slow poison. And why was the dog standing there, not making a beeline for Jamie? There was only one possibility that came to mind. Audra.

Impossible. She was having lunch with Meggie. She wouldn't have stayed long. She'd promised Jamie she would be back.

Leo shot across the street. Once he reached the tree, Leo set Jamie on his feet.

"Willie! Willie! You're b-bleeding. What's w-wrong with h-him, Leo?" The returning stutter spoke volumes.

Oh, shit. This was bad. "It's okay, boy. Let me see." Leo gently lifted his paw. Willie whimpered, but thankfully his tail wagged if only half-heartedly. A good sign. "Looks like a cut." A clean, deep cut. The bastard. "He'll be fine, Jamie. We'll get him stitched up. But listen to me. We need to find Audra. Miss Dempsey."

"He took her to a little hidey-hole he has near the tracks." The voice, feminine, was slurred and definitely pissed.

Leo's eyes moved up the woman's form where she leaned heavily against the tree. His gaze slid up over her muddied legs, over her torn dress. By the time his eyes met hers, he was reeling with fury. "Florence Payne you are not. What is your name?"

"Ginger. I'm truly sorry, Mr. Frisk. He forced me. Probably thinks me dead."

"You'll take me there."

"I don't think I can make it—"

"I'll t-take y-you, Leo. We h-have to h-hurry. Uncle Donnie ran after me."

Ginger's eyes scanned the area. "Yes, you'd best hurry. He's not here, and that can only mean one thing." Her meaning was clear.

Leo stood and brushed off his trousers and put out a hand for Jamie.

Jamie ignored him. "You'll have to carry Willie."

"I can watch him," Ginger said.

"N-no. No, t-thank you."

Of course, not. Leo dug out his handkerchief and squatted, speaking to Ginger. "The cops are two streets over," Leo said, carefully wrapping Willie's front paw. "I would appreciate your letting them know where Miss Dempsey's been taken."

"Miss Dempsey?" He cut his eyes to her at her whispered shock. "As in Lady Margaret's *daughter?*"

"I'm thrilled to know you realize how critical the situation is." Leo scooped the dog up and turned to Jamie. "Are you certain you can find this place?"

Jamie nodded and was off.

Leo followed closely, clutching Willie against his chest, his small whimpers tearing through him. *Let us get there in time.* They stole out the back of the park, winding through alleys and over cracked pavement of deserted lots, all the while heading farther south. From Leo's estimation, Jamie was leading them toward Bass

River. Jamie's tiny, wiry body showed a confidence for which Leo was supremely grateful, if stunned. Jamie's head whipped back and forth, to and fro, scanning the area for danger. What sad and appalling things had his son witnessed? Right now, however, his experience could only serve them well. The boxcars came in sight, and Leo's anxiety skyrocketed. Noise from the railroad and the stench from the river would hide a lot of nefarious activities.

Jamie took off running faster and threw over his shoulder, "Hurry, Leo. Hurry." Jamie darted from their odd path into a nearby clump of trees.

Willie let out small bark, and Leo wasted no time.

Low hanging branches slapped him in the face. The leaves beneath were soft, leaving him thankful it was spring and not fall. Without warning, Jamie came to a stop that had Leo almost tumbling over him. Leo crouched beside him.

Jamie pointed. "There," he whispered. A small shack that looked as if one hefty breeze would obliterate and send the pieces scattering to the four corners of the earth stood before them. "Come on. I'll show you how I got out." He ran to one side and disappeared.

Leo rose and followed. Not much sunlight reached through the foliage, and he slowed, allowing his eyes to adjust.

"I squeezed through here," Jamie whispered.

Jesus. The crack from the window couldn't have been a half foot high. Leo's heart raced as he surveyed the area. With a hand on Leo's shoulder, Jamie guided him to a large tree several feet away. Leo went down on one knee. "Okay, this is what we are going to do. You and Willie are going to hide here while I go in for Audra. Whatever you hear, you stay behind this tree. I'm counting on you, son."

The earnestness of Jamie's expression wrapped Leo's emotions in a fierce fragility that was certain to dissolve under the slightest touch. Leo set Willie at Jamie's feet, put a finger to his lips. "Stay quiet. I'll be just a few minutes."

Jamie nodded, fear and trust stark in his eyes.

Leo tugged him into a tight hug. Then with a last glance around, Leo crept to the front.

Chapter Sixteen

Audra pried her eyes open, temple throbbing. She surveyed her surroundings, struggling to remember where she was. Her arms ached. Light stole through varying cracks in the walls. What happened? Groaning, she spotted one window, and whether from grime or paint, not a single ray slipped through. A trickle of blood teased her skin. She struggled to move her hand, to swipe it away. Her effort failed as the memories crashed over her. Right. Her wrists were bound—above her head.

Oh, God. She was in real trouble. She wriggled her hands, but that only brought on stinging pricks from the lack of blood flow and had the thin rope cutting into her skin. Realizing the awkward position made her hurt arms more.

Audra's chest tightened, the knot in her throat constricting the oxygen. *Think,* blast it. She must think. Rationally. The pounding in her head had her gasping for breath. She had to remain calm. *Calm, calm, calm.* She chanted the word. Panic was a hairsbreadth away. She drew in a series of deep, steady breaths. It seemed to stem the rising panic...barely. She closed her eyes, inhaled again, deeper through her nose, letting the air out slowly through her mouth. As her fortitude steadied, the rank mustiness seeped in, usurping false sense of control. The rest of her breath came out in a rush.

Fighting again, she stilled, straining to hear. Nothing. Just the leaves on the trees brushing against the structure in a soft breeze. No voices, no railcars, no birds or insects—*Jamie.* She'd heard him, hadn't she? Before that monster knocked her silly. Audra was desperate to believe. Had he escaped? And Willie. She sucked in a sharp gasp. Poor Willie. He might be dead. *Please let Willie survive.* God, her arms were killing her. Getting free would require her limbs to be constructed of silk thread. *Yes.* All she had to do was relax her muscles, then maybe she could slip her wrists free. She drew in another deep breath and held it, focused on a point straight ahead, then let it out in a pursed, steady stream.

It's working. Her arms practically relaxed out of their sockets. A sliver of hope ignited. She slowly wriggled one wrist...the bindings cut deeper. Worse? Footsteps crunched beyond the door, and in a burst of panic, all hope dissipated.

The door flew back with the assault of his leg. Her lungs constricted until the black closed in around her with the lack of air.

****

"Audra." Oh, God. Leo almost dropped to his knees in prayer. She was bound with her arms above her head. He'd kill him. Strangle that man with his bare hands.

"Leo?" Her voice was a far cry from her normal, demanding confidence, coming out a croak of cracked, rasped desperation.

"Audra!" He rushed over, laid his hand on her cheek. It was hot and starting to swell.

277

"Leo? Oh, God. Leo. You. Have. To. Find. Jamie." Her words came out in a rush of staccato beats. "And Willie. Oh, Leo. Willie is…" Gulping sobs wracked her body.

"Sh. Jamie and Willie are fine. You're hurt." He could scarcely breathe as he fumbled with the bindings at her wrists, but his knee pressed down on something hard, distracting him. "What the hell?" He reached in, lifting his find. "A gun?"

"It's Daddy's. I-I took it from his desk."

"The bastard took it from you." His voice was cold. Stoic. "It's been fired."

"No," she whispered. "I-I had it. For self-protection."

"You took it from your father's desk. Do you realize how dangerous—you could have been killed. God Almighty, Audra," he bit out. Every fear he'd bottled away spewed forth in hurled fury. He shoved the small pistol to his back and set one knee on the makeshift bed beside her. "Are you hurt anywhere?" Large hands roved her legs.

"M-my head hurts."

He tugged a pocketknife from his pocket. "Don't you have a lick of sense?" He couldn't seem to stem the flow of his anger, spurred by the thought of never seeing her again. He moved his hands up her numbed arms to the bindings at her wrists and gnawed away.

"What was I supposed to do? I arrived at your house, and the phone rang. It was that woman, telling me I had to get Jamie."

If Leo didn't get hold of himself, he might saw right through her skin, his motion so violent. He clenched his jaw, working to keep his tone at a reasonable level. "I swear, you need a damned keeper."

She flinched from his harshness. "How…how can you say that? I-I couldn't ignore her. Not…not after what Mr. Stone said about what happens to little boys."

"You should have called your father, damn it." He jerked at the rope, and a part of her bindings fell free. Her left arm dropped like a piece of limp pasta. "You should have left the hard stuff to those equipped to handle it," he bit out, knowing she'd never forgive him for berating her. He would have done the same, had done the same. Still, his words dropped in the room like knives from the sky, blowing every dream he'd ever craved by her silence.

She clenched her hand in and out of a fist. He took her arm and massaged to help the blood flow. "To those more equipped to handle it?" she bit out. "You… chauvinistic—" She was so angry the words escaped her. "—ass!"

****

The door banged behind Leo, threatening the stability of the barely standing shack. Audra let out a startled squeal. Before Leo could spin around, something crashed over his head, shattering a spray of glass. The tool he'd used on her bindings thumped against her abdomen. Leo slid to the ground in a heap just as the rest of the rope gave way. Her right arm fell to her side useless as the numbness gave way to the painful stings.

Audra's eyes snapped to the monster, his pinky ring catching the thin stream of light. Over one shoulder lay Jamie's limp, unconscious body. More rope looped his free hand. Fear choked her, but she managed to croak out a small call for help. "Leo. Leo." With her left hand now somewhat functional, Audra clutched the knife and buried the small treasure behind the material of her skirt at her hip.

The creep sauntered forward, and her apprehension raised in sharp bumps over her body like a rash, only cold instead of hot. He shot a swift kick into Leo's ribs. A small grunt emitted from him, giving Audra a glimmer of hope. *He wasn't dead.* "W-what did you do to Jamie?"

"Don't you worry none about the kid. He'll survive. You, however, may be more trouble than you're worth." He rubbed a hand over the front of his trousers. The gesture was obscene, horrifying. Audra dug her heels into the makeshift mattress and pushed away. "Still, I'm tempted."

Sick. She was going to be sick.

He leaned forward, inundating her with a whiff of some pungent, sweetish odor she failed to recognize. He snatched her right arm, jerked her up, and shoved her toward the only other inside door. "So he cut you loose, did he." He let out a maniacal laugh. "Not for long."

Audra fought him with every ounce of strength she could muster. Not easy with her throbbing head and hands that barely refused to work.

"Yeah, too much trouble," he growled. He changed direction and kicked open the door to the adjoining room. He dumped Jamie on a small table, his hold on her unrelenting.

She would have only once chance. She brought up her hand, gripping Leo's pocketknife and swung. She aimed for his heart, but he turned at the last moment, and the small knife landed deep in his bicep. Blood spurted like a fountain. Bile surged up her throat.

"Bitch!" His voice shook the walls. His fist caught her in the jaw, and she flew back against the wall. The hit was solid. She sank into oblivion.

****

A bang jarred Leo. He blinked, rising slowly to a low crouch, trying to gather his bearings. He set his fingers to the back of his head. He pulled them away and looked down. Wet. Blood. Nothing familiar met him except the stench of cigarettes and...*gasoline.* Shit. Not a good combination.

He lurched to his feet, head pounding, whipping his gaze around. Audra was gone. His vision swayed and slowly cleared as he surveyed the small, dank space. A man silhouetted in the one exit stood, lighted cigarette dangling from his mouth, trail of smoke twirling upward. Light reflected off the ring on his little finger and the canister near his leg. Jamie was hoisted over his shoulder. The sight sent a murderous rage rushing through Leo. The bastard laughed. A raspy sound that sent an icy black chill up Leo's spine.

Jamie kicked out, hitting the man's arm. *Diamond Donnie.* Donnie palmed his bicep and let out a squeal that would do a startled pig justice. Jamie, the little sneak, was playing opossum. *Thank God.*

Leo rose, exhibited his full height, took a measure of satisfaction when the brute edged back. Taking him out would be Leo's greatest pleasure.

Jamie toppled to the ground and scrambled his way in Leo's direction, but he was snagged by the collar like a dog. "Not so fast, you little shit. You'll pay for that." His eyes never wavered from Leo as he hauled Jamie up and slung him against the wall. Jamie fell, landing at an awkward angle.

Leo leaped forward. "Jamie." In a sideways kick, Leo leveled the villain with a shot to his midsection. The blow was lethal and exact, just the way Leo had learned for his special service during the war. Diamond Donnie flew back, his cigarette flailing through the air as he fell and landed with his neck bent, leaving only one conclusion. He was dead.

A blaze ignited, then a small explosion.

"Leo? Where's Miss Dempsey?" His voice was so childlike, so scared. Smoke spread, turning the small shack into a firetrap.

"Hurry, Jamie. Can you walk?"

A pained cry reached Leo. *Shit.* "I-I d-don't think s-s-so!"

Leo dug in his pocket for his handkerchief. Empty. He'd wrapped Willie's cut paw. Leo tore his shirt from his head, then stooped low. He covered his nose and mouth and crawled his way to Jamie. Time was running out. Silently, he begged Audra to hold on. His fingers found Jamie's leg.

"W-we gotta g-get Miss D-d-dempsey."

"We'll get her, son. Grab onto my neck." He cradled Jamie to his chest and hurried out the door.

"Y-you'll have t-to g-go in the w-w-window, Leo. H-hurry. H-h-hurry."

Jamie was right. Sirens sounded in the distance. *Too little, too late.*

Coughing, Leo darted around the side where Jamie had pointed out his earlier escape. The window was now closed, which could only mean one thing. The bastard had thought ahead. Tripled heartbeats pounded through Leo as he went to raise the window. It didn't budge. *Shit. Shit. Shit.* Using his shirt to protect his elbow, he jabbed. After two tries, the glass cracked. He hit it a third time. Glass shattered, leaving shards in his numbed skin. He crawled through, smoke blinding him. "Audra!"

His yell yielded nothing. Again. "Goddammit, Audra, answer me!" He couldn't see an inch in front of him. Again, ducking, he squinted through the haze. Coughing while smoke sucked up the oxygen and flames leaped beneath the closed door. Leo mauled his way through the thickness toward the dark lump he spotted.

Out of time. Out of time. Out of time.

Mirage or not, he aimed quickly in what he prayed was Audra's direction, prayed the devil wasn't playing him for a fool. He hacked out her name. "Audra. Audra, answer me, darling."

No response.

He reached out. His hand met a solid mass. Hope. He felt his way up her crumpled form, clasped her arms. Threw her over his shoulder, she weighed nothing. Fear and desperation drove him back the way he'd come. The wall behind him collapsed.

Time had ceased. The window was too small for them both. With every ounce of strength mustered, Leo bashed the wall with his shoulder. It cracked. The toxic haze burned his eyes, his nose, his lungs. Flames licked his heels. One more solid hit, and the entire wall gave way. He fell, twisting to land on his back. The brush of heat kissed his face, his arms, his legs. Gasping for air that was as elusive as water for his parched throat, he scooted back, clutching Audra to his heaving chest.

He cut his eyes to the east, to the clearing. Two police cars were parked just beyond, lights flashing. Along with one Harry Dempsey with a stronghold on Leo's son. In a blurred miracle, Audra's hand fisted in his shirt. He closed his stinging eyes to a welcome abyss.

Chapter Seventeen

Tuesday, May 20

Tears streamed down Audra's face. No matter what
she told herself, she was up against the wall. What
choice had she? It was time to leave. Prove to the world
she could—*must*—make it, on her own. She snagged a
floral print, short-sleeved dress from its hanger and
threw it in her open suitcase which Jilly calmly pulled
back out and proceeded to fold.

"Audra Faye?"

Her mother's clipped accent startled Audra, and
she spun around. Meggie's brow was creased. Oh, God.
She was making her mother age right before her eyes.

"Oh, darling, you cannot leave without even
speaking with him."

Audra turned and quickly blinked back tears. More
tears. They hadn't seemed to stop once in the last two
days. "Why not? Leo made things clear enough." *You
need a keeper. Why didn't you call your father?* Ha!
She'd tried, hadn't she? Not to mention she'd heard
nothing from Leo since he'd blasted her for taking
Daddy's derringer. Sure, Leo had been in the hospital,
but Audra had learned the minute he'd been released.
Standing at doors, eavesdropping on conversations, had
a way of unearthing information. Had *he* made the
slightest effort to speak to her? No.

What did it matter? They were right. All of them. Daddy. Iris. Leo. Audra had been protected her whole life. As the infamous Lady Margaret's only daughter, her father's *baby*—Audra couldn't work her way out of a paper bag. She jerked another frivolous frock off a hanger and tossed it in the direction of her bag. "That's plenty, Jilly. Just clasp it and get it downstairs. The cab should be here in twenty minutes." Her voice shook with choked emotion. Every fine-tuned, polished bit of her shredded in the blink of an eye.

Meggie's arm slipped around her shoulders and pulled her into a hug. "Audra. You don't have to go." Audra stiffened.

"Yes, Mother. I-I do." Unable to stem them, her tears fell in a torrential storm. "Maddie invited me to London. It's time I stepped back, took my life in my own hands. See how well I fare in the *normal* world. You and Daddy have...have protected me long enough."

"And what of Iris? She's called every hour the last two days."

Audra swiped at the tears. Like that helped. For every one she scraped away, another million more surfaced in its place. At least with Iris she had a clear conscience. "I wrote her a note. I know I behaved like a stubborn, immature, spoiled brat. I was determined to prove that no one—nothing could hurt me. I know—" Her voice broke. *Again.* "I know she told Daddy about my being accosted was out of her concern for my well-being." Audra's legs gave way, and she collapsed to the floor. "I-I'm a rotten, abysmal friend..." And that was the crux of the matter, she thought, her tears overflowing, showing no sign of abating.

Meggie settled beside her. Her mother. The great Lady Margaret, sitting on the floor. Wouldn't the press love this picture, she thought, throwing her arms around her neck, hugging her tightly. But in Meggie's very British way she did not allow emotions to drive her. "If the taxi is to arrive so soon, you'd best see Jamie. He is most anxious."

Her most difficult task yet. Telling Jamie she was leaving.

Audra's chest strung tighter than harp strings at the guilt swamping her. In the past week, she'd spent her time with Jamie but couldn't bring herself to tell him she was leaving for good. There was no getting out of that, not if she was as grown up as she believed herself to be. She gave a watery smile. "They won't hold the boat, Mother. Not even for Lady Margaret's daughter." Just days ago, resentment would have choked her. Now, however shocking and despite the tears, Audra found herself teasing her mother, if only a little. Another bruise impaled her heart at the stupidity of time she'd wasted.

After another tight embrace, Meggie rose and smiled a small tip of her lips before disappearing from Audra's childhood room. She snatched a tissue and blew her nose just as Jilly latched the buckles and set her case on the floor. "Thank you, Jilly. For... everything." Blinking quickly, the maid nodded and hauled her bag out.

Nostalgia sucked the air from Audra's lungs with her one last glance around. Would she ever be home again? With an unsteady inhale, Audra straightened her spine and forced herself through the arch, dreading every question she was certain to see in Jamie's much too observant eyes. Eyes so like his father's. He was just a small child, and to leave without any explanation would be not only be cowardly but would be vastly unfair to him. Yes. It was time to be the grownup she'd been insisting she was.

Moments later, Audra stood quietly just inside the room her parents had assigned Jamie while Leo recuperated in the hospital. Jamie hadn't spotted her yet.

Willie's head and injured paw rested on Jamie's cast-encased leg. His tail thumped soundly against the mattress, and Jamie's gaze snapped to the door. Audra peeled herself from the frame and ventured in. "Hey, slugger."

The light in his face further cracked her battered heart.

Her gaze swept along the plaster. "I see you wasted no time in coveting Lady Margaret's signature."

He grinned. "I'm gonna save it forever." His fingers lightly brushed Willie's bandaged paw. "Look. She signed Willie's too."

Audra forced a smile, the rest of her heart shattering into a million pieces. "A keepsake, indeed."

"A-are you l-leaving?"

"Who told you that?"

"I heard the maid talking."

And just like that—sucker-punched to the stomach. It took every effort not to bend over at the pain. "M-my friend, Maddie, invited me to visit her. In…in London," she finished on a whisper.

"C-can't she c-come see you h-here?"

This wasn't a conversation Audra had ever imagined or…or wanted. She lowered to the mattress, grasped Jamie's hand within her own. Unable to meet his eyes, she just stared down at his small fingers. She might not see him again for many years. "Of course. But this is an opportunity. For me to see…to see—"

"It's cuz of m-me, isn't it? You g-got taken cuz of m-me."

Her eyes flashed to his. Big tears welled there and threatened to spill over. Audra scooted closer, leaned in. She cupped his face, met his earnest gaze straight on. "No! Never. I would do the same. Again and again. Anything to bring you home safe. Don't. Don't ever doubt that."

"Don't you like us? Me? Willie?"

"Oh, darling, of course I do. I truly do. I defied my father, day after day, going to South End to see you. And when you…you disappeared…" She closed her eyes. Swallowed hard.

"And Leo? Do you love—"

She grabbed his hand, squeezed. *Yes.* But what good would it do for her to move straight from Daddy's overbearing protectiveness to Leo's? "It's complicated, sweetie." How was she supposed to explain to a child who'd had the run of the worst neighborhood in Boston a good portion of his young life something she could barely understand herself? "So…so complicated."

Her eyes darted about the room, unable and unwilling to put her fears into words. She *did* love Leo. How could she not, when she looked at this child he'd taken in at someone's word? Leo would not be giving Jamie or Willie up. Not without a fight. And that only endeared him to her more.

All those years of her silent accusations, lost. Her mother and Leo. In hindsight, the idea *was* ludicrous.

Her father adored her mother, and Audra was such a fool. She leaned in, touched Jamie's head with a light kiss. "I'm so sorry, darling. Truly, sorry." She squeezed his hand. She couldn't afford to look back. Ever.

"Complicated, is right." The heavy, husky resonance, still sounding smoke-scarred, raced up Audra's spine in an awareness that stole her breath.

"Leo!" Jamie's enthusiasm sent Willie's tail thumping vigorously.

Audra froze. *Oh, God. How much had he heard?*

Leo moved into the room. "Hey, kid. How's the leg?"

"Broken. But me and Willie. We'll be okay. You need to talk to Miss Dempsey. She wants to leave."

His eyes cut to her, and she looked away. "She does, does she? Seems I have my work cut out for me." Leo reached down and pulled her hand from Jamie's, tugging her to her feet. "What do you say, Audra Faye? You gotta minute to talk?"

Leo hustled her from Jamie's temporary dwelling, urging her inside the first doorway down the hall. A closet. "So. You're leaving? Just like that?"

"You've been talking to my father?"

A disgusted snort escaped him, and he ignored the question. "Your suitcases are next to the front door."

"Oh."

Hysteria squeezed every ounce of oxygen from her body. Audra swallowed, backing away.

"Answer me, Audra Faye. Were you planning to just disappear? Without a single word to me?" Anger, hurt, and raw pain crackled from him, his voice hoarse and scratched as if he'd drunk nails for breakfast.

Her heart broke for him. For them. "Leo," she whispered. "It appears I still have some growing up to do."

He matched her, step by step, until her back was against the wall. He towered over her, flattened a palm above her head. "I was wrong, Audra Faye."

Her gaze darted side to side, but she couldn't move if God himself demanded she do so. The urge to throw her arms around his neck and never let go frightened her. She'd never been all that adventurous. Not like Sophie, Iris, or Maddie. The *only* reason Audra had risked South End day after day was to keep an eye on Jamie. Unreadable, red-rimmed eyes skimmed over her. *Wrong about what,* she wanted to ask. The words were right there, on her tongue, but her lips were parched, unmovable.

"You're the bravest girl I've ever known."

Her head swiveled back and forth. *I'm not.* Still, the words stalled in her throat.

The slightest curve touched his lips, his gaze softened. "Of course, you are. From the time you were ten years old and stomped your way past me via my foot. You've stood up to your father despite his anger and fear of your work at the soup kitchen. Day after day in the worst part of town." He lowered his hand, encircled hers.

She glanced down at the small bandages that crisscrossed the cuts and burns. Wounds he'd procured in saving her. It turned her stomach.

"I was scared, Audra Faye. Terrified of losing to you to that…" His eyes clamped shut, tension creasing his mouth, his forehead. "I can't bear thinking of what might have been." He seemed to gather himself.

Squeezed her hand, found her gaze. "I love you, Audra Faye Dempsey. Please, don't leave me. Us. Jamie and I need you."

Audra's heart lurched so hard she feared her blood would mar the carpet. "I-I can't..."

His hand fell away, pain etching his entire being.

Those ridiculous tears welled up and again obscured her vision. "Oh, Leo. I love you too. But you don't understand. I-I can't survive being treated like a porcelain doll. I'll die. I'm a living, breathing woman who craves life, not confined by a gilded cage made of glass." She blinked, and her pooled tears spilled over.

A soft touch brushed the damp away. His features gave way to hope. "Oh, love. There is nothing I want more than you living and breathing. By my side. In my bed. In my life." He reclaimed her hand, dropped to one knee.

"W-what are you doing? Leo—"

"Marry me, Audra. I've been miserable without you. For years."

Her head started that automatic swivel—

"Don't say no. Please."

"I'm having a difficult time believing you. You've been out of the hospital for two days." She jerked her hand from his, hurt. Angry that she'd almost forgotten. Frustrated that once more he'd found a way beneath her skin.

Eyes never wavering from her, he rose. Delved in his pocket, pulled out a small box. "I had a few things to take care of." He flipped the top open of the box, showcasing a large oval diamond that winked at her.

She couldn't look away. But another surge of doubt crowded in, and her eyes narrowed on him. "If you tell me that you asked Daddy for my hand in marriage—"

He snagged her waist, yanked her into his chest, his mouth crashing over hers in a hot, demanding possessiveness that triggered the onslaught of butterflies deep in her gut. There was nothing sweet or pure about his kiss, just point-blank need, inciting a tidal wave of desire crashing over her.

His lips broke from hers, yet still close enough to touch. His breath heated her skin. She lifted tentative fingers to his stubbled jaw, excited yet terrified of what he'd say. "I would never ask your father given the chance to ask you first," he whispered.

It was the perfect answer. She threw her arms around his neck. That thick neck corded with roped muscle, she murmured into, "Then, yes, Leo. Oh, yes. I'll marry you."

A word about the author...

Kathy L Wheeler, author of both contemporary and historical romance, grew up in Dallas, Texas, but migrated to Boulder then Longmont, Colorado, where she attended high school. Her degree from the University of Central Oklahoma is a BA in Management Information Systems with a minor in vocal music.

She loves the NFL, the NBA, musical theater, reading, writing—and just to scratch the singing itch—karaoke.

Kathy lives in the Pacific Northwest with her musically-talented attorney husband, Al. They have one grown daughter who has two adorable kids, and dog Angel who lives up to her name, and one bossy cat, Carly, who acts as if she was the *rescuer* rather than the *rescue-ee*!

Find Kathy at:
Web site/blog: http://kathylwheeler.com
twitter: http://twitter.com/kathylwheeler
facebook: http://facebook.com/kathylwheeler
pinterest: http://pinterest.com/kathylwheeler
email: kathy@klwheeler.com